L.O.S.T.

AND

F.O.U.N.D.

MORGAN M. STEELE

Also by Morgan M. Steele:

Recensere: The Lost Queen

O Positive

Doing Just Fine

The Averagers: a parody

Cover art designed by sjholbert of SelfPubBookCovers.com

Steele Bookcase Publishing

ISBN-10: 1732663009

ISBN-13: 978-1732663008

For Dad,

the strongest and bravest man I ever knew.

Thank you for everything you did for Mia,

and more importantly,

thank you for everything you did for me.

PROLOGUE

The Facility of Undercover National Defense (more often known as F.O.U.N.D.) has three primary rules for their field operatives:

1. Don't defy orders.
2. Don't take unnecessary risks.
3. Don't get emotionally attached to anyone outside the agency.

I, Mia Crane, in the course of a single summer, somehow managed to break all three.

MORGAN M. STEELE

CHAPTER 1

Loud gunshots ring through the parking garage. What was meant to be a simple in-and-out extraction snowballed into an absolute mess. Sure, we got the job done, mission accomplished, but we got caught. We barely got the flash drive, but as usual, we managed. What can I say? I never said being a spy was easy. If it was saving-the-world important, they wouldn't have sent three teenage operatives here anyway. Not alone, that is.

"Don't you have to be somewhere else right about now?!" Summer Laurence, a.k.a. best friend number one, shouts across the garage.

I take cover behind the nearest car and glance down at my watch. "I have half an hour! That's plenty of time!"

"You're cutting it awful close, M. Why didn't you just have us schedule this mission for tomorrow?!" Ginger Williams, best friend number two, fires a few shots before ducking down beside me.

"I thought it was just an extraction. If I'm a little late, it's no big deal. My parents will stall him."

We sprint to the stairwell, dodging the rain of bullets. The metal bits lodge into the surrounding cars, ripping holes through the tires and shattering the glass windows. These security guards have no regard for employee vehicles. Jeez.

We take the stairs two at a time, up, up, up to the roof where a large black helicopter with the F.O.U.N.D. logo painted on its side is waiting for us.

Summer shoots three more bullets behind her. I fire a few too, taking out one of their men. He yells out in pain, clutching his chest, but he'll be fine. We don't shoot to kill unless it's mission-critical. Life or death. And with aim like theirs, these guards aren't as threatening as they are annoying.

"Maybe you should thank us, M." Summer starts a conversation at the worst possible moment. As per usual. "I mean, Ginger and I did kind of hook you two up in the first place."

"Recommending an ice cream shop that Dave happens to work in doesn't count as setting us up."

We race across the roof and into the open doors of the helicopter. They slam shut behind us and lock with a loud click. The propellers roar as the copter lifts into the air, making its way across the city to F.O.U.N.D. Headquarters. Bullets ping against the metal door, but they slow to a stop as we leave the range of their guns.

Ginger sighs, holding the flash drive in her hand. She rakes her fingers through her thick black curls. "All that trouble for one little drive. There must be a hell of a lot of information on this baby."

The tips of her hair are still orange from her latest dyeing experiment. 'Latest' meaning the most recent of many. Ginger never keeps her hair the same color for longer than a few weeks before trying something new. There always has to be change or it gets boring, I guess. But it doesn't matter how crazy the color combinations seem. She always pulls them off flawlessly.

The silver stud in her nose gleams in the light from the window. It was the only piercing besides her ears her parents would let her get, though when she turns eighteen in October I'd bet she'll be sporting a few more. Nothing too crazy, but you never know. She's kind of a wild card. In her own words: "Predictable is just another word for boring."

I glance out one of the tinted windows, watching the city drift by. Skyscrapers frame busy streets filled with streams of headlights and brake lights as far as the eye can see. People move down the sidewalks in a steady flow going every which way, flitting from shop to shop or across the crosswalks.

The city of Great City, where my Headquarters is located, is pretty big, complete with tons of skyscrapers and *tons* of traffic. It's near the coast, and from all the way up here you can almost see the suburb of Seavale, the place I call home.

"Mia, are you *sure* you can't come to the party on Wednesday?" Summer takes a seat on one of the padded benches attached to the wall of the helicopter. Effortless blonde waves cascade down her shoulders. Even after a mission with her scrapes and bruises and cuts, she still manages to look stunning. It's not like she tries, she just has one of those faces.

"Can't. Camping."

"Oh, right. I keep forgetting about that."

"Well, you're gonna miss one hell of a party."

"Some of the field agents from Quebec are coming down to visit. Two words: hockey boys."

"I suppose I'll just have to meet the hockey squad another time."

"Or, you know, you could sneak out..." Ginger raises an eyebrow.

"That's a death sentence. My parents would kill me. G, your dad might be from the science department, but both of mine are field agents. Constant vigilance. 24/7. There is no escape."

The helicopter touches down on the roof of Headquarters as another one takes off. The metal doors slide open. We race across the pavement and into the elevator, riding it down into the great metal fortress that is F.O.U.N.D. Tower.

The halls are buzzing with agents going every which way, all of them dressed in their various uniforms. You can tell what division they're from by a single glance. There are the administrators in suit and tie or sensible black pantsuits. The field agents are dressed in their heavy leather, laden with bulletproof armor and a variety of weapons they have yet to turn in before clocking out. A few people from the science and tech departments walk by wearing pristine white lab coats and pushing carts of equipment and chemicals. And then there are the interns, F.O.U.N.D. limited access passes pinned to the fabric of their navy blue polo shirts or dangling from lanyards around their necks. They run like mad, carting coffee to administrators and running files to the copying rooms and records centers.

A few minutes after arriving and checking in, we make our way to the field agent locker rooms, past rows and rows of red and black lockers. They seem to be the colors of the agency. Elegant. Professional. Lethal.

The locker room ceilings are low and the air conditioning makes the room so cold a shiver runs up my spine as soon as we walk in. The cold is refreshing, especially after we've spent the last few hours of an already-hot day running around in long-sleeved leather jackets and matching pants and boots.

Thick steam sweeps over the slick tile floor, escaping the showers in the back, and then rises to the ceiling before flowing out the vents. A few agents walk around in the barebones of their uniforms: black tank-tops or tight black sports bras and black leggings or leather pants. Some are hardly dressed at all, their hair rolled up in towels or braided over their shoulders, dripping wet with water from the showers. For a top-secret government agency, the locker rooms feel very mundane, almost like a gym locker room. All of the women in here could be ordinary. Could be. But they're not. These people are weapons, my best friends and myself included.

Summer, Ginger, and I have recruit numbers very close to one another: 224, 237, and 212, respectively. Each Headquarters has all of their field agents numbered 1 to up to 1000. When agents leave, are transferred, or die, the new recruits fill the gaps so the numbers don't keep climbing higher and higher. And sometimes if an agent saves the world or something they'll retire the number, but that rarely happens. Great City HQ only has three retired numbers, but I couldn't tell you off the top of my head. One of them belonged to my great-grandmother, Margaret Everheart, which I'm pretty sure is 012, 200 numbers ahead of my own.

"Welcome back, Agent Crane." The automated voice greets as my locker door opens.

I hang up my weapons on their hooks and shimmy out of my tight leather uniform. Next, I tug a bright red t-shirt over my head and hop into a pair of jean shorts. Literally anything would be more forgiving in the summer heat than our black long-sleeved jackets.

Exhausted brown eyes stare back at me in the mirror, the dark bags beneath my eyes begging for a concealer touch-up. I run a brush through my tangled ponytail of brown waves in an attempt to bring order to the chaotic knot. Once I'm sure I at least look decent, I close my locker and grab my bag.

"See you tomorrow." I wave and walk towards the door.

"Forgetting something, babe?" Ginger holds out her hand expectantly. Oh, right, the thing that's not supposed to be in my ear.

I carefully pull the metal earpiece out, untangling the wire from my hearing aid, and toss it to her. She grins, waving a goodbye as I walk out of the locker room.

It doesn't take long to get to the parking garage and check out my motorcycle. There she is, waiting for me all shiny and fresh from her appointment with the vehicle maintenance team. I rev her up, racing down the busy Great City streets. Rock music blares through the headphones set into my helmet. The vibrations set off fire in my veins.

Traffic is heavy and the lanes are full of honking cars. I weave through a few of them, trying to make my way forward as quickly as possible, but eventually the flow comes to a stop.

I look around for another way out. There. An alley. I turn off of the street and race down the old brick passage squeezed between an overgrown church and a little indie coffee shop. The street on the other side isn't nearly as crowded as the one I came from. I'm able to dodge through cars quickly, twisting and turning to fit through the small spaces. It helps that I took my Driver's Ed. classes at F.O.U.N.D. Offensive Driving 101 is the best thing that ever happened to me.

My phone rings, and the call is displayed on the projected screen in my motorcycle helmet. I'm like Iron Man. David Bowen, the nerdy curly-haired dork I call my boyfriend, would freak out if he knew about all of the awesome gadgets I have access to.

Speaking of Dave...

"Hey, Curly," I answer. The rock music that was playing moments ago is replaced instead with Dave's voice. "Happy anniversary!"

"Happy anniversary, M. I'm on my way over now. Is there anything else you want me to bring? I've got the picnic basket and your super-awesome top-secret anniversary present."

"Just your cute self. I'll see you in a few."

I turn a sharp corner, and hit a red light, brakes squealing as I come to an abrupt stop.

"Are you out somewhere? It sounds like you're in traffic."

"On my way home from work." It's not technically a lie.

"You were at Sugar & Spice today? I should have stopped in. Those cupcakes are amazing."

"Tell you what. How about I turn around and pick up a few for the picnic? I might be a little late, but—"

"Have I ever told you you're the best girlfriend ever?"

"It might have slipped out." I smirk. It really doesn't take much to impress him. "What flavor do you want?"

"You're letting me pick? God, um...red velvet."

"Cream cheese filling?"

"You know it."

"Coming right up. See you in a few."

"Love you."

"Love you too."

After hanging up, I take a quick left turn and park in front of the bakery I work in as a cover: Sugar & Spice, the place that makes everything nice. It's a homey little shop downtown with cream-colored walls and big red hearts painted all over the tile floors, one heart for each agent that's worked here since the shop opened in the forties. In other words, there are a lot of hearts. It kind of looks like Cupid threw up, but that's alright. It's home when I'm not out arresting drug lords and taking down terrorists.

"Mia? I thought you were busy today," Greta, the kind old German woman that runs the place, asks.

She's a former agent, as are most of the people that are in charge of F.O.U.N.D. businesses, but Greta is different. Even after her fielding days, she worked as an administrator. My administrator's administrator, to be exact. She knows the agency better than anyone I've ever met.

Greta's wearing a white apron with the Sugar & Spice logo on the front pocket. Her waist-length silver hair is pulled back into a tight braid that hugs the back of her head. And while she looks like a sweet innocent old lady, I know for certain she keeps a gun under the counter. Long story short, the woman's a badass.

"I was. Just got out. I'm headed home now, but I need a dozen red velvet cupcakes for my picnic with Dave."

"Not a problem, meine kleiner Vogel." Greta winks, a smile forming on her wrinkled face. A warm twinkle shines in her wise gray eyes. When she hands me the box of cupcakes, her soft hands rub against mine affectionately. I don't get to see my real grandparents all that often, so she's practically filled that position.

"Thanks Greta. You're the best."

"Don't mention it. Anything for my girls." She gives a knowing wink before shooing me out the door.

After securing the box of sweets in place, I swing a leg over my motorcycle, pop my helmet back on, and drive out of the city into the suburb of Seavale.

I ride past the shopping district that consists of a grocery store and a few strip malls, through the housing settlement suburbia, and up the winding road along the edge of the mainland. Waves lap the shores of the east coast.

Here, away from the city, there aren't any people on the beaches. It's just the waves and the sand. Quiet. Isolated. Perfect. A little further, and I pull into the tall metal gates around Crane Manor.

The big old mansion looms over the yard like a shadow, tall and beige with brown roofing tiles and shutters. A striking contrast from the bright green yard and flowering gardens surrounding it. The lawns are freshly mowed, the hedges trimmed this afternoon. An elegant fountain sits in the middle of the little stone courtyard in front of the front door.

There's no porch or patio on the front of the manor, just the front steps, but there's a pretty big deck out back with a grill and a pool and a dining table. It has a better view of the beach anyway, which is just outside the walls around the back yard.

The first time I brought Dave here, it took an entire month for me to convince him my dad isn't Batman. I had to explain to him that it was in the family. My dad's grandparents built it with funds from the agency and passed it down through the generations. Of course I didn't tell Dave about the agency part, but he bought the rest. Though, he still eyes my father suspiciously from time to time, muttering that he's Batman under his breath and refers to the place as Wayne Manor, which is ironic because my grandfather's (Mom's dad) name is Walter Wayne.

Anyway, Dave thinks he's slick, but he's really not. I caught him in the library once, trying to find the secret entrance to the Bat Cave. There *is* a secret entrance to the training facility in the basement, but it's not there.

I park my bike in the garage alongside Isaac's and then hook it up to the power source to charge for the night. Dad is standing in the kitchen, wearing the cheesiest of his aprons. It's black with a large magnifying glass on it and in white letters it says: 'I Spy Something Delicious'. A towel is draped over one of his broad shoulders and he has an oven mitt on each of his hands.

Dad is built like a lumberjack. Tall, muscular. He's a little over forty, but he looks like he could be in his mid-thirties. Kind brown eyes sit beneath dark brown eyebrows, his thick brown hair is neatly combed, and a short but dark beard shades his sharp jawline. Despite his somewhat menacing—no, that's not the right word—*intimidating* appearance, he's about the nicest guy you'll ever meet.

If you don't piss him off, that is.

"There's my girl! What's in the box?"

"Cupcakes. For my picnic with Dave." I open the fridge and slide them in to keep them cool until after dinner.

"Nice. I hope you don't mind if I sneak one." The oven beeps, and he turns his attention to it. "C.A.I.T.L.Y.N., tell Melissa dinner is just about ready."

"*Of course, sir,*" replies C.A.I.T.L.Y.N., our AI. She's our Caretaking Artificial Intelligence Technology and Logistical Youth Nurturer. Because who needs a babysitter when you have a robot, right? Well, she lacks physical form, but you get the idea. She's like our own personal female J.A.R.V.I.S.

"Hey baby sis." Isaac walks into the kitchen, straight to the fridge. "Ooh, cupcakes!"

"Not for you." I cross my arms.

"Miaaaaaaaa," he whines. Isaac is built a lot like Dad (tall, strong jawline, very muscular), but he gets most of his looks from Mom (blond hair, blue eyes, thick eyelashes that make all the girls swoon).

Although we have a no-one-hurts-my-sibling-except-me relationship, Isaac and I are pretty close. Closer than our other siblings, that is. It's been just the two of us since Jason (who we call Jace) left to study at one of F.O.U.N.D.'s bases in England three years ago. Nicole (more commonly known as Nikki) left the year before that to be a field agent in Australia.

Isaac is very protective, but only when it matters. I really don't know what I'd do without him, but I guess I'll find out when he leaves for F.O.U.N.D. Academy in the fall.

"You can have one. *After* dinner," I compromise. "And more later if there are leftovers."

"Yessss."

"Mia, Dave is on the front steps." Mom peeks into the kitchen. Her long blonde waves are pulled back into a ponytail. Mom is, well, Mom. She's nurturing, sweet, and gives the warmest hugs. That said, she's also the one that taught me how to throw knives, so...

"Thanks."

Just as I jog into the front room, the doorbell rings. I open the front door and let the biggest dork in the world inside. His wild brown curls frame his face, and thick plastic glasses rest on the bridge of his nose. A vintage Polaroid camera hangs around his neck on a rainbow strap.

"Happy anniversary, you beautiful girlfriend, you!" He snaps a picture of me and then hugs me while he fans the black film square, waiting for it to develop. "That one's a keeper."

"Happy anniversary, dork."

"Well." Dad walks into the living room. "Nice to see you, Dave."

"You too, Mr. Crane, sir." Dave plays with his hands, eyes flitting around. An entire year and he still hasn't gotten over his fear of my father. It's kind of cute, although it might have to do with the fact that he still kind of thinks I'm Batman's daughter. That would scare the pants off of any of the nerds in Dave's circle.

"David!" Mom envelops him in her arms. He hugs her back. "How's your mom doing?"

"Mom's doing fine. Thanks, Mrs. Crane."

"How's it going, bro?" Isaac takes his hand and they perform their little handshake.

"Pretty great...bro."

The oven dings.

"I'll get the food and meet the rest of you on the patio." Dad returns to the kitchen. I grab Dave's hand and pull him along. And we, like puzzle pieces, fall into our places in this seemingly perfect cookie-cutter cereal commercial family.

CHAPTER 2

"That was an incredible meal, sir."

"Well thank you, but the chicken did all the work." Dad chuckles in amusement at his own lame joke.

I can't help but smile, rolling my eyes. The phone rings in the house. Mom excuses herself and gets up to answer it.

"Now," Dad takes a breath and looks over at the curly-haired nerd, "I'm sure Mia told you about the yearly camping trip."

"Right. You leave this week, sir."

"Monday morning, bright and early. So...Melissa and I were talking, and, since you and Mia have been together for so long, we were wondering if maybe you wanted to come with us. I know it's kind of last-minute, but—"

"For real?" Dave's face lights up with an excited smile.

I have the same question, but not with nearly as much enthusiasm. I think maybe Mom and Dad forgot that we go camping with another family of agents. In a camp full of F.O.U.N.D. spies. As if bringing Dave camping on F.O.U.N.D.'s campsite wasn't enough of a risk of blowing our perfect-cereal-commercial-family cover, sticking him in a cabin with not one, but two families of F.O.U.N.D. agents is basically handing him an autobiography by the Crane family titled: 'Hey, We're Spies!'

"Yeah bro. For real." Isaac nods, and winks.

I plaster an insincere smile on my face. How can they think this is a good idea? It's not like I ever asked to take him. As far as I know, this just popped up out of nowhere.

"I mean, I'll have to ask my mom, but I think that'd be awesome!" Dave gets up from the table and throws his arms around

Dad, who chuckles and pats his back. "Thank you so much." His voice is a muffled mumble, the sound trapped in the fabric of Dad's shirt.

"No problem." Dad smiles at me, shaking his head at my adorable boyfriend.

I look at him with a face that says 'what gives?' Or, more precisely: What are you thinking?! Have you gone insane?! Rogue?! What's wrong with you?!

'I'll tell you later.' he signs behind Dave's back. I nod, plastering a fake smile on my face once more. Mom walks back onto the patio.

"Mia, Aunt Sheila called. Make sure you call her back later." Mom takes a seat just as Dave pulls away from Dad.

And no, Sheila isn't really my aunt. That's just what we say when Dave is here. Another lie in the tangled, twisted web. It's probably just a briefing for my mission tomorrow.

"Okay, will do." I nod, folding my napkin on the table and standing up. "You have the picnic basket, Curly?"

"Yeah. It's inside. With your super-awesome top-secret anniversary present."

He waggles his eyebrows suggestively and grabs his basket off of the table in the middle of the front room. I pull the box of cupcakes out of the fridge and pick his present off of the kitchen counter.

We walk past the patio, around the pool, through the wooden gate on the back wall, and down the stone path to the beach. My bare feet sink into the sand, toes wiggling, digging deeper into the grainy shore. We set our things on the beach and I help him spread the checkered blanket.

He sits down first, crossing his legs. I take a seat in his lap. He lets out a little gasp, surprised by the sudden weight. I laugh, reaching back to ruffle his thick brown curls with my fingers. His arms wrap tight around my waist, thumbs tracing gentle circles on my hips.

For a moment, we're both quiet, just watching the waves, listening. I close my eyes and take a few deep breaths. A calm breeze sweeps by, deepening the pure beach bliss.

"You ready for your super-awesome top-secret anniversary present?"

I nod, turning my head to kiss his cheek, but my lips find his instead. "I want to give you yours first."

"Okay."

I place a large box wrapped in *Star Wars* wrapping paper in his hands. He reaches around me, tearing it open only to reveal a plain cardboard box. It's taped shut. He uses his car key to unseal it and inhales an excited breath at the sight of the contents.

Nerd. Heaven.

There are lots of movies and books and comic books, along with a limited-edition Spider-Man comic autographed by—

"Stan Lee? Is this real? How did you—?"

"Let's just say I know a guy."

"Oh my God, no way!" He kisses my cheeks and my lips over and over and over, hugging me tight while repeating his thanks a million times.

"You're very welcome."

"Okay, okay, now open yours." Dave presses a small velvet box into my hands. It's navy blue, covered in little rhinestones that glitter like stars. I open it slowly. Inside, tucked into the fabric is a simple silver band engraved with the words 'I love you'.

"Awww, Dave," I cover my mouth with my hand, "this is perfect."

"Wait 'til you see mine." Dave holds his hand in front of me, wearing a matching ring that I hadn't noticed until now. Instead of saying 'I love you' like mine, his says 'I know'. A *Star Wars* reference hidden inside a romantic gesture.

What. A. Dork.

"You nerd!" I laugh kissing his nose before holding our hands up together in front of the sea.

"Thought you might like it."

"I do. I really do."

Dave rests his chin on my shoulder, fingers lacing through mine. He hums. His camera clicks. He holds the fresh picture between his fingers, shaking it as it slowly develops.

"How did I end up with the best girlfriend in the world?"

"Oh hush." I shake my head. "Someday, you'll know everything about me, and you won't think that anymore."

"Yeah right. Nothing could change my mind. Ever."

"You and I both know I've got some skeletons in the closet. You sure you're ready for that?"

"Without a doubt." He reaches into the picnic basket and pulls out a small container of chocolate-covered strawberries. My favorite. He takes a small bite before asking quietly, "Tell me a secret."

"A secret?" I take a strawberry from the box, sucking on the chocolate. "Okay. Um..." I pause for a long time. I have tons of secrets. Just none I'm legally allowed to tell him. "I...well, I speak Russian."

"No way."

"Yes way." I nod. The words flow out fluently. "[*There's so much I would like to tell you, my love.*]"

He visibly jolts, taken aback, but also in awe. "Holy shit! That's so cool! My girlfriend is a secret badass!"

"I am a badass, but it's no secret, hot shot." I wink, taking another strawberry from the box. "Okay, now you tell *me* a secret."

"I didn't know your name was Amelia until like four months ago," he blurts quickly, his cheeks reddening from emb-arrassment.

"You what?!" I burst with laughter. "How?!"

"I don't know!" He offers a sheepish smile. "Mia just made sense! I didn't think it was short for anything!"

"Dork." I elbow him lightly in the chest.

"I deserve that."

"You're lucky you're cute."

"True." He's quiet for a minute, thinking. His clear blue eyes are focused far away, fixed on the horizon. "M?"

"Hmm?"

"I love you."

I grin, unable to resist the urge. "I know."

CHAPTER 3

Dave stays over for a few hours longer before going home. After I take a shower, get settled into my pajamas, and have a long chat with Dad about my concern with Dave coming on the camping trip (which he simply waves off and says Headquarters approved it), I call Sheila back. C.A.I.T.L.Y.N. opens up a video chat on the TV screen in my bedroom.

Sheila Dormer, my F.O.U.N.D. administrator, looks as she always does, beautifully professional. Her straight sandy locks are pulled up into a crisp bun, high cheekbones dusted with light pink blush. Her favorite shade of bright red lipstick gives her smooth tanned face a pop of color.

For an administrator, Sheila's unusually young. She's only in her early forties, whereas most administrators are well into their fifties by the time they quit doing field work. I don't know what made her give it up so soon. Maybe it was an injury she couldn't bounce back from or a traumatic experience that never really left her. Whatever it was, she never talks about it. It just kind of looms over us. Unspoken, but acknowledged.

"Hello, Agent Crane," she greets, her voice smooth and clear. "How was your anniversary?"

"It went really well, thanks."

"That's great. Now, about your mission tomorrow." Sheila doesn't stray from the point very long. She means business. She always means business. "I talked with the other girls and sent them their files. Yours should be printing out as we speak."

The screen splits, showing Sheila's face on half of it and a building from downtown Great City on the other half. It's a big place, very grand, newly renovated. A huge sign along the front of the building reads: 'The Louis Orville State Theater' in curly golden letters dotted with bright lightbulbs. It feels like it was ripped right off of Broadway.

"This is the Louis Orville State Theater, a branch of Orville Enterprises. The building, along with the rest of the company, is owned by a wealthy entrepreneur named Louis Orville II."

The slide of the theater switches to show a skyscraper I recognize from the Great City skyline.

"This tower is one of five identical Orville Enterprises Headquarters scattered around the country. He also owns a plethora of other smaller companies and businesses; namely, Lucky's Ice Cream Shop, a fishing company down by the docks, an ice skating rink, a packaging plant, and Bethany Orville Memorial Park."

"Rich-business-guy complex, huh?"

"You could say that. We suspect Orville has been out to get the agency for quite some time now, but his rumored plot has only recently been brought to light. We need you and Agents Laurence and Williams to bring back as much intel as possible. Do a full sweep of the place and bring anything you can get your hands on back to the agency for further analysis."

"Just intel, then."

"At the moment, though we suspect things won't be this simple for long." The other half of the screen slides out of the picture, leaving only Sheila standing in front of the F.O.U.N.D. logo. "Retrieve your files from the printer in your office and read up. There isn't much this time around, just information on Orville and all of the notes we have on the layout of the theater. Oh, and get some rest. You have a long day ahead of you."

"Thanks, Administrator Dormer." I offer a little salute. "Night."

"Goodnight."

The monitor fades to black. I slip into my Kim Possible slippers and head downstairs to the office. Isaac is already here, leaning against a desk while he retrieves papers from the other printer.

"You too, huh?"

"Yep." He gathers his things. "Headed to the docks to check out a place called Louie's Buoy. Apparently the agency has reason to believe it's a nest for Russian mercenaries. At least four of them. Probably more. You know how it is. There are never *just* four Russian mercenaries."

"That wouldn't happen to be owned by a Mr. Louis Orville II, would it?"

"Indeed it is."

"Summer, Ginger, and I are going to check out his theater tomorrow afternoon."

"Well, if Mr. Orville is up to no good after all, he has one hell of an ass-whooping coming his way." Isaac chuckles, shaking his head. "Who knows how many teams they're dispatching tomorrow?"

"At least two. But there are never *just* two."

"You know it." Isaac pauses, his smirk fading to a more grim expression. "Hey, M."

"Yeah?"

"Just be careful, alright?"

"Will do."

A hand drifts to my ear, fingers rubbing against the plastic hearing aid lodged there. Finally, the printer spits out the last of my papers. I slide them into a folder.

"Well, goodnight, baby sis. Sounds like we're both going to need it. May your mission be successful and your sleep be...I don't know, sleepy or something."

"Goodnight you big dork." I chuckle.

He gives my shoulder a pat before leaving me alone in the office. I glance over my papers for a few seconds before closing the folder and heading up to my room. By the looks of it, tomorrow is going to be a loooong day.

CHAPTER 4

Summer, Ginger, and I arrive at the scene wearing F.O.U.N.D. undercover uniforms: agency-issued bulletproof leather jackets, colored t-shirts, dark blue skinny jeans and knee-high boots. Since we're out in public going to watch a play, we can't be seen out in our full leather gear. It's still hot, but not quite as bad.

The woman at the door takes our ticket stubs and lets us through without so much as a suspicious glance. The lobby is incredible. High ceilings, low lighting, glittering crystalline chandeliers, and colorful murals and sculptures all around. It's very modern. By the looks of it, Orville put his money to good use.

"Holy...Wow." Ginger whispers in awe. She takes a pair of glasses out of her bag and slides them up her nose, tapping the frames a few times as she looks around. To any onlooker, they look like regular, run of the mill glasses, but Ginger has an entire super-computer in there. An invention of our brilliant friend Brian Martin, who I'm sure will come into play soon. "Nice place."

"You can say that again." I pretend to text someone on my F.O.U.N.D. phone while actually hacking into the theater's security feed. Out of the three of us, I'm the best hacker without a doubt. Summer can do some serious damage when need be, but my fingers fly across keyboards faster than anyone I know. Except my older brother Jace. He types at practically the speed of light. I'm good, but I'm not *that* good. Then again, that's why he's a hacker by profession and I am but a humble field agent.

"Three guards at the door. By the look of it, they're armed."

"Mia, can you read their lips from here?"

"The tall one said 'all clear, sir.' into his earpiece. They have no clue we're here."

"Good. Let's keep it that way." Ginger lifts her glasses off of her eyes and rests them on the top of her head. "Um, Mia?"

"Yeah?" I don't look up from my phone, still punching commands into my hacking program as fast as my fingers will move.

"Dave is here."

Everything stops. My fingers hover above my screen for a few seconds while I pick up the pieces of my shattered thoughts.

"What?" I whip around.

Sure enough, there he is, standing with his mom. They're talking as they walk into the lobby.

"Shitshitshitshitshit." I turn around before he spots me, but it's only a matter of time. "This is not happening."

"Oh, it's happening." Summer uses her compact to look behind us while pretending to powder her cheeks with blush. "He's coming. He sees us."

"Shit," I repeat. "Is it too late to abort?"

"Yes. Yes it is." Ginger sifts through the data at her fingertips, but with the glasses on, it just looks like she's squinting at everything. "I can't believe in the year since you two have been together, this is only the first time this has happened."

My heart races in my chest. Dave approaches, wrapping an arm around my waist. I kiss his cheek, quick to click off my phone and shove it into my pocket.

"Hey girls. What are you doing here?"

"Oh, just here for the show." I shrug. "Didn't expect you to be here."

"Same." He glances down at my ticket. "Where are your seats?"

"Somewhere in the back."

"Aww dang, Mom and I are down in the front."

The lobby lights flash. A signal that the show is starting soon.

"That's our cue. I guess we better head inside."

"Yeah." Dave nods. He pecks my lips, quick but meaningful. The type of kiss that still manages to make my heart do a little flip. "See you later?"

"Definitely," I lie, smiling when he peels away to walk in with his mom. Summer sighs in relief.

"That was kind of close."

"You're telling me."

We walk into the auditorium and take our seats. The chairs are plush and comfortable, laid in neat rows, rounded at the corners. A wide balcony stretches overhead. Three large sparkling chandeliers hang from the ceiling, and the stage is framed by long velvet curtains. Set pieces are scattered around: a few bales of hay, large wooden crates, wooden barrels, and a piece that looks like an old farm house, ready for the show. Soon they'll be part of Dorothy Gale's farm for the opening of the Wizard of Oz.

The theater doors shut and lock, trapping us inside. The armed guards from the lobby are stationed at each exit. Average people would look at them and only see ushers, dressed in sharp black suits, but we notice the little things: the earpieces with the coiled wires, the slight bulge in their lower jackets, where their guns are ready to eliminate us if need be.

I grab the girls' attention before signing 'Four guards. Armed. Two at each door. No way out.'

'We'll figure it out. We always do.' Summer signs back, her hands moving almost as quickly as mine. We've all had eight years to get used to using sign language and it certainly comes in handy in times like this.

'We need to look around more during the intermission and maybe sneak off for Act II. My glasses are getting a weird scan from one of the rooms attached to the lobby.'

'Great. Now we just have to avoid Dave.'

'Easier signed than done.'

The show is the best rendition of the Wizard of Oz I've ever seen. The Wicked Witch has a laugh that sends chills down my spine, Dorothy's singing voice is as smooth as velvet, and the effects are impressive to say the least. The Wicked Witch's broom flies on wires, and Glinda enters in a floating bubble. However, despite the amazing play, this place has a lot to hide, and we have to get to the bottom of it.

As soon as the curtains close and the lights come up for intermission, we book it to the lobby, desperate not to be spotted by Dave so we can sneak off and continue the mission as scheduled.

"Over here." Ginger motions. We follow her to a locked door. I look around for guards, but all of them are out of sight around the corner. "Mia, work your magic."

I kneel in front of the doorknob. It only takes a few seconds for me to get it open. The tech department has tried to hook us up with machines to pick the locks for us, but I've raced and won against every gadget and gizmo they set in front of us. It's my secret weapon, and the bane of Brian Martin's existence.

The three of us rush into the room, quickly closing the door behind us before we can be followed. It's a large room, storage by the looks of it. Brown cardboard boxes are stacked in piles that nearly reach the ceiling. Filing cabinets line the walls, and a table in the corner of the room has a dozen thumb drives laid out on a computer station.

"See what you two can find in the files and boxes. I'm going to download as many of these thumb drives as I can." I take my own personal drive out of my bag and hook it into a USB port on the computer, plugging one of the other drives in right beside it. Hopping past the firewall doesn't take too long, though it's more complicated than I expected it to be. Mr. Orville's programmers know what they're doing. Unfortunately for them, so do I.

"Hey, M?" Concern laces Summer's tone.

"Yeah?"

"Can you come take a look at this?"

"Give me a second." I punch in three more lines of code before stepping away from the computer. "What is—oh my God."

Ginger hands me a metal briefcase. There's a round logo on the side of it, not unlike the F.O.U.N.D. logo: a circular gear around a gridded earth with a microscope inside of it. On the gears there's an inscription. League of Science and Technology.

"What the hell?" Ginger looks over my shoulder.

"I'm getting all sorts of weird readings from it. There's something inside. Something dangerous." The sensor in her hand, which looks like no more than a small remote with a thin metal antenna attached to the end, beeps and whirs in what sounds like a tiny robotic panic attack.

"We should take it with us. Summer, your purse is definitely big enough, right?"

"Big enough for two. Give me another." She slips them inside the large pink bag hanging from her shoulder. I return to the computer where the same logo is displayed. Someone is hacking into the computer remotely, and this time it's not me. I eject my flash drive quickly, scooping up the others and tossing them into my bag.

"We have to get out of here. Now. Someone broke my firewall. They know we're here."

"Shit. Well, I guess we'll just have to kick some Orville ass on a later date." Ginger cracks her knuckles and rolls her neck.

"You could say that again." Summer fixes her lip gloss in her mirror. She snaps it shut with a click. "We'll have to come back and check it out when there are less people here."

"Right. In the meantime, let's take these back to Headquarters. I have a feeling Sheila will want to get her hands on these."

CHAPTER 5

"How was the mission, girls?" Greta is rolling out a ball of sugar cookie dough on the bakery counter when we walk in the back door.

"Good." Summer leans against the counter. "Found some nifty briefcases full of mystery weapons and about a dozen flash drives that somehow wound up in Mia's purse."

"I panicked." I open my purse to show her.

Greta shrugs. "Better safe than sorry. Back in my day, we stole an entire filing cabinet one time. Sounds ridiculous, but I have the records to prove it."

"Oh my God." I laugh. "That's hilarious."

"There was no one around, why not? Johnny Crenshaw bet me three whole dollars we couldn't pull it off. We did, and then he treated us all to milkshakes after." A wistful sigh. Greta looks up and tilts her head to the side. "Anyways, aren't you supposed to be heading over to HQ now, ladies?"

"We're on our way there now, Mama G. Just thought we'd pop in for a sec." Ginger wraps her arm around Greta, resting her head on our mentor's shoulder as she continues to roll out cookie dough with her trusty wooden rolling pin.

Summer presses a kiss to the old woman's cheek. "We love you."

"I love you too." Greta laughs and motions to the elevator in the back of the kitchen. "Take the tunnels. It's faster."

"That's the plan."

"And grab a cookie on your way out." She winks.

We each take a heart-shaped sugar cookie and walk towards the elevator, riding down to the tunnels.

Great City has a subway system. Great City *also* has a F.O.U.N.D. tunnel system, which is basically the same thing, just a private circuit for agents who are moving around the city. All of the businesses owned and run by F.O.U.N.D. have a stop on the grid, and then there are a few stops that are connected to the other subway stations for a broader spectrum of coverage. Four trains run the circuit all the time, so it never takes too long to catch one.

It looks like we're lucky this time. After only a few minutes of standing on the platform, headlights stream through the tunnel. Brakes screech as the train slows to a stop and the doors on the side of the car slide open.

We step on, taking seats beside the other agents on their way to Headquarters. There aren't very many. Thankfully, we've just beat the post-mission rush, and are much too early for the nightly dispatch. I have a feeling we won't be so fortunate on the way back to Sugar & Spice afterwards, though.

The bakery is one of the closest stops to Headquarters, so it only takes a few minutes to get there. The train pulls into the shiny metal tunnel and the doors on both sides of the passenger car open, letting off a trickle of agents walking up the stairs and riding the escalators into F.O.U.N.D.'s Great City Headquarters, our second home.

We find ourselves in the lobby. Three floors with walkways overlook the ground level. Bright white lights make it feel surreal, a little bit unnatural, like something straight out of a dream. There are receptionists stationed at each desk and security guards at each door. We sign in with our favorite receptionist, Cathy. She was never a field agent before this, just an intern, but she always offers us Twizzlers from her top-secret candy drawer. She's awesome.

After signing in, with licorice in hand, we take the elevators up to the administration department and walk into Sheila's office.

"Good afternoon, girls," she greets.

Large glowing holograms are projected above the glass table in the center of the office. She waves her hands, dismissing whatever she was working on and motions for us to sit down and give her our follow-up. I empty the contents of my purse onto the table, straightening the flash drives into a neat row. Summer and Ginger each set a metal briefcase in front of them. After we hack into the electronic locks, they pop open easily.

Each case has four syringes embedded in foam and filled with liquids of varying colors. Both of them contain a matching color sequence: pink, purple, orange, lime-green. They're labeled beneath as R-1, R-2, R-3, and R-4. A series. Medication perhaps? Or something much more potent? A chemical meant to alter life as we know it, meant to bring civilization to its knees? Or it could just be the cure for the common cold. What do I know?

"Woah."

"Yeah." Summer's eyebrows crinkle in concern. "Administrator Dormer, what do you think they are?"

"I have no idea." Sheila's lips press into a thin line, her face stern, eyes fixed on the syringes full of God-knows-what.

She's silent for a long time, thinking. We don't dare touch them, scared of the endless capabilities contained in these plastic tubes.

Sheila drums her red-painted fingernails on the case of her tablet a few times before tapping and swiping with her stylus. The printer at her desk hums to life, spitting out a pink lab slip and a drop card for the intelligence department. She fills both of them out before scooping the flash drives into a bag and handing them to us.

Summer skims over the lab slip.

"I want you to take the briefcases to the science wing. Just stick the drives in the intel drop box at the end of the hall."

"Will do." I nod. "Thanks, Sheila."

"No, thank *you*. I have a feeling you girls might have brought home all the answers we need. Or at least a few of them."

We leave the office, dropping off the flash drives and continuing downstairs to the science wing. We check into Lab 32, walking past rows of science agents hard at work, mixing chemicals, testing compounds, creating weapons like knock-out gas and technological enhancements for our gear.

All of the scientists are dressed in pristine white lab coats with their IDs hooked to lanyards around their necks. Some are wearing rubber gloves and goggles, concentrating on the work in front of them. Others read papers, sift through binders while bouncing their legs against their stools or drumming their fingers on the table.

In the very back of the room is our favorite resident nerd, Brian Martin.

"Not one, not two, but three field agents at my station. Surprised you didn't get lost. Science wing isn't exactly your area of expertise," he teases, pushing his thick plastic-rimmed glasses further up the bridge of his nose, magnifying his light brown eyes. Brian's bright red hair is slicked over, and a bright green bowtie adds a much-needed pop of color to his plain outfit consisting of a white dress shirt, khakis, and a pristine lab coat.

"Oh hush. We come here plenty." I roll my eyes.

He only grins. Admittedly, Brian is one of the only science nerds I have the pleasure of talking to on a regular basis. He's our assigned specialist, so we see him at least once a week when he has to analyze all of the junk we bring him.

"What wonderful field agent finds do you have in store for me today, ladies?"

"Unknown chemicals recovered from the Louis Orville State Theater." Summer opens the briefcase.

Brian wiggles his rubber-gloved fingers, eager to get to work. "There's four of them."

"I know how to count, Agent Laurence." Brian remarks, earning a smirk and a smack in the arm.

"I told you, we're the same age. It's just weird. Call me Summer like everyone else."

"I only call you that because it bugs you." He pauses and a sly smirk creeps over his lips. "Agent Laurence."

Another smack in the arm.

"We found about a dozen flash drives there too, so the intel department should have some files for you soon regarding whatever the hell that is." I set the other briefcase on the table. Brian's eyes drift to the logo on the front of it.

"League of Science and Technology? Never heard of them before. You found this in the theater?"

"Hopefully the flash drives will have something about that too."

"Well, it's been nice, but we should get going...anywhere but here." Ginger jabs a thumb towards the door.

"Glad to see I'm loved, guys." Brian chuckles.

Summer pecks his cheek playfully, causing his face to flush bright red and rendering him speechless. "You are very much appreciated, Bri. We just have places to be and things to do."

"Um, b-bye." he stumbles when Ginger and I start to walk back towards the door. Summer jogs to catch up, blonde waves bouncing with each step. What a flirt.

"I can't help but get the feeling that whatever was in there isn't good." I glance back at Brian.

He waves a flustered little salute before we leave.

"Well, if anyone can figure it out, it's him."

CHAPTER 6

"**W**ait, Dad and Mom are *what*?!" Nikki asks incredulously.

She and I are in the middle of our weekly video chat, and I just told her that Mom and Dad invited Dave to come on the yearly camping trip. Her face looks exactly the way I feel about the whole thing.

"You're kidding. No way."

"Yes way."

"Nope. I don't believe you. No possible way our parents, Agent Crane and Agent Crane, or the agency they work for, for that matter, would ever let a civilian teenage boy onto the camping site. They would never—"

"I know. It's crazy. I talked to Dad about it and he said he already talked to Aunt Valentina and Uncle Romero, but still. Dave in the woods with two families of operatives isn't exactly what I'd call vacation. I mean, he's already suspicious of me, this is definitely not going to help matters. Anyway, they already invited him and he's really excited, so it's not like we can just un-invite him."

"Very true." She nods.

Her dirty blonde hair is pulled up to a messy bun and her necklace with a silver 'N' glares in the light of her lap-top. In the background, the real reason she's stationed in Australia walks through. Her fiancé Ethan.

Ethan Shipp, my sister's soon-to-be husband is incredibly attractive. A muscular surfer in his mid-twenties with seafoam green eyes, dark brown hair, and a dusting of stubble across his chiseled jawline. However, despite his gorgeous looks, he doesn't have a lot going on up there, if you know what I mean.

"Oh hey Mia!" He jogs over to the laptop and sits on the couch beside Nikki, pressing a kiss to her cheek and taking her hand in both of his. "How's it hanging, littlest Crane?"

"Not so well. Dave is coming on the camping trip."

"Isn't that good news?"

"Dave isn't an agent, babe," Nikki reminds him.

"Oh yeeeah..." Ethan nods, remembering. "Well, good luck with that. The waves are picking up. I'll be out on the beach." It might be 9 pm here, but it's not even noon there.

"Bye, Ethan."

"How's the packing coming?" Nikki asks once her fiancé leaves.

I roll up another t-shirt and shove it into my suitcase. "Pretty well. I'm almost done."

"Hey, um...You heard from Jace lately?"

"Not this last week. Why?"

"Nothing," she lies.

"Nikkiiiiii,"

"Okay, okay. Ethan and I were assigned the other day to check out this café by the harbor. Apparently, some guy named Louis Orville owns it. Jace is a hacker, so I was wondering if he had heard anything else about it or the larger plot going on here. My admin is being weird and secretive."

"Louis Orville is from Great City. He owns a bunch of businesses here. Summer, Ginger, and I were sent to his theater and we found these metal—"

"Metal briefcases? Yeah. Us too."

Chills run up my spine, goosebumps prickling my arms. There's something offsetting in my sister's words. This is bigger than we thought. No wonder Sheila was so relieved we brought back so much intel.

"With what inside?"

"Four syringes with this weird liquid. A series or something, I don't know. The science division is checking it out, but I haven't heard anything."

"Same here."

"Shit." Nikki rakes her fingers down her face, exhaling a long breath. "If this guy, thing, League, *whatever* is international, then—"

"Yeah. This is bad."

"Well, on that happy note, I've gotta go. We're supposed to be at Headquarters in half an hour and we haven't even had lunch yet." She glances out the door of their beach house where her fiancé is catching waves instead of being productive. "Sometimes I think his brains are in his biceps. But I love him."

"See you soon."

"Yep."

The screen fades to black, displaying 'call ended' and a frowny face. I stare at it for a long time, thinking. Maybe Nikki was right to try to get ahold of Jace. This is bigger than any of the administrators probably wanted us to know. If there's anyone who's willing to poke his nose where he knows it doesn't belong, it's my eldest brother. He's not a field agent, but rebellion runs in his blood.

I snap out of it, shaking my head. After rolling a few more t-shirts and shorts and packing them away, I make my way down to the kitchen to grab granola bars and trail mix. Isaac is perched on the counter, tending to his arm with the first aid kit, stitching it up on his own.

"What are you doing?"

"Got shot. Didn't notice 'til I got home." He doesn't look up at me when he replies, carefully using the tweezers to guide the needle in and out of his skin.

"Doesn't that hurt? Like a lot?"

"Nah," he lies casually. "It's just a scratch."

"Bull shit."

"You talk to Nikki?" A quick subject change.

"Yeah."

"What'd she say? Anything about the League?"

"Yeah." I nod. "She and Ethan found briefcases there too. Same four syringes full of the same four chemicals."

"That's not good."

"No." I pause. "Isaac, can I ask you for advice?"

"Sure, baby sis. What's up?" He sets down the medical supplies, giving me his full attention.

"You've had lots of girlfriends before, right?"

"More than I can count. Believe me, I've tried."

"Okay, but...all of your girlfriends have been agents."

"Yeah. Well, not Emily. She was from the science division."

"You know what I mean, dumbass." I smirk. "You've never...Dave isn't exactly—"

"I know it's hard, M. It's hard not telling him everything. I get that." He pauses, chewing his lip. "But, you've been with him for a year. You love him. I know you do. Whether you were trying to or not, you broke rule number three."

"It's not about me not loving him. I do. A lot. But, someday he's going to find out. He's not stupid. He'll figure it out eventually, and when he does...He's going to hate me for lying to him."

"Do you really think Dave, *your* Dave could ever hate you?"

"Well, no. But—"

"Your Dave. The one that's obsessed with super heroes and *Star Wars* and all things nerdy. When he finds out his girlfriend, his *girlfriend* is a super-spy, I don't think he'll hate you. He's going to probably bombard you with questions and ask to try out all of our gadgets, but I don't think he could ever come close to hating you. Especially since you've been protecting him this whole time."

"You really think so?"

"I know so." Isaac chuckles to himself. "And I bet you ten dollars that the first thing he asks is if you know James Bond."

I shake my head, laughing.

"You laugh now, but you know I'm right."

"We'll see about that." I hop off of the counter, walking to the cupboard to grab granola bars for my backpack. "Thanks. I needed that."

"I know you did." He shrugs, resuming his stitches. "That's my job, right?"

"Maybe if we're lucky, we won't completely blow our cover on this trip."

"We'll see about that." Isaac chuckles and shakes his head. "I guess we really have our work cut out for us, huh?"

"You could say that again."

CHAPTER 7

A three-hour drive north takes us to F.O.U.N.D.'s camping grounds: Secret Falls, so named for the waterfalls at the mouth of the river that runs into the lake. Dad pulls into the driveway in front of cabin 317, parking the car. Dave jolts awake, slowly removing his head from my shoulder. A chuckle slips from my mouth.

"Morning, Sleeping Beauty." I tease, poking his cheek. He groans and stretches like a cat, a yawn escaping him.

"Are we there yet?"

"Mmhmm." My hand slips into his, his large but gentle fingers clumsily lacing between mine.

A small and tired smile tugs at his lips. I sneak a kiss to the corner of his mouth before tugging him out of the car after me. Dave uses one of his hands to shield his eyes from the sun and looks up at our cabin.

"Woah," he murmurs, eyes searching the huge wooden structure. He lifts his Polaroid to his eye, snapping a picture. Dave hands the dark sticky square to me and I shake it as it slowly lightens.

From the outside of the building, it looks almost rustic with a log cabin feel. Long windows stretch over the walls, floor to ceiling, and a stone chimney sticks out of the brown-tiled roof, billowing smoke from the fireplace inside. A large patio wraps around to the back of the building, connecting to the docks on the lake. From here, I can make out thin zip lines that connect the four tall wooden towers around the campsite. The shooting range isn't far from here, and the obstacle course is closer yet.

I know this place like the back of my hand. We've been coming here every year since before I could walk, and though I'm a bit afraid to show Dave around for fear of blowing everything I've worked so hard to hide, I can't deny that I'm excited to be back.

"Come on, Curly." I pull him towards the path. He tucks the picture of the cabin into his pocket and slings his duffle bag over his shoulder, adjusting to its weight. We walk toward the front door, his hand tightening ever so slightly in mine. My free hand closes around the silver doorknob and pushes the door open. Ah, cabin 317. It's good to be home again.

Tall orange flames crackle in the stone fireplace set into the back of the cabin. The windows on the wall around it give an excellent view of the lake. Plushy couches and chairs are arranged in a U around the coffee table. To the right, there's a kitchen complete with nice wooden cabinets and stainless steel top-of-the-line appliances. Along the left wall is the staircase to the second floor, where all of the bedrooms are.

We drop off our bags in our rooms and meet Mom, Dad, and Isaac back in the living room. Isaac motions me over and starts signing, which generally means something related to the agency is going down and we can't exactly tell Dave about it. But a perk of my hearing problems is this: a secret form of communication that Dave still struggles to understand.

'Aunt Valentina called Dad. They ran into a little trouble on the way up, but they'll be here in time for lunch.'

'I'm going to take Dave out for a walk through the woods. We'll be back in like an hour.'

Dave watches, eyes fixed on our quickly moving hands. After so many years of practice, it's practically my second language, though in my case it's more like my fifth. Maybe Dave might catch a word here or there, but for the most part, he has no idea what's going on.

'Sounds good. Don't get lost. Avoid the secret spy base if you can.'

'No shit.' I chuckle, signing goodbye before taking Dave outside.

"Aren't your aunt and uncle coming?"

"They're on their way here. Ran into traffic." I explain simply. I mean, technically, if you count a car chase as traffic, it's not a lie.

"Well, in that case," Dave bends down in front of me, facing forward. His arms reach back towards me. Then, in the worst British accent I've ever heard: "Fancy a piggy-back ride, milady?"

"Don't mind if I do, you huge dork." I climb onto his back, his hands gripping my thighs to hold me up.

Dave's old tennis shoes sink into the soft dirt path beneath us. Bright green leaves rustle in the trees overhead, not yet touched by the amber hues of fall. God, I missed this place. I missed the simplicity of the woods; owls calling in the firefly-filled evening, the sunsets reflecting on the lake, bright and orange and so alive. When you spend enough time in a dead metal skyscraper, you start to miss the life this place has. And if it were my choice, I would live out here full-time.

"You okay? You zoned out on me." Dave checks, a soft smile tugging at his soft lips.

Oh, what I wouldn't do to pin him to a tree and kiss him senseless. Maybe later we can sneak off, but at the moment, there are too many agents and too many cameras for us to pull off something like that in broad daylight.

"Oh, yeah, sorry." I shake my head, ignoring my burning cheeks.

He laughs. I don't fluster easily, but when Dave's around, I'm like putty in his hands. A good kind of vulnerable.

"So what do you guys usually do on this huge camping trip anyways? Your dad makes it sound like a big deal."

"Oh believe me, it is. Aunt Valentina, Uncle Romero, and their three kids share the cabin with us. They're a ton of fun, but we don't get to see them very often. Lucia and Mateo are around our age. They're all really excited to meet you."

"You told them about me?"

"It might have slipped out. Along with the fact that you're a dork."

"But I'm your dork."

"Yes. Yes you are."

We walk around the woods for a while, down a few paths, past a few places we'll visit later in the week. I show him some of my records on the scoreboard at the shooting range and take him by the giant obstacle course. It's always full of agents, so we usually head down there at night or really early in the morning when it's not as crowded.

After about an hour and a half, we make our way back to the cabin, immediately taking notice of the red SUV sitting in the driveway. The Hernandezes have arrived. They're not really family, just family friends. Mom was Valentina's partner back in the day. Our families have been camping together for ages. But since my real aunts and uncles live so far away, it's nice to have an agency family that I get to see a few times a year.

I hop down off of Dave's back and race into the house, my feet pounding against the pavement.

"Aunt Valentina!" I nearly tackle her to the floor.

She laughs. "There she is!" Valentina swings me around, my feet dangling in the air.

Valentina Hernandez is a very strong woman physically, mentally, and emotionally. She's tough as nails, not afraid to do whatever it takes and never willing to back down from a fight. But there's also kindness in her warm brown eyes.

"This must be David." Uncle Romero shakes Dave's hand, large biceps bulging when he reaches forward. One of his tattoos sticks out of the sleeve of his black t-shirt. It's a red rose with 'Valentina' written beneath it in fancy cursive letters.

"It's Dave, sir. Nice to meet you." Dave plays it cool, but I can see the fear in his eyes. No pep talk could have prepared him for this.

"What a cutie," Lucia Hernandez, my "cousin," grins, raising an eyebrow. "I'm Lucia. This is my bone-head hermano Mateo, and the most precious little girl on the planet, Marisol."

When she introduces the youngest sibling (only three years old) she pulls her up onto her hip, bringing her closer to Dave. He smiles, immediately going into Baby-Mode. Dave loves kids. Loves them. He babysits his little cousins a lot, so he knows exactly how to talk to them and get down to their level.

"So you're the boyfriend we've heard so much about." Mateo (my age, roughly. Younger than Lucia, but not by much) squints and takes a few steps closer. "Just do me a favor. If you're gonna make out with mi prima, do it while I'm not watching."

"I-I wasn't thinking about it." Dave coughs and takes a timid step back.

I grab his hand.

"Knock it off, Teo." Lucia punches her brother in the arm.

He scowls, still giving Dave the stink-eye.

"Well then, on that happy note," Mom interjects, motioning towards the kitchen. "Who wants lunch?"

CHAPTER 8

Large flames flicker in the campsite's shared fire pit late at night. I can feel the heat hot on my face, but it's not uncomfortable enough to make us move further away. Fireflies flash in the woods like little winged Christmas lights and the stars in the velvet sky reflect on the glassy lake. I missed this more than you could understand. Nights like these are one in a million, and with a job like mine, you can't take these moments for granted.

The fire pit is a melting pot full of other families here on their yearly getaway. It's a twenty-minute walk from our cabin, but worth the trip. Even the outsiders are welcome. Dave's clothes, a bright green shirt and orange shorts, give him away as a non-agent, whereas most of the others are dressed in red and black, the agency's preferred color palette. It's a wordless signal to the others not to talk about agency matters around him. It also broadcasts his colorblindness to the world.

Dave plops down onto the padded bench beside me. He sets a s'more on a plate in my lap and wraps a blanket around my shoulders. Gentle lips graze my cheek and his large hand envelopes mine, his thumb spinning the silver 'I love you' ring around and around and around my finger.

"So who are all of these people? You know them?"

"Some of them." I rest my head on his shoulder. "My parents' friends from work, mostly. The company gives them each a cabin out here for a few days so they can intermingle and unwind."

"Oh cool." He looks over at Lucia and Mateo, who are socializing with other agents. "Your cousins are pretty hardcore."

"Just wait for tomorrow, Curly. You haven't seen anything yet."

"Really?"

"Yeah." I take a bite of a gooey s'more. Melted marshmallow and chocolate drip onto the plate and stick to the corner of my mouth.

Dave's eyes drift to my lips. He stares for a long moment, mouth slightly agape and blue eyes drifting half-shut.

"You okay?" I laugh. I think I know exactly where his mind was wandering. Mine was headed in that direction too.

"Yeah, I just—"

I lean forward and capture his lips with mine, stealing a long kiss and then pressing a quick one to his nose. When we separate, he's got a stunned grin on his face. His glasses are crooked. The light of the campfire dances in the large rounded lenses that frame his eyes.

Out of nowhere, Marisol Hernandez tottles through the crowd of people and clambers up onto my lap. Her black hair is pulled up into two short pigtails and her big brown eyes look into mine. She sucks on her thumb.

"What are you doing here, sweetie?" I ask, poking her nose.

"Canny go cabab," she states, words muffled around her fist.

I raise an eyebrow.

"Cabin?" Dave seems to understand her without even having to think about it. He's like a baby translator. "You want to go back to the cabin?"

"Yeah." She nods.

I toss my plate into the trash and hold her on my hip. One arm holds her up and the other hand finds its way into Dave's. On the way up the stone stairs out of the fire pit, Lucia rests a hand on my chest, stopping me in place.

"She wants to go back to the cabin." I explain.

"I can take her if you want me to, chica."

"Nah, that's all right." I lean closer, keeping my voice low. "Dave and I might benefit from some alone time, if you know what I mean."

Lucia wears a dark smirk. "Oh, well in that case, by all means. Her bed is set up in our room."

"Okay. Thanks."

"And don't be...too loud when you—"

"Lucia!"

"Sorry, sorry," she laughs and then adds with a wink, "I'll see you tomorrow morning..."

"See ya."

Dave and I take Marisol through the woods, up the paths, and back into the cabin. I tuck her into bed, kiss her forehead, and plug in her sun-shaped nightlight before meeting Dave downstairs.

He's sitting on the couch, paging through one of the magazines from the coffee table, pretending like he's not waiting for me to get back.

"Marisol's out." I walk over and stand in front of him, looking down at him for a second before straddling his lap.

He tosses the magazine to the other side of the couch, gentle hands resting on my hips as mine sneak up to the soft skin of his neck. His pulse races against my fingers.

I press a chaste kiss to his lips and slip my hand into his thick brown curls. "And now that we're alone," I purr into his ear, "I was thinking: you, me, this couch...and a movie."

"Aw sweet, movie night? Cuddles included?"

"You know it." I kiss his nose. "And Lucia thought we were having sex. How boring is that?"

"Pretty boring." Dave nods. I get off of his lap and start to walk away from the couch, but he grabs my wrist. "Popcorn? Please?"

"That's where I'm going, silly."

"You're the best."

"Believe me," I wink before walking off towards the kitchen. "I know."

CHAPTER 9

Lucia and I get up bright and early the next morning and go for a run around the lake. We certainly aren't the only ones. The paths are filled with agents on their daily jogs, keeping in shape and on their workout schedule even on vacation, though not as vigorously as they would if they were still at Headquarters.

The morning fog floats over the lake, thick and hazy. The sun hasn't come up yet, but it's starting to peek over the horizon, just barely shining through the thick line of pine trees. The air smells like freedom. So clean and fresh, as opposed to the faint scent of car exhaust that always seems to linger in Great City.

By the time we get back to the cabin, Mateo and Isaac are leaving to go for a run too, and Dave is sitting at the dining room table, sipping coffee so tampered-with I can practically smell the sugar from here, out of a mug I painted when I was like seven years old. It's blood red with my name brushed onto it in sloppy black first-grade letters.

Property of Amelia Elizabeth Crane. Don't touch unless you want to lose a finger.

God, I haven't changed much. Little me was a tiny badass.

"Where'd you find that?" I tilt my head, laughing.

He smiles, setting it down and holding it between his hands. His curls are lopsided, a messy bedhead that I can't help but smile at. He's still in his pajamas, a light blue t-shirt and green plaid pajama pants.

"It was in the cupboard. My new favorite mug." His voice is still thick with sleep, noticeably deeper than it usually is. "I'm not gonna lose a finger for drinking out of it, am I? For the record, it was all I could find, but I hid the knives just in case."

"Hush, you." I give his curly head an affectionate shove. "I made that when I was in elementary school."

He smiles. "I know. It's a masterpiece."

"Dork."

"Do you wanna go for like a walk or something?" Dave points out the window. "I know you just got back, but I don't want to wander out there and get lost and then end up getting mauled by a bear or kidnapped by a band of wild wombats or—"

"This isn't Australia. If you wanna meet a band of wild wombats, I'll take you to visit my sister. Now go get changed." I give him a shove up the stairs and a few minutes to get dressed while I put my tennis shoes back on, and then we leave the cabin.

"All right, where are we going?" Dave stretches out his legs and twists his torso. "Shooting range? Obstacle course?"

"Nope."

He raises an eyebrow at my answer.

"It's a secret. Follow me." That seems to be enough to satisfy him.

He shrugs and then takes my hand as I take the lead.

I pull Dave down the mossy paths, taking a few turns here and there. The woods get darker and darker as we travel into the thickest circle of trees. I push hanging branches out of our path. It's a long, complicated journey, but I know the way like it's an extension of me. A lost part of my soul left behind here, a piece of my childhood, a shard of my being.

You can't find my secret place on any of the campsite maps. It's been long-forgotten, ignored and overgrown. The path isn't even a path anymore, just a set of footprints through the dirt. My footprints. And Nikki's. And now Dave's.

The familiarity of the marked paths are far behind us now, putting more and more distance between us and the lake at the center of camp. We step over dead branches and fallen leaves, swat at bugs that hover in little swarms. Finally, after our shoes are nice and dirty and we can barely see each other's faces in the blackened shadows of the trees, we arrive.

Nikki and I found this little safe haven, a vine-covered gazebo, when I was five and she was nine. It was an accident. We were really lost, but stumbled upon the not-as-overgrown wooden structure. Needless to say, it was perfect for adventuring. We were princesses living in a wooden castle, pirates sailing the forest green, or aliens on the way to a distant planet called Earth.

When we got older, it became a good spot for reading and talking about boys. We brought Christmas lights and strung them through the railing, hung an old metal lantern from the hook in the center and covered the wooden ceiling with cheap green glow-in-the-dark stars we found at the camp store attached to the Outpost.

I walk to the railing and plug the Christmas lights into the endless line of extension cords that stretches like tree roots beneath the ground all the way to the F.O.U.N.D. Outpost. The gazebo springs to life like something out of a movie, ripped from a world of whimsy and wonder and dropped down into ours. It's still covered in moss and leafy vines but it feels like a real life fairy tale.

"What *is* this place?" Dave walks in slowly, as though he's afraid it'll shatter at his touch. I trace the old wooden railing with the tip of my finger. He snaps a few pictures on his Polaroid and then tucks them away for safe keeping.

"Nikki and I found it a really long time ago. We think it was part of a park or something and just got so overgrown that no one cared to fix it up." I walk along the edge of it with Dave following timidly. "It's a good place to read or just think."

There's a long pause. The only sounds are the distant calls and whistles from the campsite behind us. A slow smile tugs at Dave's lips.

"May I have this dance, milady?" Dave sweeps into a deep and somewhat awkward bow and offers his hand. I slip mine into his, resting the other on his shoulder. His other arm wraps around my waist. He tries to start a waltz, but ends up stepping on my toes. We laugh, fumbling to find the footing. Eventually, we get the hang of it, stiff at first. It doesn't take long to fall into the pattern, stepping and turning fluidly through the seemingly-enchanted gazebo. It doesn't matter that there's no music aside from Dave's out-of-tune humming and the rhythm of our tennis shoes against the old wooden boards. We don't need anything but ourselves.

It feels like we're frozen in time, stuck in a perfect moment. There are no agencies. No guns and bullet wounds. No hand grenades and ticking time bombs. No deadlines. No requirements. Here, we don't have to be anything we don't want to be. I don't have to be Agent Crane, trained assassin and lethal field operative. Instead, I don the identity of Mia Crane, high school senior and ordinary teenage girl that owns way too many pairs of sweatpants and watches way too many Channing Tatum movies.

But moments like these are fleeting.

My phone buzzes, shattering the brief illusion of normalcy. A text from Isaac. There are pancakes waiting for us at the cabin. I tell Dave and immediately it becomes a race to get back first. Unsurprisingly, I beat him. I was considering letting him win, but in a house full of teenagers and spies, pancakes wait for no one. You either get there on time, or you don't get any at all.

Aunt Valentina stands at the stove, flipping pancakes like a pro. Uncle Romero stands beside her, catching them on a large plate and then distributing them to the rest of us.

"Mama, toss one over here," Mateo calls. Valentina rotates the pan in her hand, sliding it around a few more times before flipping a large, floppy pancake through the air and right onto Mateo's plate. Dave's face is one of pure unabashed amusement.

"Send two over here!" Lucia challenges, itching to one-up her brother. Valentina picks up another pan and delivers two flying pancakes in record time. Lucia catches both of them in the center of her plate seconds apart, one on top of the other in a perfect stack.

"Oh yeah?!" Mateo stands up. His hands slam down on the table, shaking the dishes and glasses full of orange juice in a sudden jolt. They clink against the wooden surface. I flinch. Not again.

"Yeah!"

"I'm just gonna stay out of this one," Isaac takes a not so subtle scooch away.

"So am I." Valentina rests the pans on the stove, taking off her oven mitt. "Save that energy for the obstacle course, hijos."

"The what now?" Dave asks.

Mateo rubs his hands together, raising an eyebrow. "Oh newbie, just you wait."

CHAPTER 10

The obstacle course stands tall above us, shining stainless steel and polished wood, ready to kick our asses. It was put together by the best agents there are, filled with spring traps and jets that shoot water to throw everyone off their game.

A deep pool sits beneath the course, full of agents who fell off or simply want to enjoy the cool water in the summer heat. A red buzzer is at the very top, gleaming in the sunlight in an almost teasing way. Anyone who makes it to the top gets a medal. Let's just say, barely anyone gets a medal. Not to brag or anything, but I have three.

Dave whistles, looking up at the spinning metal beast that looks like it's just itching to tear us to pieces.

"It's even more terrifying from this angle."

"Yeah."

"Wow."

"Yeah."

"Oh, it's not so bad." Mateo rolls his neck and cracks his wrists. "Race you to the top."

"You're going down, Hernandez." Isaac stretches.

"In your dreams, Crane."

"Hey boys, try not to cry too hard when Mia and I beat both of you, all right?" Lucia smirks, putting her hair up.

"What do I do?" Dave's wide blue eyes flit from agent to agent. Obviously he stands no chance against this hellish course. Even I've only beaten it a handful of times in all of my years. And while it is very challenging, I can't deny that it's pretty fun. Sure, you get bruised and beaten and thrown around some, but it's never killed anyone. That I know of. It's harmless, mostly. And besides, it's a tradition.

"Do your best and forget the rest."

"I-I'll try." He gulps, causing his Adam's apple to bob. A mischievous smirk pulls at my lip. I can't resist the urge.

"Do or do not. There is no try." As soon as the *Star Wars* line slips out of my mouth, his towering fear seems to slowly dissipate, replaced instead with naïve determination. But a nerdy reference and an adrenaline rush can only get you so far. I give him two minutes. Tops.

I switch my hearing aids off and hand them to Mom. Sure, they're agency-engineered, but they're not completely water proof, so wearing them on the course is just asking for repairs and a very grumbly Brian Martin.

Without them, the world is swimming in silence. Muffled. Faint. It feels like my ears are full of cotton. But if my damaged hearing is good for anything, it's getting me to focus. No one can trash-talk me. No noises will make me jolt or scare me off the course. Now, it's just me and my instincts. Just the way I like it.

Isaac waves a hand in front of my face, grabbing my attention. He motions forward, signing 'let's go'. I follow to the starting line. When the confetti gun fires, the five of us dash across the shaking steel bridge over the water and onto the course. Our bare feet slide against the wet metal, causing us to waver, but we make it to the base of the tower. Here, we're met with the first of five rings. The course's layers (or as Isaac refers to them, the Rings of Hell) are stacked vertically, getting increasingly harder the higher you go.

I ignore Isaac's attempt at trash-talking in sign language (keyword: attempt) and make my way through the obstacles of the first level. Spinning metal poles covered in foam. They stick out of the wall, jabbing and stabbing and trying to push us off of the platform, but I stand my ground, hopping over the low poles and ducking beneath the tall ones.

Agents bobbing in the water cheer, but I can't hear them. I can't hear anything except my own heartbeat, thump, thump, thumping in my head. There's movement to my left. I turn my face just in time to watch as Dave splashes into the pool, wild wet curls sticking to his sun-burnt skin. As predicted, he was taken out by the first ring. But you have to give him credit for trying.

Dave joins the others in the water, cheering on me and the others as I use one of the poles to climb up to the next level.

Immediately, I'm blasted with water straight in the face. I almost lose my grip, but manage to cling to the slick platform, clawing and kicking to stay on. I pull myself up and look at what lies ahead. There are metal rings suspended overhead without anything beneath them. More jets are lodged in the wall, squirting timed streams of water at unsuspecting people. On top of that, some of the rings are fake, and will fall out as soon as you grab them.

I take a leap of faith, grabbing two rings. One falls out, but the other doesn't. Kicking my legs buys me the much-needed momentum to get to another ring. The next doesn't fall, but I get blasted in the thighs with a high-pressured blast of water and lose my grip on one of them, swinging wildly on the one I manage to hold on to. I grab it with both hands instead, clinging on until the flow of ice-water stops. Shivering and dripping wet, I soldier on to the third level.

While it looks harmless, the third wave is among the worst. The metal platforms shake, retracting into the wall randomly. Water pours from above making it slippery and hard to move across. Cannons imbedded in the tower shoot out pool noodles to knock us over the edge. Finally, I get a glimpse of one of the others. Isaac is ahead of me, climbing on to level four. Mateo is behind me, still stuck on level three, and as far as I know, Lucia is ahead of us all.

I step onto the first metal slab, only for it to retract beneath me causing me to dive and sprawl onto the next one, holding on for dear life. One of the cannons above me fires three noodles in a row. If I were upright, they would have taken me out for sure.

Scrambling to my feet, I run across the shaking platforms, dodging under and hopping over a few flying pool noodles. I make it to the end with a few close calls and climb up to level four, just in time to watch Isaac take the fall into the pool waiting below. He had a good run.

Level four is a climbing wall. That's it. Well, except for the fact that it's angled slightly back so it feels like you're falling off. Oh, and it spins. Fast. No safety net, no harness. On top of that, there are more foam-covered poles and water jets just waiting to ambush us. The tech guys have too much fun running this course, to be honest.

Sweaty hands, wet feet, and all, I start making my way up the climbing wall. Water blasts me in the face. Again. I sputter and shake my head, coughing it up. A few more feet up and I take a foam pole to the stomach. And it hurts. It does, don't get me wrong, but I've endured worse on this course.

My knuckles are white from gripping the climbing wall rocks so hard and I'm pretty sure my fingers are going numb. I imagine Dave and Isaac yelling out to me, cheering me on. I wonder if they are, but I don't look back to check. I have bigger fish to fry. Namely: level five.

The final level of the tower spins faster than the climbing wall. It's on a slight slant upwards leading up to a circular platform in the center. Sounds like it'd be easy, but it's dripping wet due to the constant downpour of water on it and it moves so fast you'd be lucky not to get spun right off. The only way to stay on is to use the very small finger-holds scattered up the smooth surface. The red buzzer stands atop a metal pedestal on the center platform. Lucia is almost there, directly in front of me, but she slips, sliding directly backwards. I grab her hand when she's close enough, holding her on.

"Together." I say, though I can't hear my own voice. She nods and we help one another move towards the center, slowly inching ourselves further up the deathtrap. It's hard, tiring, and we're both soaked to the bone with strings of wet hair clinging to our faces and shoulders, but somehow we make it. And for the fourth time in my short, spy-filled life, I slam my hand down on the buzzer. God, does it feel good.

More colored confetti rains down, exploding from the tower like fireworks. I can't hear the other agents and Dave cheering, but I can see them going nuts, shouting and screaming. I can only smile, holding Lucia's hand high in the air with our fingers intertwined. Against the odds, we made it, even when no one else could.

She says something, but I miss it so she points. Oh. The diving board. She gives my hand a squeeze before jumping off and diving gracefully into the pool below. I leap off as soon as she swims out of the way, adding a twist before I splash down into the water.

I still can't hear anything, but I feel people patting me on the back and slapping my hand and rubbing my shoulders, congratulating me on a job well done. Dave swims over as fast as he can, speaking way faster than I can comprehend. I shake my head, pointing to my ears.

'Oh yeah, sorry.' He slows way down so I can read his lips. 'You are an amazing incredible woman, and I think I just fell even more in love with you, if that's even possible.'

"Dork." I kiss his nose and give his shoulder a little shove. He slips his hand into mine and I tug him to the edge of the pool with me to retrieve my hearing aids from Mom.

Mom and Dad are ecstatic. So are Aunt Valentina and Uncle Romero. I jam my hearing aids back in and turn them on. The sound swells, surrounding me. One of Dad's strong hands comes to rest on my shoulder, shaking me around some.

"That's my girl! I am so proud of you!"

"Thanks, Dad."

Isaac walks over from the tech booth, holding a medal in each hand. He tosses one to me and hands the other to Lucia.

"Congrats, little sis."

"Thanks." I pull my hair through the medal's red, white, and blue striped ribbon, letting it dangle around my neck, a mark of victory. A reward from a mission accomplished. It's large, gold, round, and has my name engraved on it. Mia Crane: Obstacle Course Champion. I have to admit, it certainly does have a ring to it.

CHAPTER 11

"I swear M, you moved like a ninja or something. It was incredible. You were everywhere, jumping and flipping and dodging and taking hits like they were nothing!" Dave rambles as we walk through the woods back to the cabin after a long day. Cricket chirps and toad croaks fill the night air with forest music, accompanied by the occasional owl hoot or snapping branch. Fireflies light the path like little flickering stars. God, I love the woods. "You're like Natasha Romanoff! Or Wonder Woman! Or Supergirl! Or—"

"I got lucky is all." I brush it off like it's no big deal. But it is. A really big deal, as proved by the shiny new medal dangling around my neck. "Usually that course kicks my ass and everyone else's."

"Well, it kicked mine." Dave shakes his head. "I didn't even make it to the second round."

"You'll get it eventually. All you need is more practice."

"You think so?"

"I know so." It's a lie and we both know it, but he seems content, so I don't say anything.

Dave twirls me around, wrapping me up in his arms from behind. He peppers tiny little kisses all over my cheeks and jaw and neck, trapping me in his grip. I can't help but laugh when he wiggles his fingers and tickles my waist, causing me to double over and buckle at the knees. My one weakness. Ticklishness. It's turned a dangerous, lethal, weapon of a girl into a vulnerable, giggling mess. This is why I love him so much.

Dave is only a few inches taller than me, maybe half a foot at most. And despite the fact that he's about twenty pounds heavier than I am, it doesn't take much effort to flip him on his back, pinning him to the dirt path. He laughs, sparkling eyes searching my face. Even with my hair in a messy ponytail and a bit of mud on my face, he still looks at me like I'm made of stardust and magic, some ethereal supernatural creature who just so happens to be his girlfriend.

"What's that look for?"

"You're amazing."

"And you're a dork." I crawl off of him and pull him upright. We look up at the star-filled sky through the canopy of trees. A squirrel scurries by overhead and something stuck in a branch glares in the light of my flashlight. Something that shouldn't be there. Something metal. "Hey Dave, give me a boost, would you?"

"What? Why?"

"There's something up there."

"Like what? Leaves?"

"Just give me a boost!" I rest my hand on the trunk of the offending tree. Reluctantly, Dave laces his fingers together, creating a step. I place my foot in his hands and use the extra height to latch onto the lowest branch.

"Please be careful."

"I've climbed trees before, you know." I tilt my head, looking down at him.

"I know. I was there."

I climb a few feet higher, out of his line of sight. Almost immediately, I find what I was looking for. A chunk of metal stuck in a knothole, caked in dirt and mostly hidden by some dead leaves. I reach in and take it out to look at it. A little metal ball. I brush away the muck with my thumb so I can read the inscription. Four letters: L.O.S.T.

My heart pounds, fingers trembling so much I almost drop it. I furrow my eyebrows. The pieces fall into place. L.O.S.T. League of Science and Technology. The label on the briefcases. Everything suddenly makes sense. If Nikki was right about this being an international issue, then maybe this is more than just a coincidence. This is a threat. They're real. They're here. Maybe they always have been. And someone who names his organization L.O.S.T. must not be very fond of F.O.U.N.D.

"Everything all right up there, M?" Dave calls after a long moment of quiet. How long have I been up here?

"I'm fine. Give me a sec." I pray that he can't hear the slight waver in my voice. The worry. The fear.

I don't know what to do with this thing. I don't even know what it is. But I know it can't be good.

The light from my phone shines on a seam in the stainless steel sphere. I rest the phone on my thigh and cup the little ball in both hands, trying to twist it open. It doesn't work. I glance down at Dave. I can't leave him there forever. Dammit. Okay, new plan. I'll go to the F.O.U.N.D. Outpost tomorrow and send it to Brian so he can figure it out. That seems like a better plan than whatever I'm trying to do now.

I stick the ball and my phone in my backpack and start cautiously climbing back down the tree.

"Did you find whatever was up there?"

"No. I must be seeing things."

"Hmm," he hums. A few seconds later, I hop down in front of him. He jolts, a hand slapping over his heart. Wide blue eyes are framed by his thick plastic glasses. "Jeez. Scared me."

"I see that, scaredy-cat." I reach out and poke his nose with the tip of my finger, earning a somewhat embarrassed smile.

"Let's get back to the cabin before the mosquitos eat us alive, alright?" he scratches at his arm, which is amassing more and more irritated red bumps the longer we're out here.

"Alright, alright." We start walking back down the path the way we were headed. Without any warning, he picks me up and carries me over his shoulder. I hit his back a few times weakly with my fists, kicking and laughing at him. "What are you doing, you dork?"

"I'm taking my beautiful girlfriend hostage!" he breaks into a run.

"You're an idiot."

"I know."

"But you're my idiot."

"I know."

CHAPTER 12

"**A**re you absolutely sure this is safe?" Dave wobbles on unstable legs, looking down in horror at the flowing rapids beneath us. Ah, River Rush, the only thing better than the infamous obstacle course. It's a beautiful afternoon. Clear skies, sunny, not even a chance of rain. "I think now is a bad time to mention my fear of heights, right?"

"You'll be fine." I strap into the large inflatable raft. There's room for five. Once the raft is filled, the F.O.U.N.D. technicians will open the gates and send us down the river. Think of it as a giant crazy water slide, but it was designed by Mother Nature. And spies. "It's the best thing at camp, Dave. If you don't come, you're missing out."

"Yeah buddy. We've all done it tons of times." Isaac nods, buckling in between Mateo and I. "And we're still around to tell the story. Right?"

"Yeah, but you're all crazy. No offence."

"None taken. Just get in." Mateo points to the vacant seat to my right. "Because right now, your girlfriend has more balls than you do."

"I don't know, guys. I feel queasy. I think I'm gonna get sick." Dave looks down the steep hill. The falls are directly above us, and the water streaming down feeds into the river and down to the lake.

"Oh, come on, Curly Fry. You gotta live in the moment! No regrets!" Lucia buckles in beside her brother. I tug my ponytail through a rubber headband and secure it around my ears to protect my hearing aids. Lucia looks to the others before starting a chant.

"No regrets. No regrets. No regrets! No regrets!" it starts quiet, but slowly gains volume as more and more of us join in. "NO REGRETS! NO REGRETS!"

"Okay, okay, fine. I'll do it. Just make sure I have a nice funeral, okay? Lots of flowers and a good organist and for the love of God, don't let them bury me in a suit. I'd prefer my *Star Wars* hoodie. The one with the lightsabers, not—"

"Shut up and strap in." I smirk.

He sits (more like collapses) down beside me, buckling into the harness with shaky hands and short, shallow breaths. I lace my fingers through his and give his hand a reassuring squeeze. Dave offers a weak smile before looking over the river with a mix of terror and anticipation. Mostly terror.

He presses two fingers together and touches them to his forehead, sternum, and then each shoulder in the shape of a cross, silently praying. His Adam's apple bobs and he clenches his jaw, swallowing thickly. Dave's fingers grip my hand so tight I fear he'll break something. The techies open the gates and the raft drifts forward.

"Oh God. Ohhhh God. Is it too late to get out?"

"YES!" all of us shout at him. There are a few seconds of silence, quiet excitement. The only noise is the water roaring in the pool under the falls and rushing down the steep hill. In an instant, my stomach drops and we take the nearly-vertical hundred-foot plunge. Our screams shatter the quiet.

It's an exhilarating race down the river, full of twists and turns. Every bump causes a splash. By the time we get to the lake, all of us are soaking wet, yelling loudly, and running purely on the generous amounts of adrenaline coursing through our veins.

"We lived! Oh my God I lived!" Dave raises his fists in the air. "Whooooo! I'm alive!"

"Of course you are, Curly. I wouldn't let you die on this thing, you know."

"Can we...could we go again?"

"Yeah. We can." I knew he'd love it. "Actually, uh, Isaac and I really need to run to the Outpost. You stay here with Lucia and Mateo. I'll meet up with you later?"

"Uh sure. I'll see you later." he agrees.

"Don't worry, M. We'll keep your boyfriend safe." Lucia winks and leans back against the inflatable raft. We unbuckle ourselves and get out. I walk up the steep paths with Isaac. Once we get all the way up the hill and wave goodbye to the others, we make our way down the other side, towards the F.O.U.N.D. Outpost.

About twenty minutes later, we arrive at the log cabin style building. From the outside, it looks harmless, but inside is the most high-tech building in a five mile radius, filled with hackers and scientists and field agents called to last-minute missions. The Outpost is like a mini Headquarters smack dab in the middle of the campgrounds. Just when you think you can get away from F.O.U.N.D., it sucks you right back in.

Isaac and I scan our badges at the door and walk inside. Cold air from the air conditioning prickles goosebumps up my arms. It's so nice compared to the muggy summer heat waiting just outside the door. A few agents and interns hustle around the three-story building, but for the most part, it's pretty empty.

A large stone fireplace lies directly in line with the front door, surrounded by plushy couches and chairs. There are bookshelves lining the walls and chessboards on the tables so agents can sit back and unwind even while they're here at the brains of the operation. Over to the right, there's a reception desk, to the left is a dining area and a café. Everything else is upstairs.

After signing in with the receptionist, we walk upstairs and down the hall to one of the computer labs. Isaac wanders off to meet some friends and I scan my access badge and log onto one of the computers, firing up a video chat with the one and only Brian Martin. Tired brown eyes and messy red hair appear on the screen almost immediately. The light from the screen glares in his glasses and his pale freckled face is illuminated in the dim lab.

"Are you okay, Brian?" He certainly doesn't look okay. Dark rings under his eyes tell me he hasn't gotten much sleep as of late, and it might be the screen, but he looks like he's shivering. Brian takes a long sip from a mug of coffee before replying. There it is. Brian hates coffee. Hates it. He must have been up all night. Or for several nights. Probably the latter.

"No." His voice is thick and heavy with sleep. "This stupid chemical won't respond to any stimuli. Tried to freeze it. Didn't work. Tried to boil it. Didn't work. Tried to mix it with other chemicals. Didn't work. All it seems to bond with is human blood cells, which is kind of terrifying to say the least. 'Kind of' is an understatement."

"How did you think to—"

"I got a paper cut and a little blood just kinda—you know what? Never mind. It's not important. What do you want?"

"I found this in the woods." I set the ball on the digital scanner. A few seconds later, the hologram is projected in front of Brian. He reaches out and takes it in his hand, spinning it around to look at it.

"Are you kidding me? Where did you find this thing?"

"Up in a tree."

"Why were you—? Never mind. I don't care." Brian enlarges the hologram with his fingers. "What I *do* care about is the inscription. Did you try to open it?"

"Won't budge."

"Send it to me. I'll have the tech guys have a whack at it if I can't figure it out."

"Will do. Thanks."

"Don't mention it. Oh, and Mia?"

"Yeah?"

"Please, please promise me you'll steer clear of any more of this L.O.S.T. stuff until you get back to Headquarters. It's dangerous and I really don't feel good about it."

"Aww are you worried about me?"

"I'm serious." He wipes his hands down his face. "The further we look into this case, the deeper it seems to go. Just don't do anything stupid. Please."

"Oh come on; have I ever done anything stupid?"

"Do you want me to answer that question?"

"Shut up." I smirk. "I'll be careful. I promise."

"Good." He takes another long sip of coffee, wiping his mouth on the back of his hand. He grimaces at the aftertaste, but I can tell he needs it. "Wouldn't want to lose my favorite field agent,"

"Favorite, huh? I thought that was Summer..." I bite my lip, twirling my *Star Wars* ring around my left ring finger.

Brian's cheeks burn bright red and his finger hovers above the button to end the call. "Okay bye." He hangs up before I can fluster him any further.

Isaac pops back in. "Mission accomplished?"

"Just about. I need to send this to Brian and then we're good to go."

"Okay good. I don't know about you, but I don't want to leave Dave alone for too long. Wouldn't want him to overhear something he's not supposed to."

"Right. We haven't blown our cover so far. Let's see if we can keep it that way."

CHAPTER 13

Russian Roulette is a dangerous game. One gun. One bullet. Six chances that someone will die. And yet, the thrill is tempting. Maybe that's why so many versions of the game have emerged over time. Safer, less deadly versions for those who want an adrenaline rush without putting their life on the line. For example: there's a pepper in one of the chocolates, some of the chips feel like they set your mouth on fire, half of the jellybeans taste like horrible nasty things.

And then there's the Crane version.

Crane Russian Roulette is a mix of the aforementioned game and a drinking game. Ten plastic shot glasses are placed on a spinning slab in the middle of the table. Half of them are filled with water, and half of them are filled with a watered-down F.O.U.N.D.-engineered torture chemical compound that stimulates brain freeze. We call it Frost Bite.

Frost Bite isn't deadly. It's only dangerous if you ingest large quantities of it, and even then the worst it can do is make your feet go numb. As far as I know. I'm sure if you drank the whole bottle, there'd be problems. But really, the only harm it does is sting like a bitch, right between the eyes, a twisting pain that takes forever to fade.

"Okay, so I know you said I can't die from this, but has anyone ever passed out from it or anything?" Dave's nervous blue eyes flick around the room at the spies prepping our traditional game. Tonight is our last night at camp, so as we do every year, we opt out of the big bonfire and instead spend a night in, playing spy games. With Dave here, we can't play most of them, but we can play this.

"You're a scaredy cat, Curly Fry." Lucia's ruby red lips pull into a smirk and she leans against the couch, sipping from her red solo cup. "We do this every year and we're all in one piece."

"I...don't know about this." Dave settles uncertainly. I take a seat in his lap and turn my head to kiss him. Mateo groans on the other side of the couch.

"Get a room!" He tosses a pillow at us, but I catch it without even turning to look. I press another soft kiss to Dave's pink lips while tossing the pillow back.

"You'll be fine."

"Okay." He still doesn't sound so sure of himself.

Aunt Valentina comes down the stairs after just having put Marisol to bed. She takes a seat on the couch as Dad and Uncle Romero finish setting up. I itch at a mosquito bite. God we're a mess, covered in sunburns and awkward tan lines, bug bites and bruises, scratches and scrapes and cuts from our many camping adventures. Our battle scars, in this sense, are almost normal.

"Do you know the rules, David?" Mom asks.

Dave nods, his hand finding mine. He stretches his fingers and grips my hand a little bit tighter. "I think so, yeah."

"Everyone's in until they tap out. Last man standing wins."

"Wins what?"

"Wins the pot." Valentina sets a black velvet top hat in the middle of the spinning table. Everyone stuffs a few dollars or a handful of change into it, causing the metal to clink with every move. Dad rubs his hands together with anticipation.

"Let's get going. Who's first?"

"I'll go." Isaac volunteers, giving the wheel a spin. He wiggles his fingers, watching the shot glasses spin around the table. Suddenly, he plucks one off of the wheel and drinks it in a quick and fluid movement. We wait for a reaction, but there isn't one. "Guess it's my lucky day."

"We'll see about that…"

Mateo volunteers to go next, puffing out his chest and flexing his biceps in a feeble attempt to one-up my brother. Their little competitive streak gives me life. Mateo cracks his neck before picking up a shot and drinking it. His reaction is very subtle, very focused, but it's there. He clenches his jaw, dark brown eyes locked on a brick above the fireplace. The veins in his forehead and neck pop ever so slightly as he strains to keep a straight face.

I can't help but grin, amused by his effort.

"What? You think you could do better, chica?" He crosses his arms and cocks an eyebrow.

I rest a hand on my hip, using the other to grab a shot. "I'm pretty sure I can." I tip my head back, taking it in.

The cold, cold liquid runs down my throat, and immediately I feel the pinching, twisting pain between my eyes, but I don't flinch. I don't move. I just let my face go blank, staring straight into Mateo's eyes with a silent challenge. I'm not going down without a fight. And I get the feeling that neither is he.

Over the course of an hour, the playing field is narrowed down to Isaac, Mateo, and I. Dave was eliminated first, then our parents, and then Lucia only a minute ago. I take another, larger shot. My face scrunches up and I stare at the ceiling, trying to blink it away. After so many of these, it hurts so much. My toes and fingers start to tingle, going numb.

"You okay, M?" Dave wraps an arm around my shoulder and scans my face with concern. I nod silently, clenching my jaw and squeezing my eyes shut.

"All done, baby sis?"

"No way!" I try to get up but fall right back on the couch. "Okay. Yep. I'm done."

"Just us then." Mateo picks up a cup and hands another to Isaac. They count down from three and drink them at the same time. Mateo just about passes out from the large dose of Frost Bite, stumbling onto the table. He knocks over all of the remaining shots, arms flopping over the edge like useless noodles. I can't help but laugh.

"Bro, does that mean I win?!" Isaac kicks his legs up, smirking.

"Yep. Yep. You win." Mateo rolls off of the table and falls to the floor with a thud and a groan. That'll leave a bruise. Isaac lifts the now-squashed top hat and pours the cash onto the couch, counting the crumpled ones and handfuls of change.

"Sweet. I wonder what I can get in the camp store for $6.13."

"Probably at least a few candy bars or something," Lucia suggests.

Dave pulls me further into his arms, rubbing little circles on my shoulder and the small of my back. My fingers flush with heat, reddening as the feeling gradually trickles back into them. I don't think I've ever made it this far in the game before. Maybe I was wrong about this stuff not being dangerous. I feel pretty endangered. And dizzy and partially numb.

"You good, Mia?" Dave checks again. I stretch my fingers and wiggle my toes. A groan escapes my lips and I mumble a reply. Yes. I'm fine. Just dazed. I'll live. I've been through way worse. Hand grenades and tasers and scary men with guns and sharp knives. I leave out that last part.

Dave helps me up the stairs to the second floor hallway and by this point, I'm almost back to normal. The fog seems to have lifted, leaving me in a sort of limbo. Tired, but still on my feet. Different than usual, but still me. And yet, there's a feeling inside I can't yet describe, but I feel it rising closer and closer to the surface.

"Your family is kind of wild," Dave chuckles softly, a hand reaching up to scratch the back of his neck. He takes my hand with his free one and the sleeve of his soft green hoodie brushes against my wrist.

"Yeah, I uh, guess they kind of are. But I grew up with it, so I never really noticed how—"

"Hey, I never said that was a bad thing." Dave is quick to reassure me. His earnest smile shines through his blue eyes as they carefully search mine. I push some of the brown curls out of his face. "I really had fun this week."

"I'm glad you came."

"So am I." His voice is low, almost a whisper now. He pushes forward slightly, gently guiding me towards the door of the spare bedroom. Dave's large hands have no trouble finding my hips and pulling me closer. A bold move, confident. There's not a falter in his gaze, not even a single hint of hesitation. Our chests are pressed up against each other, heat from his body melding with my own. God, he's so warm.

Dave takes another step forward and I reach back for the doorknob, twisting it in my hand and pushing the door open behind me. As soon as we're inside, Dave sheds his green sweatshirt, leaving him in his red t-shirt, a testament to his colorblindness even in an intimate moment like this. I stifle giggles as we walk together, my feet beside his, our legs moving in sync as we inch through the doorway of the bedroom.

There's a moment of silent needing and anticipation, of locked eyes and bated breaths before my lips come crashing onto his like waves onto shore. His lips are warm, sweet, coated in Cherry Coke. My fingers get tangled in his thick brown curls. I tug gently, earning a quiet moan from him. With unexpected strength, Dave lifts me up onto his hips, hands gripping at my thighs. My lips leave the warmth of his and instead find a place on his jaw, then his neck. Not hard enough to leave a mark, but enough to make him whimper like putty in my hands.

"Mia," he whispers, a hitch in his voice. I press a quick kiss to his jaw before returning to his lips. I feel him smile against me, hands giving my thighs a squeeze. He pushes me against the wall, his mouth leaving mine and travelling down my neck, but not being quite as gentle as I was with him. I will probably have to wear a scarf tomorrow.

I arch my back, inhaling a sharp breath as he sucks a mark onto my collarbone. He chuckles as my fingers dig into the fabric of his t-shirt. I tilt my head back against the wall, sighing in bliss. We've been quiet so far, but I know if we're any louder, someone will hear. He kisses my lips a few more times before stopping to rest his forehead against mine. His warm breath ghosts over my cheeks. Our faces are red and our breathing is heavy, shoulders rising and falling with each labored lungful of air.

He laughs softly, smiling. I can't help but smile too, taking in his scent. Cologne and bonfire and hints of the woods.

Dave sets me back on my feet. I lean into his chest, taking another deep breath. He wraps his arms around my body, pulling me tight against him. His brown curls start to stick to his face, moist with sweat. Warm lips brush against my forehead tiredly. I have a feeling we're both going to sleep well tonight.

"Goodnight, Mia." His voice is barely a hoarse whisper at this point.

I look up at him, gently running my fingers down his cheek. "Goodnight. See you in the morning."

CHAPTER 14

Only a few hours later, the alarm goes off. I barely even notice the muffled noise without my hearing aids, but the thick black band around my wrist vibrates; a nifty little invention of Brian's to keep me in the loop because my hearing aids are just way too uncomfortable to wear to bed.

Sleepily, I slide the bits into my ears, wrapping the large plastic base around the back and turning them on. At first, I mistake the alarm for Lucia's phone telling us to get up for our run, but I soon recognize it as something else. Something much more sinister, much more important. The intruder alarm.

"Lucia!" I throw a pillow at her, causing her to groan and roll over.

"Let's just skip the running today, M. I'm exhausted."

"It's the intruder alarm."

"The intru—Dios mio..." Lucia sits up, pulling the gun out from under her pillow. I grab mine from the top drawer of the nightstand. "He's out there in the front yard." Lucia points out the window to a man dressed in black, prowling through the lawn like an animal, just waiting to pounce on his first victim. Unless he brought some of his buddies, this asshole is about to learn a lesson he won't soon forget.

Lucia and I run down the stairs, practically kicking the front door open. Before the guy can even aim his gun, I shoot him twice in the thigh. Blood spurts into the grass, thick and red. He shouts out in pain. Lucia springs ahead and locks him in a chokehold. He coughs a few times, struggling against her. She kicks the back of his knees, forcing him to the ground.

Another guy jumps out of the shadows, lunging at me fist-first. I grip his wrist with both hands and flip him over onto his back, pinning him to the lawn. A third man tears me off of the second, throwing me aside as if I weigh nothing. I hit the back of my head against a tree. Pain jolts through my body, exploding like fireworks. Sparkles cloud my vision. I groan, squeezing my eyes shut in a feeble attempt to make the world stop spinning.

After taking a second to compose myself, I use the tree to get back on my feet. By this time, Isaac and Mateo have woken up and made their way out to fight not three, not four, but five attackers. A sixth creeps around the corner of the cabin, drenched as if he had come out of the lake, which, at this point, I can only assume he did.

Lucia punches one in the face. Hard. He slumps to the ground, knocked out. I pull a knife off of the leather-clad man's belt, flinging it at one of the others. It lodges into his right bicep, causing him to let out sharp yelp. A few quick strides and I'm standing in front of him. I wrap my fingers around the handle of the knife, twisting it in his arm and then I use my foot to push him back.

Mateo and Isaac double-team a third guy, both getting in a few hits before he drops, eyes lolling back into his head. Two down, four to go. The next guy grabs me from behind, trying to choke me. I ram my elbow into his abdomen as hard as I can, and he doubles over, emptying his stomach onto the grass.

"Mia!" Isaac shouts. I move my head just in time to dodge a tranquilizer dart. They're not here to kill us. They're here to take us in. Aunt Valentina and Uncle Romero emerge, followed very quickly by my parents. Valentina uses her taser rods to zap the living daylights out of the nearest guy. With our parents added into the mix, the remaining three don't stand a chance.

It doesn't take long to whittle them down to one guard. I pin him to a tree with my new knife pressed against his neck. My gaze locks on his, eyes narrowed, teeth gritted. The pointed metal tip pokes into his flesh the slightest bit.

"I'm going to ask you again. And believe me, if anyone else has to ask, they won't be so nice about it. Who sent you, and why are you here?"

"Orville told us about you..." Blood trickles from the man's nose and his eye is swollen, surrounded by dark bruises. "He said you were...what was the word he used? Hopeless. Brainwashed practically from birth. You think you're saving the world, but all you are is a virus. A sickness," he hisses, sneering at me. "F.O.U.N.D. thinks they're helping you by turning you into weapons..." He laughs, a horrible, stomach-churning howl. "Soon you'll know. You'll all know. Stay out of our business, or we'll pick you off one by one, killing you like the pests you—"

I clock him in the face. The back of his head slams into the tree and he passes out. I sigh, running my fingers through my hair.

Shit.

"M-Mia?" a very scared Dave walks out of the front door of the cabin, playing with his hands and visibly trembling. His blue eyes are wide, looking around the lawn at the unconscious bodies. Heavy breaths enter and leave his lungs, shoulders heaving. Uncertainty and fear flash through his gaze, eyebrows knitted together. He can barely look into my eyes. I wonder how much he saw.

Shit.

"This isn't real." I lie, staring directly into his eyes as Isaac walks up behind him and jabs a syringe into his neck, thumb slowly pressing down on the plunger and forcing the concentrated sleeping drug into his veins. His eyes shut halfway and he struggles to stay on his feet. I rush forward, catching him as he slumps unconscious into my arms.

Shit.

"They're from the League." Mateo kicks one over and finds a badge stashed in his black leather uniform.

"No shit." Lucia holds up one of the badges she picked up.

Isaac plucks the syringe from Dave's neck, shoving it back into his pocket. We've always kept it on hand in case of an incident like this, but this is the first time we've ever been forced to blow our cover.

"Romero, help me get these guys to the Outpost's detention ward." Dad yawns, bending over to drag one of the attackers to the big black F.O.U.N.D. truck as it pulls into the driveway. Its yellow light flashes like a police light, spinning around and around, but no siren is heard.

I pull Dave into the house, which is easier said than done, and get him to the couch, using it to reposition him in my arms like a baby. Speaking of...

"Bad guys?" Marisol asks, looking at me with worry.

"It's okay, Mari. We got 'em. You can go to bed, sweetie." I tell her, putting on a smile. She sucks her thumb and gives me a blank expression. "You want me to tuck you in?"

She nods.

"Okay. Let me tuck Dave in quick."

I set Dave on his bed in the boys' room and pull the covers up to his shoulder. Snores escape his lips. He's out. Marisol lingers in the doorway a few feet away, watching silently as I brush the curls out of his face and press a gentle kiss to his forehead.

"Hey kiddo," Isaac rubs Marisol's head affectionately, "you okay?" She nods wordlessly, looking up to my brother, who's a giant compared to her tiny frame. "Good. How's Dave, Mia?"

"He'll be out for a while. How big of a dose did you give him?"

"Nine hours. He'll sleep like a baby." Isaac is quiet for a few seconds. He takes a long breath and leans against the doorway with that older-brothery look on his face. The softness in his eyes, the way his lips move before he finds the right words. Something he perfected by watching Jace, a.k.a. the master of older-brothery looks. "It's not your fault."

"I know."

"It was just a matter of time until this happened."

"I know."

"He won't remember it."

"I *know*, Isaac."

"Are you okay?"

"Yeah. I just..." Tears cloud my vision, but I don't let them escape my eyes. "I've never seen that look on his face before. He...he looked at me like I was a monster."

"It's okay. It'll be okay." Isaac rests a hand on my shoulder. I succumb to his comforting embrace. He rubs my back a few times before I pull away, remembering that I have to put Marisol to bed.

"I know." I put on a brave face. Because it happened like this, he'll have to find out all over again. He won't remember this. He'll think it was a nightmare. But sooner or later, the day will come when I can't just wipe it from his mind. I'll have to deal with it. Forever.

"No cries." Marisol says simply, reaching up for me with her tiny, tiny hands. I lift her up and hold her on my hip. Her palms press on my cheeks, squishing them forward into a fishy face. I can't help but smile.

"Thanks, sweetie." I kiss her cheek, carrying her back to the girls' room. I set her in her little bed and pull the blankets around her, securing her into a soft little nest. "Goodnight, Mari. Get some sweet dreams, okay?"

"Okay."

"Well that was a mess." Lucia walks into the bedroom, flopping onto her bed as I crawl into mine.

"Understatement of the year."

CHAPTER 15

I've been at home for 0.5 seconds, and I already miss the cabin. Yeah, an awesome high-tech mansion is great, but home means—

"Miss Crane, Headquarters called." C.A.I.T.L.Y.N. speaks in her automated British voice. I roll my eyes. Vacation is officially over. "You have a mission scheduled for tonight. Brian is waiting to discuss the properties of the chemicals found in the briefcase and the metal capsule you recovered at camp. Dave's mother has an appointment in the bakery this afternoon, and Sheila has to brief you and Agents Laurence and Williams for the mission. Also, three of your files for submission were rejected and need to be filled out again, you need to pick up your fresh uniforms from the textile department, and you have 54 unanswered emails."

"Thanks, C.A.I.T.L.Y.N." I drag my fingers down my face. "Anything else? Actually, I don't want to know."

I drag myself up the stairs and flop onto my bed. My screams of frustration and stress and bottled-up emotions from last night are muffled by a pillow. When I'm done, I brush out my hair, touch up my makeup, and don my uniform. And yeah, I look like a badass with the smoky eyes and the tight black leather, but I feel like a stressed, pathetic teenager.

Shouldn't it be the other way around? Shouldn't the lethal killer be hiding behind the cheerleader, waiting to pounce on anyone who underestimates her? I feel so fake. Am I a fake? Have I always been fake? I don't feel like Amelia Crane, Dave Bowen's girlfriend. I don't feel like Agent 212, a human weapon working for the government. Maybe I'm something in the middle, a happy compromise of the ends of the spectrum.

What's happening to me? What's wrong with my brain? Did last night's events trigger a chemical imbalance? Was it the horror in Dave's eyes when he saw me press my knife to the L.O.S.T. agent's neck, or was it the adrenaline rush of finally being caught? For three seconds, he knew. Did I want him to? Did I want him to know everything? Rip it off like a Band-Aid and deal with it there? No. I couldn't. I can't want that. I *shouldn't* want that. But it would have been so easy. It would have been so easy to spill everything instead of locking up all of my secrets and throwing away the key again for God-knows-how-long.

All my life, I've abided by the agency's rules. I've been careful to keep my mouth shut. I've never been captured, never left anything behind. I've always followed orders, never taken unnecessary risks. But one civilian teenage boy, a weak, dorky, nerdy one at that, has managed to turn a sharp assassin into a confused emotional mess.

Love is a weakness. The only power on earth so strong it brings civilizations to their knees. A bond so powerful that if it's broken, it can shatter hearts like glass or harden them to stone.

Theoretically, what would happen if someone killed Dave? I would either a) lose my shit and go on a killing spree or b) become a horrible sobbing mess that no amount of mint chocolate chip ice cream could ever fix. Neither of those options are good for business. And that, my friends, is why the third rule is in place. But I've already broken it, so now what?

Maybe the agency is just waiting for me to crack. To go Rogue. To break the other two rules and throw everything into chaos.

"Mia? You okay in here?" Mom walks through the open bedroom door, a look of maternal concern on her face.

"Yeah, just...thinking."

"About what?"

"Madness." I shake my head. "Deranged and utter madness."

"So, Dave then?"

"How'd you guess?" I try to force a laugh, but my fake smile fades.

Mom wraps her arms around me from behind, meeting my gaze in the mirror. She and I look completely different. She's blonde, I'm brunette. She has blue eyes, I have brown. But there's something in her face that looks like mine. The way her eyebrows crinkle, the soft smile that tugs at her pink lips.

Mom pulls my hair behind my shoulders, braiding it with her fingers the way she used to when I was a little girl.

"When did you get so old, baby?" Her voice comes out as a whisper. She shakes her head. "Seventeen with a boyfriend and an impossible quest to prove everyone wrong."

"What do you mean?"

"You're not afraid to fall in love despite everything that means in our line of work."

"Should I be?"

"Maybe." Mom tilts her head to the side. She finishes my braid and wraps the end in a hair tie. "I know I was when I met your father. Nikki was when she met Ethan. But you're different, baby. Nikki and I fell in love with people from the agency. You were the only one brave enough to screw the rules and take a chance. I admire you."

"I'm not brave. I'm just stupid."

"Maybe." She pauses, hands resting on my stomach, chin resting on my shoulder. "Maybe not. I guess time will tell. Anyway, you should get going. Don't want to be late."

"Right. Yeah. Thanks."

"Now go kick some ass for me, would you?"

I chuckle and offer a quick nod. "Yes ma'am."

CHAPTER 16

I stop in at Sugar & Spice before taking the tunnels to Headquarters. Greta is terribly understaffed, so I promised to come in for Mrs. Bowen's appointment to help out, and I told her I'd bring the girls with me. I mean, besides the million things I have on my schedule today, there's nothing better to do, right?

After checking in at the front desk, taking care of my filing problems and wading through my sea of emails, I find the girls in the lounge. Ginger is sporting pink streaks in her hair along with and in place of the orange, which is new. God, she's hot.

"I like the pink." I twirl one of the soft strands around my finger. She smiles, proud. "Looks good."

"Thanks, babe." Ginger winks and pokes my stomach. "We have a briefing with Sheila in abooouuuut..." she checks her watch. "Five minutes. Then we gotta check on Brian in the lab and make sure he hasn't put himself into a work-induced coma, and *then*—"

"Then we have to help out Greta in the bakery because I promised and because Dave's mom has an appointment."

"Aww I love Mrs. Bowen!" Summer beams. She fiddles with the zipper on the pocket of her leather jacket as we walk into Sheila's office.

Our administrator extraordinaire is sitting behind her desk, typing at the speed of light. But surprisingly, she's not alone. There's a young woman sitting at a makeshift desk in the other corner of the room, doing work on Sheila's tablet and sifting through papers. Short red hair just barely brushes her shoulders, and large emerald eyes are magnified by a pair of thick black glasses. She's dressed in a navy blue polo shirt with a F.O.U.N.D. limited access pass dangling from the lanyard around her neck.

"Ladies, meet my new intern, Elise Ellivro." Sheila motions to her and she gets up from her desk to meet us. Elise gives each of us a firm handshake, using her finger to push her glasses further up the bridge of her nose.

"I've been reading over your files for the past two hours. You three are remarkable for field agents of your age bracket."

"The best in their division," Sheila brags before getting straight to the point. "Girls, tonight we're sending you to do another search of the theater. Your priorities this time are to plant cameras, retrieve any data you can get your hands on, and bring in more briefcases for analysis."

"So just in and out?" Summer asks.

"Just in and out." Sheila nods. "But be thorough. At this point, we can't afford to miss any critical details."

"Um, Administrator Dormer?"

"Yes, Mia?"

"How much do we know about L.O.S.T.?"

"At the moment...not much. We have no idea what they have planned or how it'll be accomplished. We're not even sure what the chemicals you found are for or what they do. All of the flash drives crashed and wiped themselves as soon as the hacking team tried to pry their way in. With any luck, you'll bring home the answers."

"But no pressure, right?" Ginger smirks.

"Right." There's a long pause. "You're dismissed. Just do me a favor and make sure Agent Martin isn't dead."

"We were headed there already." I wink. "You know how he gets when he's 'determined.'"

"I'm pretty sure his blood is seventy-five percent coffee at this point." Sheila shakes her head, laughing. "And he hates coffee."

"That's how you know he's in the zone." Summer says with mock intensity. "And then he gets paler, if that's possible, and starts shaking uncontrollably. And then he passes out."

"I had a video chat with him from camp and he was already trembling in the light of his computer."

"Then there's no time to lose is there?" Sheila laughs, waving as we dash to the science division to stop our favorite little genius from crashing. By the time we get to the door of Lab 32, it looks like we're too late. Brian is sprawled over his station in the very back of the room, glasses crooked and hanging off of his face. Soft snores escape his lips; a testament to how exhausted he is. Summer shakes her head.

"We should take him to the Crash Room, right?" Ginger tilts her head as she looks down at the little sleeping nerd.

"Yeah. We should." I agree.

"I've got him," Summer volunteers. The way she scoops him up into her arms like a little baby is almost routine. I tuck his arms into his chest so they don't dangle and take off his glasses. He speaks in a sleepy gibberish, resulting in us shushing him. It's not our first rodeo.

A lot of F.O.U.N.D.'s scientists are like Brian: they work until they drop. To remedy this problem, they set up the Crash Room, a large space with rows and rows of beds for sleepy little agents that need a bit of a nap, or in Brian's case, a lot of a nap. Not all field agents do, but most are careful to take care of their resident nerds.

Here's a secret: we put on a big bravado and act like we're all cool because we're field agents and that must make us special, right? Well, without these pasty little nerds sitting in this damn lab until they can't feel their legs anymore, we wouldn't be anywhere. Actually, we would be somewhere. About six feet under. A good field agent is only as good as their engineer. Don't let anyone tell you otherwise. I know for a fact that Ginger, Summer, and I would all be dead a thousand times over if it weren't for Brian Martin.

Once we're in the Crash Room, Ginger writes Brian's name and info on the white board beside his favorite bed. I pull the covers aside so Summer can set him down and tuck him in. Before we leave, I set his glasses on the nightstand and strap a pair of wireless headphones onto his head. Faint ocean noises escape them.

Brian's eyes open and he squints up at us tiredly. Confusion is quickly replaced with the realization of where he is. He nods wordlessly and closes his eyes, snuggling deeper into the warm blankets. Usually he puts up a fight, but the dark rings around his eyes win the battle, tugging him down into dreamland.

Summer ruffles his hair playfully, causing a smile to tug at his lips before fading back into a blank, sleepy expression. He rolls over, his face turned towards the wall. I close the curtains around his bed. They're light green and decorated with little colorful test tubes and beakers and microscopes. There's a muffled 'thank you' from the other side of the fabric and we chuckle at him. What a dork.

Ginger glances at her watch.

"If we hurry, we might make it to the bakery on time for Mrs. Bowen's appointment."

And with that, we leave.

CHAPTER 17

We walk past the elevator doors and into the warm bakery. Instead of the usual flock of agents working at every station, there are about four, Greta included. Understaffed was an understatement. I peel off my leather jacket and replace it with an apron, immediately setting to work.

"Where is everybody?"

"Where do you think?" Greta shakes her head as she rolls out a sheet of cookie dough. "They're all busy investigating L.O.S.T. That's where you're going tonight, isn't it?"

"Yeah." Summer picks up a bowl of frosting and starts mixing it before scooping dollops onto red velvet cupcakes.

Ginger spreads the sweet icing around, spinning each cupcake in her hand as she does so. When she's done, I sprinkle each one with red sugar sprinkles and load them into boxes.

"Seems like the whole agency is upside down trying to get a handle on the situation. It's crazy."

"Threats and enemy agencies come and go as commonly as passing storms. This will blow over soon enough." A tired laugh. "Believe me, I've been around long enough to know."

"I hope." The phone rings. I pull the red landline off the wall. "Sugar & Spice, the bakery that makes everything nice! How can I help you?"

"Mia? Is that you? This is Linda Bowen. Dave and I are on our way, but we got caught by a boat on the way there. I just wanted to let you know in case we're ridiculously late."

"Oh it's no problem, Mrs. Bowen. Take your time," I twirl the curly phone cord around my finger, leaning against the counter.

The foghorn blares in the background, accompanied by Dave's faint voice. Though it feels like a month ago, it was only this morning we got back from the cabin. He must be beyond exhausted.

"Thanks honey. See you in a few."

"Yep! Bye!" I hang up. "Mrs. Bowen and Dave are going to be a few minutes late. They got stuck by a boat."

"Okay." Greta points to Ginger. "Ginger, get the sample plate ready for them."

"Aye-aye, captain!" Ginger begins to put together a tasting plate of seven or eight of our most popular cake flavors: chocolate, vanilla, red velvet, and marble to name a few. I work on frosting cupcakes for about fifteen more minutes until the bell over the front door rings. Greta grabs my hand, pulling me into the lobby with her.

"Hey, babe." I lean against the counter. Dave slips both of his hands into both of mine on the glass barrier between us. "Long time no see, huh?"

"What's it been, four hours?" He glances at his watch, grinning. "Four hours too long."

"A wild David appears." Summer emerges from the kitchen. "Fancy seeing you here. Oh, and hi, Mrs. Bowen."

"Hi Summer, Mia." Mrs. Bowen greets. Judging by her pink pastel scrubs, she must have just gotten out of work, or maybe she's on her way there. Her long curly brown hair is pulled up out of her face, a few stray strands hanging loose.

"I'm here too!" Ginger comes out and sets the sample plate on the counter, handing Dave and Mrs. Bowen a fork.

"Hello, Ginger." Mrs. Bowen smiles at Greta. "Thanks for the sample plate, Mrs. Hertz, but my mom wants red velvet."

"Grandma's favorite."

"The woman has good taste." Ginger smirks, plucking the little square of marble cake off of the plate and popping it into her mouth. "I can help you over here, Mrs. Bowen."

Mrs. Bowen walks over to the register to fill out her order form, but Dave stands at the other end of the counter with me, his large hands still fastened around mine, gentle fingers rubbing circles on my wrists.

"I had the weirdest dream last night." Dave states, smiling.

I crinkle my eyebrows. "Oh yeah?"

"Yeah. So like, you were a badass assassin chick or something and you kicked some guy's ass when he was trying to break into the cabin." Dave rubs his eyes. "God, I'm so tired. I thought I got a lot of sleep, but..." He yawns. "I guess not."

"I think you should take a nap." I mess up his hair, causing him to chuckle. "Weird dream. I think I could pull off the assassin look, though. Maybe for Halloween? We could go as Kim Possible and Ron Stoppable."

"Yes. We should," Dave agrees. "Or Black Widow and Hawkeye."

"If we're going as comic characters this year, I've got dibs on Storm." Ginger chimes in from the register. She hands Mrs. Bowen her receipt. "She's my girl."

"You'd be a perfect Storm, G. You'd look pretty hot with white hair." Summer agrees from the doorway. She must have snuck out of the kitchen while I was preoccupied.

"I think I could rock a white Mohawk." Ginger sticks out her tongue and playfully flashes rock hands.

Mrs. Bowen tucks away her receipt and her change and then turns to Dave. "Well, thank you very much, girls. You always make it easy." Mrs. Bowen slides her Minnie Mouse wallet back into her big flowery purse. "Come on, Dave. We've got three more stops before I drop you off at work."

"Duty calls." Dave takes my hand and kisses it. "Until next we meet, milady."

"Bye, Dave." I smile and shake my head at him. The bell over the door dings on their way out. Dave blows a kiss from the other side of the large front window and I pretend to catch it in my fist, holding it to my cheek.

"He's a keeper, that boy." Greta rubs my shoulder affectionately, watching as Dave climbs into his mother's car.

"Believe me Greta, I know."

CHAPTER 18

The transition from teenage bakery employees to lethal secret agents is quick and seamless. It's a mental switch. Instantaneous. Painless. I can go from high school cheerleader to grade-A assassin without a hitch.

Sometimes it scares me. In times like this, yeah. It scares me a lot. More than I'd care to admit, me being, well, 'me'. Fearless Mia. Courageous Mia. Agent Mia Crane, F.O.U.N.D. Operative GCNYHQ212. But I don't know another way to live. It's all I've ever known.

After picking the lock to the maintenance door in the garage adjacent to the theater, Ginger, Summer, and I creep into the large empty building. Our motorcycles are hidden out of sight, stowed away in the garage for safekeeping. My belt is heavy with gadgets and gizmos of all shapes and sizes.

"We need to do a sweep of the back room." Ginger states. "There wasn't enough time last time."

"Right." We slink down the back hallway past the stairwells and elevators and out towards the lobby, which we need to cross to get to the room on the other side of it. I suppose we could go through the theater, but we'd run the risk of tripping an alarm.

"Shit." Summer's arms hold Ginger and I back just before we step into the elegant high-ceilinged lobby. Red lasers sweep through the large space and two guards pace back and forth.

'Summer, take the guards. Ginger, come with me.' I sign with quick precise movements. My face is stern, determined. We know what we have to do. Summer nods, carefully slinking across the lobby, dodging the lasers and disarming the guards from behind. She's quick to knock them out, barely making any noise as she drags them out of sight of the lasers.

Ginger takes her F.O.U.N.D. glasses out of the pocket inside her leather jacket, pushing them up her nose and looking around. When we get to the door of the mysterious storage room, we're met with another problem.

"A fingerprint scan? What the—? When did this happen?" Ginger's amber eyes narrow and her nose scrunches up as she reads the data presented to her. "Can you hack it, M?"

"I can try." I stare at the metal panel embedded into the wall. I need a screwdriver.

"What's the problem?" Summer leans against the wall, slightly out of breath.

"Fingerprint scanner." Ginger answers. I pull my Swiss Army Knife off of my belt and use the screwdriver to open up the box.

"Can Mia hack it?"

"Working on it." I scan over the wires. God, it's dark in here. Almost too dark to see. "Summer, hold this," I hand her the panel and point to Ginger's glasses. "Ginger, give me those."

"Here." She pushes them up my nose. Immediately, the interface flashes to life in front of me, pointing out different things in my surroundings. Thermal scans, foreign chemical signatures, anything that the air filters detect; it's kind of overwhelming. Swiping up the length of the right temple causes them to focus on the wires, and thankfully, the reading gives an estimation to the purpose of each one. Keyword: estimation.

"M, we don't have much time."

"I know." My eyes flick from cord to cord, and I use the knife to snip the connection between the scanner and the alarms. Seems important. There's a few seconds of anticipation waiting for the wailing sirens and flashing red lights, but fortunately, they never come. Job well done. I screw the metal plate back into place and pick the lock as normal, popping the door open only a few seconds later.

Ginger takes her glasses back, adjusting them as we walk into the small room. Things have been completely rearranged. The computer is gone. The briefcases are gone. And yet with all of the changes, the filing cabinets haven't moved. They're still up against the wall, just waiting to be searched.

"Full of files," Ginger reports, her index finger resting on the temple of her glasses. "That man cares more about his computers than he does his records apparently."

"Or maybe they're planted to throw us off track." Summer takes a step forward, opening the top drawer of the nearest cabinet. "Either way, we've got work to do."

All three of us set to work, flipping through the files quickly, but there's not much to work with. Meaning: the files are blank. Every page, every label, nothing. We open every drawer and thumb through every folder, but there's nothing...Until there is.

At the very back of the last drawer is the one file Louis left.

"Um..." Ginger moves uncertainly, looking at the file sitting on the table in front of her. "Summer, I think you're right. This can't be real."

"What is it?" I glance over her shoulder. At first, it's all fuzzy, as if my eyes are protecting my brain from whatever information the papers hold, but it's real. It's terrifyingly real. A chill runs up my spine and I swallow thickly, a bad taste settling in my mouth. I feel like I'm gonna throw up.

Dave.

It's Dave.

My Dave.

What the f—

I lean over the file, reading every word. After triple checking the name and picture, I'm sure it's him. David Thomas Bowen, 5'9", brown hair, blue eyes, colorblind.

"Shit." My heart races a mile a minute, pounding in my chest. It feels like it's trying to escape, run down the street and leave me in the dust. I don't blame it. I wish I could escape too. "Oh my God."

"What does it say?" Summer takes a peek over my shoulder. Our activity has come to a halt, stalled by the bomb-drop of my boyfriend crossing paths with my workplace for the second time. And though the first little mix-up was harmless, I sense this one will leave a longer impression. Come to think of it...the other run-in was in this very building...

"David shows potential for greatness. Although he's lacking the skills required physically and mentally, Dave has been seen around town on several occasions with suspected F.O.U.N.D. agent, Mia Crane. Using him as a means to get to her could be his greatest use to us."

"Shit."

"Yeah. Shit."

"What are you gonna do?"

"I don't know." I close my eyes, setting the file off to the side. Tears cloud my vision, but I ignore them and keep working. Summer and Ginger look to me with empty stares. They don't know what to say, and frankly, neither do I.

After a long patch of thick silence:

"M...Aren't you gonna scan Dave's file to HQ?"

"No." I shake my head. "They'll take him out. He's a liability."

I don't tell them what really runs through my mind. Dave being a liability makes me a liability. There's a crack in the bulletproof exterior that's supposed to be guarding my heart. Love is power, but it is also weakness. And in this moment, it feels like an anchor tethered to my ankle, ready to drag me down with it.

"Right." Ginger states. Her usual carefree devil-may-care party girl attitude has faded away. Her face is serious, sad even. "It's just—"

"Mia..." Summer takes my hand. "You can't hide it forever. You know that. They'll find out. They always do. And when they find out that you hid it from them..."

"I know." I sigh. "I know, but it's not like—"

"Come on. It looks like there's something under the stage." Ginger is quick to change the subject, using her glasses to pick up a signal from three rooms over. I tuck the file into my jacket and follow her. Good thing about being a spy is that we're light on our feet. It makes dodging through the security lasers almost fun in an adrenaline-pumping sort of way. The rush of potentially getting caught pushes us forward, daring us to take a risk.

I pick the electronic lock on the grand golden double doors to the auditorium. We're careful to step over the trip wires at the ends of the aisles and hurry down to the stage. Summer forces the trap door open, shining a flashlight down into the dark hatch. To be honest, I don't know much about drama, but I'm pretty sure normal stages don't have an arsenal under them.

Hand guns, grenades, throwing knives, smoke bombs, bullet-proof gear, gas masks...You name it, it's probably down here. One of the walls is lined in metal briefcases identical to the ones we recovered last week and a crate in the corner of the room is filled with little steel balls like the one I found in the woods.

We take some pictures, but as soon as I reach out to touch anything, an earsplitting screech tears through the building. Ginger and Summer slap their hands over their ears to block out the noise. I flick off my hearing aids, causing the sound to disappear almost entirely.

I can't hear her, but I see Ginger spout a string of curse words, squeezing her eyes shut in pain. Summer is in similar shape, though she's not as verbose. As a thick unidentified fog sweeps across the floor, it becomes apparent that we need to get the hell out of here while we still can. I scale the ladder, pulling myself out and helping the others after. After sprinting through the dark theater, we make it to the lobby, which is no longer patrolled by lasers. It's completely empty. But based on Summer and Ginger's reactions, it's still loud.

We retrace our steps, leaving the lobby the way we came in and reaching the back maintenance hallway. One of the metal doors takes us out to the garage where our motorcycles are faithfully waiting.

Ginger slams the door behind us, heaving a sigh of relief and resting her hands on her knees.

'It's safe.' Summer mouths and points to one of her ears. I click my hearing aids back on. City noise swells around me accompanied by the muffled siren on the other side of the door. We made it. I give a half-hearted glance to the file peeking out of my leather jacket. It's pretty thick, so I'm sure there's plenty to go through tonight while thoroughly debating giving it to Sheila. I probably won't, but I know there are consequences.

There are consequences either way.

"You okay?" Summer checks. Her eyes meet mine in the silence that follows.

Ginger doesn't say anything, only moving to wrap an arm around my shoulders and rest her head against mine for a long moment.

I nod, shoving the file further into my leather jacket and zipping it up to keep it safe. I'm not okay. She knows that. They both know that. But I keep up the act anyway, pushing all of the negative feelings, the doubts, and the crippling need to read this file word for word at least seventy times deep inside until I get home. I just have to get home.

And then I'm going to explode.

CHAPTER 19

Screaming into pillows works wonders for stress, as I've recently discovered. I'm realizing now as I'm sitting on my bed surrounded by papers about Dave that I really don't know that much about him. Never figured I'd need to run a background check on the cute nerdy guy that works at the local ice cream place, but here I am. This is what happens when a spy doesn't do her homework. Well, that and failing APUSH.

So basically, I spent twenty minutes screaming into a pillow, five minutes staring at the contents of the file but not really reading it, ten more minutes convincing myself to just dive in, and then thirty minutes actually reading. Long story short, it's not as bad as I thought it would be. There's no big red stamp that explicitly says Dave works for L.O.S.T. No signs point to the fact that he's one of them. He's not, as far as I know.

It's just—I think it's a sort of recruitment file. Is that how to put it? Like not quite an application 'here-join-my-evil-agency' sort of thing. It's more like a 'this-kid-could-be-great-in-our-evil-agency-because...blah blah blah' sort of deal. They want Dave. Not for his skills. Not for his intelligence. They want him because of me. They want him because I need him.

To make matters worse, there's not anything I can do about it. If I tell the agency, I'll be punished for withholding information, number one. Number two, Dave would be put on a watch list and if he did join them he would have to be apprehended. Or...worse... Three, I'd not only be punished (refer to point one), but if anything did go wrong with Dave, I'd rather just nip it in the bud, take care of it myself instead of letting the agency handle it. And four, I love him. I love him. Sweet, naïve, innocent teenage love, yes, but love nonetheless.

The more I stare at these damn papers, the more I want to rip them up and toss them in the fireplace in the living room. But I don't. I compose myself, nicely gather them into a folder, and tuck them into the drawer on my desk.

Immediately following this, I scream into my pillow again.

That's when C.A.I.T.L.Y.N. speaks up.

"Mia, would you like some hot chocolate?"

"Yes." I mumble a weak reply. The glow-in-the-dark stars on my ceiling are mocking me, watching my life, my relationship, my sanity wither away. I need to go to bed before I do something stupid. I don't know how many minutes pass before there's a knock on the doorframe.

"Knock-knock." Isaac smirks, two mugs of hot cocoa in his hands. The whipped cream is spiraled high, and there looks to be an abundance of cinnamon, marshmallows, and chocolate chips.

"Who's there?"

"An awesome older brother with hot cocoa."

"An awesome older brother with hot cocoa who?"

"An awesome older brother with hot cocoa who...wants to make sure you're okay. If our robot is concerned, you know something is wrong."

"She's not a robot, she's AI."

"Whatever." Isaac hands me a mug and takes a seat on the bed across from me. "Do you want to tell me what happened or do I have to guess what happened? Because my first guess has to do with a certain curly-haired civilian dork, but—"

"Sheila sent us back to further investigate the theater and we found a lot of messed up shit. One of the messed up shitty things is a file about Dave and the very detailed ways the League plans to use him to get to me. So yeah, life is great. Also, I not only decided to *not* turn in the file to the proper authorities, but I can't really do anything about it. It's not like I can just say 'hey Dave sorry to bother you, but um, I'm a spy and you're kind of in trouble because of me.'"

"Sounds like a mess."

"Understatement of the century." I take a long sip of the warm cocoa, whipped cream settling on my lip in a foamy mustache.

"It'll work out."

"Maybe."

"I've seen you pull out of worse."

"Have you?"

"No." He pauses. "Yes."

My ears, he means. I have pulled out of worse. But that was a long time ago. I was young, and I certainly wasn't in it alone. Not like I am now. My choice to protect Dave from the agency was my own. My choice to defend him from the League is my own too. Whatever happens to him now is on me. Not anyone else.

There's a knock at the door. Not very loud, barely loud enough to hear over the pouring rain pounding against the roof, but it's there. I take another sip from my mug before I set it down, step into my *Kim Possible* slippers, and walk down the stairs. Who could possibly be here this late?

As soon as I open the door, a very tired, bruised, soaking wet Dave stumbles into the manor and trips over the threshold. I catch him, heart racing at the sight of his beaten form. One of his eyes is dark, swollen. His lip is split, there's a cut on his forehead, and one of the legs of his shorts is soaked in fresh crimson blood.

"Dave, oh my God are you okay?"

"I-I've been better." He coughs weakly, trembling wildly and clutching me like a lifeline. Isaac helps me get him to the couch.

"Isaac, get the first aid kit."

"I'm getting Mom," he replies. She's better than a first aid kit.

"What happened?" I ask. He leans back against the couch, squeezing his eyes shut and wincing at the pain. "Where does it hurt?"

"E-everywhere. I got mugged on the way...home from work...walked here..." He takes a big breath, looking at me through the cracked lenses of his glasses. Tears well up in his blue eyes. "Guy with a knife...stabbed me...in the leg. Mom can't...see me like this. She'd freak."

"Let me see."

There's a great big gash on his thigh caked in blood and gravel, but by the looks of it, he got lucky. The cut isn't too deep. Not deep enough to do serious damage, but deep enough to hurt like hell.

"David, what are you doing here? What happened?" Mom carries the huge red first aid kit down the stairs with Isaac trailing behind her. She sets to work immediately, unpacking medical supplies on the coffee table. Dave explains what happened as best as he can and tells her what hurts and how bad. She concludes that he has a very minor concussion and, besides the cut on his leg and the black eye and split lip, only minor bruising and battering. He's going to be sore, but he'll live.

I hook him up with an ice pack wrapped in a towel to press to his eye. His leg has been disinfected and wrapped in gauze, propped up on the coffee table. Isaac loaned him some of his sweatpants and a t-shirt so he didn't have to wear his soaking wet clothes. Dave finishes off a few cookies from the bakery, which seem to make him feel a bit better, though he still looks like he could burst into tears at any second. I don't blame him.

He's been through a lot for one night. Something like this wouldn't even faze me, but even in a place like Great City, Dave's never had problems with anyone except the few bullies at school who are brave enough to mess with him knowing that I'd kick their asses if I ever found out. This probably rocked his world.

"You okay?" I ask once Mom's gone. He nods. "Do you want me to drive you home?" He shakes his head. "Do you wanna stay here?"

"I- is that okay? I d-don't want to be a burden—" His voice is impossibly small, uncertain, almost afraid. His hands fiddle mindlessly, eyebrows furrowing. His eyes can't seem to find mine.

"Yeah. Of course." One of my hands wraps around his and the other removes his broken glasses, setting them on the table.

"Is my face messed up?"

"Mmhmm,"

"Is it bad?"

"Yeah. You're still a cutie, though. The black eye makes you look like a badass."

"I bet." He chuckles. "I texted my mom on the way here. Told her you needed emergency cuddles because your cat died."

"I don't have a cat, babe."

"I know." He exhales a large breath, blowing the wet hairs out of his face. "I'll figure out how to explain the black eye and...everything else I guess."

"Are you really okay?" I check, resting a hand on his knee carefully. He looks me in the eyes, a small smirk finding his lips.

"I am now."

"Cheeseball."

"A very tired cheeseball."

"I love you." I lay down on the couch.

"I love you too." He cautiously lays down on top of me.

We've been together for a year. Cuddles are commonplace in our relationship, but sleeping together is untouched territory even in its most innocent sense. Once he overcomes the timid touches, Dave snuggles up to me, burying his face in the crook of my neck. I wouldn't dare call him out on it, but I feel his shaking breaths and his fresh-forming tears, wet against my skin. All I do is hold him tighter, pulling him as close to me as I can without hurting him.

It's quiet. The lights are dim. It's just him and I, holding each other on my couch. My heart swells with so much love and so much compassion for the lanky nerd curled up in my arms that soon I feel tears forming too, dripping down my cheeks. I could have lost him tonight. I could have lost him and I wouldn't have been able to do anything about it. Wouldn't have been able to stop it, prevent it, protect him from it. He would have just been gone.

So I just lay here, softly crying and holding him until we're both asleep.

CHAPTER 20

It's still dark out when I wake up. The living room is pitch black, and the only noise is the rushing waves against the shore outside and Dave's deep breathing. The fact that there's sound at all means I forgot to take my hearing aids out before bed. I guess I was kind of too preoccupied to remember something like that. I press a long kiss to Dave's forehead. He lets out a sleepy hum, still drifting in dreamland.

It takes me a few moments to notice the piece of paper jutting out of his back pocket. My fingertips brush against it. Eyebrows furrowing, I tentatively pull the paper out and unfold it. It's way too dark to actually see it, but I pluck my phone off the table, using the dimmed light from the screen to make out the blood red letters.

A chill runs up my spine and goosebumps prickle up my arms the moment my muddled sleepy mind finally strings the group of words into a sentence. It's very short, very precise, but it does its job.

Miss Crane, stay out of this. Or else.

PART 2

CHAPTER 21

When I wake up for real, it's bright outside. For a few precious moments, I think that what happened last night was a nightmare. I wish it was, but it wasn't. None of it. Not the mission to the theater, not Dave's file, not Dave showing up in the middle of the night, and not the note warning me to back off "or else." The weight on my chest and the arms tight around my waist are reassuring. He's still here. He's still safe.

For now.

"Morning, babe." My voice is soft, thick with sleep. A glance at the clock tells me it's noon. God, I overslept. Dave groans, attempting to bury his head deeper into my shoulder.

"Morning." His voice is barely audible, muffled by the couch. He looks around, blue eyes finding mine after searching the living room. "I'm so sore."

"I bet. Black eye is looking a little better though."

"Yeah?"

"Yeah." I try to get up, but he weighs me down in an attempt to keep me here. "Come on Dave, it's noon."

"Five more minutes."

"I have to go to work."

"Stay," he pleads, his voice soft.

"How about..." I press a long kiss to his forehead. "I make lunch."

"Lunch?" He turns to look at the clock, squinting to read the numbers without his glasses. "Oh right. Lunch. Do you by any chance have mac and cheese?"

"I think we do. Stay here. I'll go check." I untangle myself from him and get off of the couch, walking to the kitchen. It seems we have an abundance of the cheesy noodley goodness in the cupboard. Like a lot. At least ten boxes. I grab one and set it on the counter. Dave gets up and makes his way to the kitchen table, limping there in a stumbling mess. "Dave!"

"What? I'm fine!" He plops down onto the wooden chair. I shake my head before bending down to fish a pot out of the cabinet. Dave fiddles with his phone. Seconds later, music starts playing. Cheesy, upbeat '80s pop music. I can't help but dance along, filling the pot with water and setting it on the stove. A wooden spoon becomes my microphone as I slide around the smooth wooden kitchen floor in my socks. Dave doubles over with laughter, clutching his chest. "You are stunning."

"With no makeup on, making dumb faces in my kitchen?"

"It's a good look for you."

"I bet."

I finish making the mac and cheese and set a bowl in front of each of us just as Isaac walks into the kitchen.

"You're still here?" I shovel a spoonful of cheesy noodles into my mouth. "Thought you had work."

"I do, but I was kinda up 'til 3 a.m., so..."

"Right."

"Ooh mac and cheese!"

"Help yourself." I chuckle.

He fills a bowl and takes a seat at the table with us. "How're you holding up, buddy?"

"I'm alright." Dave nods. He's still a little squinty without his glasses on, but it's cute. "Still sore."

"Before I take you home, I've gotta change your bandages, okay?"

"Okay." He nods.

"I'll take you two," Isaac offers. I look at him skeptically. He doesn't usually offer rides. "No really, I can."

"Thanks." I take my empty bowl to the sink and rinse it out before sticking it in the top shelf of the dishwasher. "I'm gonna go get changed. I'll be down in a few. Put some ice on that black eye."

"Yes, ma'am." Dave tilts his head back towards me as he usually does when he's expecting a kiss. I press my lips to his and let them linger for a few seconds before leaving the kitchen. My phone blares the Kim Possible theme song just as I'm halfway up the stairs.

"Hello?"

"Where are you, babe? Sheila said you haven't checked in. Are you even at Headquarters?" It's Ginger.

"Not yet. I'm on the way, I swear. There's just...there was a situation last night that I'm still trying to get a handle on."

"Uh, 'situation' meaning what, exactly? Is everything okay?" Summer takes control of the phone.

"It's fine now. Dave got mugged on the way home from work."

"What?!" they both shout.

"Oh my God, is he okay? Do you know who it was?" Summer fires questions at light speed.

"I'll explain when I get there." I walk into my room and stick my hand into the pocket of my sweatpants to take out the crumpled paper with the bright red warning.

Even now, the words make my stomach drop. They know who I am. That much is clear. They know what Dave means to me. I don't know what they want, but the fact that he was hurt the night we dug up his file and set off the alarm at the theater is in no way anything close to a coincidence. This is a threat. Stay away from L.O.S.T. or they'll make it personal. A warning I can't heed, given my current occupation.

"Okay," there's a pause, "see you then." The girls hang up.

I change as fast as I can. My pajamas are exchanged for a pair of red short-shorts and a black thick-strapped tank-top with lace-up black ankle boots. Once I'm dressed, I rush through my makeup routine at a speed the Flash would envy and head down the stairs as soon as I'm done, sliding down the railing.

Next, I change the bandages on Dave's leg, apply more ointment to the wound, and hook him up with a portable ice pack that he can take home with him. I think he's good to go.

"All aboard the Isaac Express, kiddos!" Isaac jingles his keys and pushes his shades up his nose. He and I slip into our leather jackets. Dave raises an eyebrow.

"It's like eighty degrees outside. I swear, your whole family is cold-blooded."

"We must be." I shrug.

Dave leans on me for support, limping to take weight off of his injured leg. I help him into the front seat of Isaac's red convertible and take a seat in the back. The engine hums to life, headlights illuminating the garage until Isaac turns them off. The sound of Taylor Swift telling us to 'shake it off' fills the car, but Isaac is quick to flick it off, replacing it with Green Day instead. I eye him suspiciously.

"Isaac?"

"Hmm?" He pulls out of the driveway, hiding his eyes behind his shades.

"Why do you have my Taylor Swift CD?"

"Hmm?"

I do my best to hide my amusement, but Dave is straight-up cackling. "Why. Do you have. My CD."

"Sorry baby sis! I can't hear you over the music!"

I shake my head and Isaac continues to drive across town to Dave's house. Dave tries to jam out to the rock, but he's too sore and too tired to put his heart into it. In a little over twenty minutes, we pull into Dave's driveway. Isaac parks the car and I walk my poor, sweet, injured Dave to the front door.

"Let's get you to the basement, okay?"

"I can handle it. I'll be all right." Dave stops me at the front door. He smiles weakly, his squinty, tear-filled blue eyes meeting mine. His right eye is bruised and slightly swollen, but it looks like it's cleared up a bit since last night. His lip is still split, and there's a purpling bruise on his left cheekbone, not to mention the cut on his forehead or the one on his leg, wrapped tight in gauze. "But thank you. For everything. Seriously, I don't know what I'd do without you."

"I love you." My arms wrap tight around his body, holding him close. I bask in his warmth, in his smell. I could never get enough of it. I feel him trembling, shaking as he embraces me. "I love you so much, okay? I'd do anything for you. You know that."

"Are you okay, M? Are you...crying?"

"No...No. My allergies must be acting up again. Just please be careful. If you ever need a ride home from work, call me. I'll pick you up in a heartbeat."

"Okay. I love you too."

"I'm gonna come check on you later, okay? Maybe keep you company for a few minutes during my break?"

"Okay." He nods.

I pull away to look at him. There's a long moment of silence. Just him and I. He takes my hands slowly. My fingers rub against his calloused palms, and his thumbs gently stroke circles on my skin.

He inhales a long breath and holds it for a few seconds before letting it out. "I'll see you later then."

He cranes his neck down, meaning he wants a kiss. I press my lips to his, leaving red lipstick behind, a bright, rich mark. Pink creeps across his cheeks. Even after a year, he still gets flustered when we kiss in front of other people.

Once we've exchanged our goodbyes, I climb into the passenger seat of Isaac's convertible. We drive down the street towards the city, leaving Dave's house far behind us. I just have to trust that he'll be okay on his own, at least for now. A girl can hope.

CHAPTER 22

Upon reaching the agency and checking in, Ginger sends me a text that she and Summer are in Lab 32 with Brian, so I head there instead of Sheila's office as I had originally planned.

"What happened? Spill. Tell us everything." Ginger demands as soon as she lays eyes on me.

"Dave got mugged, but I'm pretty sure it was a set-up. They're using him as bait to get to me. This was in his back pocket. I don't think he noticed, though. Fortunately." I hand them the note.

Summer takes it, unfolding it and reading it quickly. Her eyes meet mine, full of concern. She shows it to Ginger and Brian, both of whom wear similar expressions.

"L.O.S.T. knows about me. I don't know how, but they know who I am and they know how to get to me."

"Shit."

"Yeah. You're telling me," I shake my head. "I'm screwed."

"What was in the file about your boyfriend?" Brian glances into his microscope and adjusts the lens, eyes flicking up to mine nervously before returning to his work. An escape from my intense gaze.

"How do you know about that?"

"We kinda told him?" Summer explains. "Sorry. It's just easier to not keep secrets from our engineer."

"Whatever. It's fine. I trust Brian."

"Thanks."

"I trust that you know I'll kick your ass if you tell anyone." I clarify. "Because I can and I will."

"You don't need to flex your muscles around me, Mia. I know what you're capable of. I've read the files."

"Okay good." I relax the tiniest bit. I know he's right. I know he wouldn't tell anyone. I'm just so stressed and worried and all of the pressure is getting to my head. I need to chill. "So, basically, Dave doesn't work for L.O.S.T., but they've suspected me of working for F.O.U.N.D. They want to use Dave to get to me to get to the agency."

"Why?"

"Because they hate us." Ginger adds.

Summer points to her. "True."

"They think we're a virus. A sickness. I think 'brain-washed' was the word the guy at camp used." I flash back to the intruders that attempted to ambush a household of agents and horribly failed. "Orville is the brains of the agency. Louis Orville. Sheila told us about him."

"Louis Orville the Second?" Brian perks up. "That guy owns like half of the city. A theater, a park, this fire safety foundation thing. He owns Lucky's Ice Cream Shop and—"

"Lucky's." I stop him. "Dave works at Lucky's. No wonder he knows who I am, I go there all the time. A second grader could have made that connection."

"Don't beat yourself up about it. It's not like you can just stay inside forever. Like me." Brian shrugs and switches the slides on his microscope. "You actually have a life. I've never even been to the mall in this town."

"We can take you there whenever you want. Or you could, I don't know, take the train or a bus or a cab there like a normal person."

"No thanks. I'm good." Brian looks up at the three of us. The dark bags are still present under his eyes, but they're not as bad as they were. It looks like his rusty red hair has seen a comb and some gel recently so I assume he's showered.

Summer puts a hand on his shoulder in an attempt to get him to refocus. "Tell Mia about the chemical."

"Right. That's why you're here isn't it?" Brian pulls out a thick file of papers. "This was with the stuff you guys found last night. Apparently, L.O.S.T. calls this stuff Chemical Rebirth, and they're supposed to be taken in a sequence, hence the numbers on the labels, but besides that we have no clue. All of the files the field department's combined efforts recovered were encrypted, written in code. Intel is trying to get a handle on it, but until then...I'll be here with a microscope and some test tubes. Fun times."

"It's your favorite place to be."

"That it is. Lab, sweet lab."

"I'm gonna get you a shirt that says that." Ginger grins.

Brian looks amused by the idea. "You do that. In the meantime, I'll be here. As usual. Kinda takes the fun out of looking for me, huh?"

"Well it certainly takes away the surprise. Thanks for the info, B. I don't know what we'd do without you." Summer kisses his cheek, sending his face into a flustered frenzy of red. "Next stop, Sheila's."

Sheila's office is inhabited by three people. Sheila is at her desk. Her new intern Elise is seated on the couch, attending to business on the tablet, and a tall sandy-haired field agent stands with his back to us.

He stands up straight, stiff as a board with his hands clasped tightly behind his back. An array of weapons is strapped to the belt of his black leather uniform.

"Ah, there you are. Girls, I'm sure you remember Archer Reynolds." Sheila motions to him.

Archer turns around to face us as we walk in. Puberty has been kind to the once average-looking agent we worked with a few years ago. Piercing green eyes, a strong jawline, broad shoulders and muscular arms. His chest is thick with muscle, as are his thighs. Hopefully his personality has gotten a similar makeover. If I remember correctly, he was always kind of an asshole.

"Archer, agents Mia Crane, Summer Laurence, and Ginger Williams."

"It's been what, three years now?" Archer's British accent is as thick as ever. I nod. So far so good. He smirks. Uh oh. "Hopefully your skills have improved since then." Whoop, there it is.

"Good to see you too, Archer. What are you doing here? Shouldn't you be, I don't know, on the other side of the ocean?"

"My partner John and I were transferred here temporarily to help with your L.O.S.T. infestation." Archer smirks, taking a small step forward. "But believe me, Crane, the three of you wouldn't have been my first choice. It was Hodge's decision, not mine."

"Let's get down to business, shall we? Elise, the presentation, please." Sheila is quick to cut off the conversation before Summer and Ginger can join in the sarcastic banter and snide remarks.

"Yes, ma'am." Elise swipes up the length of the tablet and the projector kicks to life, showing a picture of the man of the hour, Louis Orville. I've seen his face before, briefly, but seeing it now after everything that's happened since then makes all of this much more real.

"Agents, this is Louis Orville II, possibly the wealthiest man in Great City and the director of L.O.S.T. Orville is known for many things, but L.O.S.T. has only surfaced recently. We don't know how long their agency has been established, but their footprint is international. Briefcases of Chemical Rebirth have been recovered in Europe, North America, South America, Asia, and Australia, all in or near businesses and buildings connected to Orville Enterprises."

The screen changes, fading into an image of one of the nicest hotels in Great City, Le Doux Rêves Hôtel.

"Orville's non-profit organization, the Orville Fire Safety and Prevention Foundation, is holding a fundraiser gala at his prized five-star hotel tonight. Your job is to infiltrate. Get close to Orville. Monitor his conversations. Investigate his staff. Plant bugs wherever necessary."

Sheila hands each of us a card for the textile department.

"Ginger, you'll be taking on the role of concert cellist, Veronica Wilson. You'll need to pull your hair back to hide the pink streaks, but the nose ring can stay."

"Yesss!"

"Summer, you'll be infiltrating the waiting staff as a red-haired waitress named Sara. There's a wig waiting for you in textile."

"I can work with that."

"Summer, Ginger, both of you need to arrive at the back door of the hotel around 5pm for gala prep. You'll be dropped off in separate vehicles to eliminate a connection. Mia, Archer, the two of you will be attending the gala as Scarlett and Theodore Cress, wealthy young newlyweds from Legacy, Florida. Mia, you'll need a blonde wig. Archer, the stylist downstairs will temporarily darken your hair."

Archer reaches up in concern, his fingers raking through his upswept sandy locks.

"Don't worry. The dye will wash out in the shower."

"Alright, good." He tries to hide his relief, but is not very successful.

"You two don't need to be at the gala until 7:30. A limousine will transport you to the front doors of the hotel. Report to the textile department at 6:30 sharp."

"Will do."

"You're dismissed."

We leave Sheila's office. Archer walks down the hall.

"God, why are the hot ones always such asses?" Summer asks as soon as he's out of earshot. She tries not to, but she watches him go. We all do. That boy's rear end is just as fine as his front.

"You're not the one fake-married to him!" I hiss.

"Yeah, but you *are* the one with a boyfriend." Summer states. "What if he has to kiss you? Or worse? What if you like it?"

"One, I won't. Two, not my type. Three, it's not like Dave will ever find out. It's fine. It's not real. We're practically actors. And you know what they say: the show must go on."

"Well in that case," Ginger glances down the hall after the attractive British agent, "break a leg."

CHAPTER 23

Even after clocking in a few hours at the bakery, I still have a little over three hours before I have to report to textiles. Upon hearing about Dave, Greta gives me two dozen red velvet cupcakes and sends me out the door to check on him. I had planned on checking in before, but the cupcakes will definitely lift his spirits. After all, they are his favorite.

I borrow a motorcycle (because mine is in the garage at home) from F.O.U.N.D.'s arsenal of vehicles and pull into Dave's driveway in the suburbs just under half an hour later. His mom isn't home, but there are a few other cars here. An old white minivan is parked just in front of my bike, its back window decorated with various nerdy car decals: a Superman symbol, Captain America's shield, Thor's hammer, and the Flash's logo.

Whoever owns this car is shamelessly mixing Marvel and DC like they don't know what they're doing. I don't know as much about comics as Dave, but I know that if you're going to go around mixing the two universes, you should at least organize it, not stick them around like they belong together.

With two boxes of cupcakes in my arms, I unlock the back door and walk down the stairs into Dave's Nerd Cave. Over the loud noise from the speakers, I can make out four distinct voices. Dave must have some friends over. Admittedly, I haven't met very many of Dave's friends. Every time he's tried to do something with them and I, a mission or something comes up. What can I say? I'm a busy girl.

"Babe! I brought cupcakes!" I shout, pushing through the Spider-Man curtains hanging in the entrance of Dave's Fortress of

Solitude. Sure enough, there are three teenage boys in addition to Dave spread out in his awesome center of entertainment.

It's been a while since I've been down here. Dave's rearranged a bit. A large round Death Star rug sits under the coffee table. Several superhero action figures and bobble-heads are locked into battle poses on the shelves, arranged by team and universe. Dave has an arsenal of books, comics, movies, and video games. There's a large traffic-cone-orange couch sitting in front of the TV with a long Doctor Who blanket draped over the back of it.

A Mjolnir night-light sticks out of the wall beside a framed *Avengers* poster, and the ceiling is covered in the same brand of glow-in-the-dark stars that are in my bedroom. A pair of lightsabers are mounted on the wall, locked into an eternal clash by super-glue and some bolts and screws. The walls are covered in tons of posters and things from the internet, a few pages of comics that Dave drew (they're not half bad, if I do say so myself), and beside the screen, there's a picture of the two of us. Dave's prized Polaroid camera rests on the table nearest to him.

"Who are you?" asks the closest member of Dave's nerd brigade: a lanky Asian kid wearing a pair of neon green headphones around his neck. The smartphone in his hand has a case that matches the very loud shade of green, as do a pair of sunglasses resting on his head. I kinda dig it.

"I'm Mia. Mia Crane," I state. I'm greeted by unbelieving expressions and a very smug-looking Dave. "Dave's girlfriend?"

"She exists!" gasps the kid in the middle. He has twice as many freckles as Brian (which I didn't think was possible until now) and he's wearing a Flash shirt and a pair of Captain America socks. If I had to guess, the minivan is probably his. "This last year, I thought Dave was just really good at character-building and compulsive lying."

"And Photoshop." Adds the other guy.

Freckles nods. "That too."

"Well, let's look at the data. Dave is Dave, and this girl is gorgeous. And she brought cupcakes. Maybe she's a robot."

"Not a robot. Sorry to disappoint." I chuckle, holding the box in front of each of them so they can take a cupcake. "I work at Sugar & Spice, so this is one of the many job perks."

"I need to get a job at a bakery..." mumbles the third guy, a curly-haired blond, as he takes a bite of one of the red velvet cupcakes. "These are so good, holy shit."

"My favorite." Dave smiles. "Thanks M."

"No prob. Thought it'd cheer you up." I drop into the seat next to him and look around at Dave's buddies who are just as thrilled as he is.

"It worked." Headphones nods. "I'm Mark by the way. Freckles over there is Tommy, and the blondie is Nick." each of the boys offer a nod and a 'sup' as Mark introduces them. Their X-Box controllers rest on their laps, the game paused, and their attention turned instead to the supply of cupcakes and Dave's not non-existent girlfriend.

"Are you sure Dave didn't hire you?" Tommy asks.

"What?" I laugh incredulously. "I'm pretty sure, yeah."

"It's just...Dave is so...*Dave*, and you're so not."

"Woah, whose motorcycle is that?!" Nick peers out the window while standing up to get another cupcake.

"Mine."

Shocked silence from all parties but Dave, who is chuckling to himself. Nick's mouth is agape, and all of them have wide eyes.

"Dave, where did you find her and can you find me one?"

"Sorry guys, she's one of a kind." Dave wraps an arm around my waist, pulling me closer.

"Oh hush," I mess with his hair, "cheeseball."

"Are you out of work?"

"Hmm?"

"Are you done today?"

"Nah, I've gotta go back in at 6. But I'll be in the back, not at the counter."

"Oh, okay." Dave nods.

I look over his injuries. His mom must have changed his bandages on her lunch break because they look fresh. An ice pack rests on the table, but it should be on his eye.

"Babe, keep this on your eye. It'll help the pain, trust me." I press the cold bundle into his hand. He nods, exchanging his glasses for the ice. I pause. "I can come check on you after work if you want. It'll be late, but—"

"The window's always unlocked." He smirks. His guy friends ignored us long ago, plunging into a deep conversation about *Star Wars* so they wouldn't have to be caught in our lovers' talk. It's not even really flirting. It's just me checking up on him as any good girlfriend would.

We sit there for a couple of hours. I watch the boys play their games on Dave's X-Box. There are a few conversations going at once, one about the game they're in the middle of, and another still stuck on the topic of *Star Wars*.

Nick whispers into Mark's ear. He laughs before passing whatever they're talking about on to Tommy. He nods, chuckling.

"What?" I ask.

Dave rolls his eyes. He seems to know what they're going on about.

"Mia, we need a female opinion."

"Shoot."

"Dave needs help dressing himself, right?" Tommy laughs. "He's a train wreck."

Dave shakes his head chuckling. "This again."

"He's colorblind." I laugh. "Sure, he's a mismatched mess, but it's adorable."

"Thanks, babe."

"And on that happy note, I have to leave." I get up off of the couch. "Nice to meet you guys. Dave, I'll be back later, alright? Stay off that leg and keep ice on that eye."

"Got it. See you later." Dave leans up for a kiss. My lips meet his, and once again I leave a red mark.

"Oooooooooh," the guys coo teasingly. They make kissy noises and whistle. I roll my eyes. So mature.

"Shut up." Dave's cheeks are almost as red as the mark I left on his lips.

"Bye, guys."

"Thanks for the cupcakes!" Mark calls as I walk through the Spider-Man curtains at the base of the stairs.

"I'm still not convinced you're human!" Tommy's final declaration makes me laugh on my way out the back door.

The sight of my motorcycle on the driveway is almost jarring. I think that's honestly the longest period of time I've spent with a group of non-agents, and for that short amount of time, I didn't have to be anything I wasn't. I just had to be me. Now, I have to go put on a wig and infiltrate a charity gala with my fake husband and my real best friends in an attempt to find information that will bring a corrupt organization of science and technology to its knees before anything else can go wrong. It's about as simple as it sounds, meaning it isn't simple at all. But who said simple is fun? Predictable *is* another word, for boring, after all.

I strap my motorcycle helmet onto my head and pull out of the driveway. The low rumble of the bike is soothing. It's home. My safe place. Normalcy was nice for a while, but if I don't accept reality now, I never will. I am not a normal girl. I never have been. I never will be. I am an undercover teenage operative of a government-run facility of defense. I can't change that. And if I want to keep my cover and finish my mission, I have to embrace it.

CHAPTER 24

"You're four minutes and 17 seconds late." Archer taps the watch on his wrist a few times, standing in the lobby of the textile department. I roll my eyes.

"I checked in eight minutes early."

"But you're *here* four minutes late."

"Shut it, Reynolds." I drag him to the counter. We set our cards from Sheila on the desk and the attendant, a forty-something named Jodi, returns with our assigned outfits. They're zipped up in long black suit bags.

The textile division is really nice. There are ten advanced dressing booths on either side of the room, all of them closed off with rich red curtains. Inside, the walls and floor are smooth oak wood, a bold contrast from every other division in the agency. I step into one and pull the curtains shut behind me. Let's take a peek at what we're dealing with here.

Sparkling silky red fabric tumbles out of the dress bag. Strapless, floor-length, and absolutely stunning. I can work with this. I can *definitely* work with this. The dress fits like a glove. Comfortable, it breathes, and I can barely feel the bulletproof corset. I spin. It twirls like a dream, effortless and light with just enough swish. This might possibly be my favorite cover to date. Scarlett Cress, you may not exist, but I love you.

On either wall of the changing room, there's a wall of electronically organized accessories and other items in automated drawers for our use. Ladies' on the right, men's on the left. I scan my ID and check out a short pearl necklace and a pair of sparkly ruby earrings. As a final touch, I step into a pair of open-toed glittering golden pumps. Damn. I look good. But I'm not done yet.

After changing and tucking my normal uniform into a cubby in the lobby, I walk past the counter, and into the back room where the stylists are. These people are magical. I mean it. They can use makeup and prosthetics to make us look like just about anybody. It's kind of incredible.

I sit down in one of the chairs in front of the long mirrored vanity. One of the stylists, a tall woman probably in her early-twenties, sets to work, wiping my face completely clean so she can start from scratch. Her long purple and black hair is pulled up into a bun, and she twirls a pen between her quick fingers, biting her black lipstick-covered lips. She jots a few things down on the log, looking me over critically.

As soon as she knows what's she's doing, her hands move at the speed of light. Foundation, concealer, eyeliner, eyeshadow, mascara, blush, and bronzer, all done in a matter of minutes. She tops off the look by contouring my cheekbones more dramatically, elongating and thickening my eyelashes the slightest bit, and rubbing a rich velvety matte lipstick on my lips. The color matches my dress perfectly.

Finally, the stylist pulls my hair up into a cap and arranges the soft blonde wig so it looks natural. Several golden pins hold it in place. I've been transformed. Scarlett Cress might not exist, but damn, does she look good?

I assume Archer is on the other side of the wall that divides this stylist station from the one beside it. He's probably been through a similar transformation, though I doubt his was as thorough.

"You're all set, Agent Crane," says the stylist, Rose according to her nametag. She winks, showing off her spectacular sparkly pink and purple eyeshadow. God, she's stunning. "Have fun out there."

"Will do. Thanks for this. You're spectacular."

"It's my job," Rose smirks, taking a seat on her stool as she waits for her next appointment. It's kind of late, so I don't expect she has much to do. She twirls a blush brush between her fingers and starts sketching something in a notebook. I realize I've been staring a smidge too long and turn to go back out to the lobby.

Archer is standing in front of a mirror, his long fingers fumbling with a red tie. He can't seem to get it right.

"Need some help there, Reynolds?" My heels click sharply along the gray and white flecked tile of the lobby floor.

He looks up. For once, there's something besides snarkiness and contempt in his piercing green gaze. His usually sandy blond hair is a dark chocolate brown, pretty close to my natural hair color. Fake stubble covers his chin and jawline. I'll give it to him, the guy cleans up nice.

"Uh, yeah." He releases the tie, letting the smooth red fabric hang limp around his neck. I take both ends of it and quickly tie it properly, being careful not to choke him when I wiggle the neat knot closer to his throat. "Thanks."

"Mmhmm."

There's still something off about the way he's looking at me. Something warm in his eyes where there's only ever been coldness, something soft. Maybe it's this dress or the wig or something he's never seen about me until now that seems to be melting his heart of stone. I snap my fingers in front of his face a few times in an attempt to break him out of it. He coughs, clearing his throat.

"Oh sorry."

"What's wrong with you?"

"Nothing, just..." He stops, eyes gliding over my face. We're so close. Inches apart. I feel his warm breath ghost across my cheeks. A chill runs up my spine. That look in his eyes. I don't like it. "You look rather good in red."

"Thanks." I take the smallest step backwards.

Archer pats the pockets of his sharp black suit. He retrieves a long rectangular navy blue velvet box. Inside are two wedding rings. Right. We're "married." He slips the gold band onto his ring finger and plucks mine out with his index finger and thumb. My left ring finger already has a ring on it. The silver "*I love you*" ring from Dave. I forgot to tuck it away with my belongings earlier.

"What's that from?"

"My boyfriend." I reply, sliding the silver band off.

Archer slides the stunning diamond ring onto my finger, and I put my *Star Wars* ring in the vacant slot in the velvet case. It'll be safe there.

"Boyfriend?"

"Dave."

"Boyfriend." Archer repeats, as though the word is foreign to him.

"Yeah. Boyfriend."

"Oh."

"Oh?"

"Ignore me. I must be daft. Sorry." Archer shakes his head and then offers me his arm. His British accent is smooth, suave. A nice recovery from the choppy awkwardness of our previous conversation. "Let's go then. Shall we, Scarlett?"

I slip my arm through his. God, we look like a married couple. Our reflections gaze back at us. His tie matches my dress perfectly, and the wedding ring on my finger dazzles like a star. Archer's suit is neatly pressed, not a wrinkle in sight. It's black, spotless. He's a few inches taller than Dave, but the tousled chocolate brown locks keep making me second-guess. At first glance, he looks just like my dorky nerd of a boyfriend, but he's not. Unfortunately.

"Right. Let's go. Theodore." God, help me.

CHAPTER 25

I have never seen so many fancy dresses in one place before in my life. Sure, I've been to events like this on missions in the past, but Orville's crowd is the highest of the high end. The people here donating tonight are some of the richest in the world, and as far as they know, so are Archer and I.

We talked over our story in the limousine. We're twenty-two years old. We met in the Bahamas when we were seventeen and both of our ultra-wealthy families were vacationing there in our summer houses. Of course, our families had been friends through the years, our fathers were former business partners and we had seen each other when we were younger, but we didn't fall in love until I saw how handsome he had gotten after all of those years.

God, the thought if it makes me feel sick to my stomach.

It takes a lot of work to pretend to be in love with Archer, let alone his wife. But despite all that, I cling to his bicep like a lifeline as we navigate the hotel's elegant ballroom. High ceilings are adorned with glittering crystalline chandeliers. The cream-colored walls shine with painted golden accents and trim, and the rich red carpets remind me a bit too much of the agency. Bright red. Blood red.

It hits me when Summer (wearing a short red wig with bangs) comes around with a platter of champagne glasses that Scarlett and Theodore are legal to drink, despite the fact that Mia Crane and Archer Reynolds are not. Well, not in America, at least. I take a few sips of the tangy sparkling liquid before abandoning it on a nearby table.

The socializing is the hardest part of this mission. I smile brighter than a Barbie doll, laughing at jokes I've heard a million times and learning about the families of the rich businessmen and their spouses. Grandsons that play golf, family yachts that are in need of a remodel, new wings on mansions I didn't know existed. Do I care? No. Do I think this information is even remotely useful? No. But small talk with the 1% is the only way to get a one on one conversation with the man of the hour, Mr. Louis Orville II.

Archer and I glide across the dance floor, waltzing smoothly to the elegant string choir. Ginger is in the front row, dragging her bow across her cello. She has a knack for that sort of thing. She can play just about any string instrument from a ukulele to an upright bass and everything in between. A hidden talent. Her movements are full of such grace that watching her, you wonder if her bow is a part of her arm, if her cello is an extension of her body. It seems so natural.

One of Archer's hands grips the small of my back, holding my body up against his. I snap back to reality. The other hand is firmly around my own, giving reassuring squeezes in response to my anxious sighs. He leans closer and his breath is warm against my ear.

"Orville is at your six, coming this way. He's got his eye on us."

"Perfect. I've been meaning to talk to him."

"That makes two of us." Archer presses a kiss to my cheek and stands upright again. A chill runs up my spine. The feeling of his lips against my skin is so, so wrong. I am acting. This is acting. I can do this.

There's a tap on my shoulder. I turn to look, pretending to be surprised. Louis Orville is a lot shorter than I expected. With these spectacular golden pumps, he's only just about an inch taller than me. The monster who's been terrorizing me and my family and my boyfriend is surprisingly human, startlingly so. The sparkle in his gray eyes seems almost genuine, though I know the smile he's wearing is probably the fakest I've ever seen. As fake as a beauty pageant contestant that just won second place. Dazzling, bright, but empty.

Orville's suit is black, crisp. His red tie is only a few shades darker than the one around Archer's neck, a deep cranberry instead of blood red.

"Hello there, I don't believe we've met. Louis Orville. Nice to meet you."

"Scarlett Cress. This is my husband Theodore. Goodness, have we heard a lot about you."

"Is that so?"

"Of course we have. You're the man of the hour, aren't you? You're the founder of this organization. The man that put this event together? God, I don't know what Great City would even be without you." Archer adds a truckload of flattery for good measure, resulting in a hearty laugh and a hand on the Brit's shoulder.

"Ah, yes. That." Orville offers a smile and a nod. He seems to be a soft-spoken man, very polite. But looks can be deceiving. This is the man that sent a threat in the form of a group of guys hurting my boyfriend. The man that had him beat up to send a message. If he's willing to go to that length to protect his secrets, he must have a lot to hide. And if he sends others to do his dirty work, he must be a coward. "Theodore, would you mind terribly much if I stole a minute with your wife?"

"Not at all, Mr. Orville. It was nice to meet you." Archer's arms leave my waist. He presses a long kiss to my lips and walks off towards Summer, who's stationed at one of the tables serving little finger foods.

Orville offers his arm and I take it, letting him escort me into the hall.

Several paintings adorn the walls outside the ballroom. A sunset over the glistening Great City waves. The emerald hues of the sun shining through a leafy canopy. A wintry forest, full of pine trees dusted in snow. They're all beautiful, but he stops me in front of the scene with the most character. It's a bright sunny spring day. Flowers are blooming all around, pinks and yellows and oranges blending into the teal hues of a pond. The grass is thick and green, and there's a woman wearing a lavender bonnet that hides her face from view. Long blonde hair flows over her shoulders and I can't help but be reminded of Summer.

There are two children beside her, both girls. They're young and have the woman's blonde hair. Their faces are hidden too, their backs turned away. Long, meaningful strokes of color and light fill the canvas with love, with passion, with life. A golden label is stuck to the frame. 'Spring Picnic,' it says.

"Do you know what I love about this painting?" Orville asks, motioning with his hand to the woman in lavender. "The innocence. The beauty. The mask of happiness that hides all of the imperfections of our world."

"It's beautiful."

"That's my wife Bethany there in the bonnet. The young ones are my daughters, Lila and Charlotte. Twins." A chill runs up my spine. There's something hidden in his words. Silent contempt. Hatred. It's subtle, but it's there. "Of course, this was about fourteen years ago. Only three months before the fire that killed them."

"I'm so sorry, Mr. Orville. I can't imagine—" My words are genuine. I didn't know. All I knew was that he's rich, owns half the city, and has a personal vendetta against the agency I've pledged my life and allegiance to. I suppose this is the reason he started a fire prevention and safety organization. And maybe it's the reason he started an illegally functioning undercover agency.

"It's quite all right. It was a very long time ago, and as I'm sure you know, time goes on whether we want it to or not."

There's a long pause.

"Who painted this?" I admire a little white butterfly flittering around the painted lilac bush.

"I did, many years ago. Lost my touch now, I'm afraid."

"I didn't know you were a painter."

"I didn't know that you were an heiress, *Ms. Crane*." he hisses as though my name is acid on his tongue. "Listen to me very closely. I pity you, I truly do. I pity you for the things your agency has done to you, but despite those horrors, I cannot let you disturb my work. I know your friend Ginger is playing the cello in the front row of my string ensemble, I know the new waitress 'Sara' is your friend Summer, and I know your 'husband' is Mr. Archer Reynolds from F.O.U.N.D.'s Headquarters in London."

My heart races, brain becoming muddled with noise. I can't string words into a sentence, so I don't. My jaw just hangs open, my eyebrows furrowing. He knows. But how? My best guess is that he has someone on the inside. Someone who fed him all of the mission information. That is a very bad problem that we will need to take care of later while he's not directly threatening us with immediate death.

"If any of you even so much as plant a single camera or snatch a single file, I will make what happened to David Bowen look like child's play. Let me make myself clear. Stay away from me and my work or you will be trampled like the bugs you are, starting with your boyfriend. Do you understand?" His voice is a soft growl. Threatening. Personal. Slightly condescending.

"Yes," I mutter, "I understand."

"Good. Now, I suggest you take your 'husband' and leave my hotel before I give my snipers their new targets."

"I don't think you know who you're dealing with, Mr. Orville. You might come to regret this."

"Believe me, Ms. Crane. I know exactly what F.O.U.N.D. is capable of. Frankly, I know more about your agency than you do." He chuckles. A smug grin forms over his lips. "There's something about you that reminds me of Bethany, and I'm not sure what it is. Maybe it's the determination in your gaze, the unwillingness to back down from a fight. Or perhaps it's the brainwashed naïvety that comes from being what you are: a child sick with love."

"In opposition to what? Being an angry adult with a heart made of stone, so sick and tired of his own life that he decides to hire people to beat up a weak nerdy seventeen year old ice cream shop employee for no reason other than to scare his girlfriend into leaving you alone? If you want to send me a message, there are better ways to do it. As for Archer and I, we'll be out of your hair in a few minutes. Don't worry about it."

I tug my arm away from his and stalk back into the ballroom, heels clicking angrily against the wooden floor every step of the way. Archer is still over by Summer, and Ginger isn't too far off.

"We have to get out of here. Now."

"What? Why?" Archer's eyes dart around, searching the room for a source of danger. "What did he say?"

"He knows who we are. He knows why we're here. We have to get out." I glance back at the entrance to the ballroom just as Orville returns.

"I don't think we've achieved the objectives of this recon." Summer looks around as she pours champagne into glasses and pretends to make small talk.

"We know he has a mole in F.O.U.N.D., I think that's all the information we need."

"True. How else would he get ahold of that information?" Ginger joins the conversation, plucking a shrimp off of one of the serving trays and popping it in her mouth. God, she looks hot in a suit. I wonder if I could pull something like that off. "Saw we were congregating and snapped one of my cello strings. The conductor decided we needed to take a short 'recess'."

"And you know what we were talking about how?" Archer raises an eyebrow.

"We're all really good at reading lips." I tap one of my hearing aids. "Kind of comes in handy."

"Right." He nods. "Forgot about that."

"You look hot in that dress, babe." Ginger grins. "I didn't know how you would look as a blonde but damn—"

"Can we focus here?" Archer snaps, green eyes flicking between the three of us. He looks at us as though we're a bunch of toddlers he's been stuck babysitting. "We don't have much time to lose."

"I contacted HQ. There's a limousine headed our way to take us back." Summer informs us. The fakest smile I've ever seen is still plastered on her face. It's not as over the top as my Scarlett Cress smile, but it's pretty damn close.

"Great. Perfect." Ginger grabs a handful of shrimp and in the most subtle way possible, shoves them into her bra. "Let's get the hell out of here."

CHAPTER 26

Twenty-two. Ginger can fit twenty-two shrimp in her bra. I thought it was pretty impressive, but maybe that's just me.

We all get out of work later than expected after an extended debriefing with Sheila and a very long shower. It takes forever to wipe off the layers and layers of makeup, but after a while, Scarlett Cress runs down the drain and my reflection looks like my own again.

It's too late to drop by the bakery, and I know that Dave is definitely asleep by now, but I decide to check in anyway. Especially with Orville's threats still fresh in my mind. I need to see for myself that he's okay, that Orville hasn't done anything to him in the hours since I left the hotel. I don't trust him to keep his word and I certainly don't trust him to leave me alone.

Dave's house is quiet, dark, drifting in a sea of sleepy houses and silent streets. In the distance, the lights from the buildings in the city are still on. They always seem to be. No matter how deep into the suburbs you plunge, there's always light from the skyscrapers that fill Great City. Always the gleaming beacon that is Headquarters. There's no escape from it, not even here, in my safe haven from the spy world.

I hop over the metal fence around the backyard and stand beneath Dave's second-story bedroom window. Thick vines cling to the bright green walls of the nice two-story suburban home, but they're too haphazard to support my weight. I know. I've tried. Instead, I opt for the nearest tree, scaling its height until I can just about reach the window. And then, I pounce like a cat, gripping the window sill with one hand and forcing it open with the other. As promised, he left it unlocked.

The bedroom is dark, the only light streaming in through the window. Clothes litter the floor, scattered in piles everywhere. His desk is a nightmare, assorted papers scattered about and pencils strewn every which way. I've never seen it this messy, but then again, he usually has some warning before I come over and if I know my Dave, I know he forgot I promised to pop in after work.

He's snoring, sprawled all over his mattress like a starfish. One arm is dangling off of the bed, the other is buried somewhere beneath his pillow. His brown curls are absolute chaos, sticking out in every direction, and the sheets and blanket are tangled around his legs.

Once I'm sure he's alive and breathing and not bleeding out on the linens, I swing a leg over the window sill, ready to leave again, but Dave slaps blindly at the base of the lamp until it clicks on. I pause mid-movement, turning to look at him. He squints, hastily shoving a pair of new glasses onto his face.

"Mia? How did you get in here?" His words slur.

"Window, remember? I wanted to check in and make sure you were alive and stuff. Work got out way late. I didn't mean to wake you up, babe."

"It's okay." There's something in his eyes, something sad. "I, uh, I actually had a nightmare, so maybe it's good you're here."

"What happened?"

I walk over to the bed and take a seat in front of him. One hand moves to cup his jaw and the other finds a spot on his thigh. I take a moment to thank the good Lord that Dave doesn't sleep naked or this would have gotten really awkward really fast. Instead, he's dressed in an old navy blue *Star Wars* shirt and a pair of white and blue plaid boxers. For once, his clothing isn't plagued by his colorblindness. Or maybe it's an accident that he actually matches.

"It was the zombie apocalypse and there were zombies everywhere and we got separated, and then when I found you, you were already—"

I pull him in for a hug. He grips me tight, holding me closer than I ever thought possible. The tips of his curls brush against my neck as he buries his face in my shoulder.

He mumbles, "I love you."

"I love you too."

"Is everything okay, Mia?"

"Yeah. Why?"

"You seem stressed," he states, pulling out of the hug. "Don't lie to me. I can always tell when you're stressed."

"Just worried about you is all." It's the truth. Mostly. "How are your injuries? Your leg doing any better?"

"A lot better, actually. Mom took a look at it. She said it's not infected or anything. She said the black eye will go away soon enough, and the split lip will probably be fine."

"Good." I pause, a long sigh slipping from my lips. "Just please be careful. Please. I don't want you to get hurt again."

"I will. I promise." His blue eyes are sincere, and his large hands encase mine, fingers weaving together. His warm lips brush against my mouth. It's a long, meaningful kiss. After kissing Archer tonight, I feel like I needed this. I needed something real. Not a fake kiss from my fake husband. I needed Dave. "I don't know what I'd do without you, Mia."

"Likewise." I glance at the clock. "It's really late. I better go before my parents send a search party."

"Oh yeah." He scratches the back of his neck, one hand still wrapped around one of mine. I pull his hand to my lips, kissing it seven or eight times. He laughs. I press a final kiss to the back of it before getting up and walking back over to the window.

"One for the road." He blows a kiss.

I catch the imaginary token of love in my fist. "Dork." I wink, swinging a leg over the sill, leaning out into the chilly night air. "But my favorite dork."

"I better be."

"Goodnight Dave."

"Night, Mia."

I make my way down from the second story. Dave shuts the window behind me. It locks with a reassuring click. As I get on my bike, I see his bedroom light flicker off. Now, my only companion is the soft hum of my motorcycle and the warm, fuzzy feelings of Dave that flutter around my heart like stray rose petals.

If there's anything I've learned so far, it's that warm fuzzy moments like these don't last long.

CHAPTER 27

Dave isn't the only one with nightmares tonight. I try to shake off the dark thoughts, but the stress muddles my mind, dragging me down into the deep. I'm sinking, drowning in images of Dave and Orville. Twisted threats and beaten boyfriends. Each dream is worse than the last, but somehow after each of them, I manage to fall asleep again.

The final time I bolt awake is not a result of the hellish dreamscape haunting my sleeping brain. It's because of the band of rubber vibrating around my wrist. The intruder alarm. Red lights flash, and as soon as I put on my hearing aids, I can hear the blaring siren that goes along with it. Someone broke in. I don't know what they want, but I have a sinking feeling I know who they work for.

I reach into my nightstand drawer and grip the handle of my emergency gun tightly before slinking out into the hallway to face whoever was dumb enough to break into a house full of trained assassins.

Someone is standing behind me.

I snap around to face them, but it's just a very confused Isaac. He looks as tired and disoriented as I feel. Messy sandy hairs stick up every which way, and dark bags have formed beneath his blue eyes.

We move towards the living room with cautious steps. Overturned furniture litters the room and shattered glass is scattered across the floor. It's chaos. A wreck. The bookshelf has been tipped on its side, and papers drift in the breeze from the broken window to the front door hanging wide open. Whoever was here is long gone, but it looks as though they cut themselves on the jagged window on the way in, given the fact that there are streaks of crimson blood on the hardwood floor.

"Shit." Isaac whispers.

"Shit." I agree.

"C.A.I.T.L.Y.N., assess the damages." Suddenly, Mom and Dad are standing behind us, each of them equipped with a gun of their own. A quick green laser sweeps through the room before C.A.I.T.L.Y.N.'s robotic voice replies.

"*One broken window, the door is ajar; several pieces of furniture have been damaged and will need to be replaced. The office suffered severe attacks, and there is human blood on the floor and a few other surfaces. The intruder seems to have left.*"

"Bring the lights up." Dad's voice is thick with sleep. He rakes his fingers through his thick brown hair and lets out a long sigh. First Dave, now this. If these late-night emergencies become a trend, we're never going to get a full night of sleep.

If possible, the room looks even worse under the bright lights. Pools and puddles of crimson blood are beginning to soak into the floorboards and the edges of the rugs. Four exhausted, disgruntled spies trudge down the stairs to investigate further. Mom scrapes a piece of glass off of the floor, holding the pointed shard in front of her face.

"It looks like they came in through the window and went out the door." She motions to bloody footprints leading out of the house. Painted on the wall is a scarlet warning. My gun clatters to the floor, jaw dropping as my eyes trace the menacing red letters.

Two words: *Or else.*

At first I don't understand, but suddenly it clicks. The note in Dave's pocket. The note I gave to Brian to analyze. Stay out of it or else. I didn't stay out of it. This is 'or else'.

I dash back up the stairs to my room and rummage through my desk in a desperate attempt to find Dave's file. But it's not there. I remember. I stashed it in the safe...down in the office. The office that was wrecked in the attack. The thought of it makes me move down the stairs a little faster.

C.A.I.T.L.Y.N. was right. The office suffered severe attacks. The computers are out of commission. It appears a fist was driven right through each of the screens, leaving gaping holes and loose wires in their wake. Sparks jump through the air like tiny fireworks, celebrating their own destruction. Ripped, tattered, and crumpled papers litter the entire space.

I sift through the mess carefully. A tint of red sticks out among the paper and ink. I reach for it. Red lipstick is scrawled on three of the papers from Dave's file, a different word on each page.

YOU WERE WARNED

The 'A' from 'WARNED' covers the colored image of Dave's face. My heart sinks, tears welling in my eyes. I feel like I'm drowning. I can't breathe. This is not okay.

I am not okay. I wonder if all of the other spies on this case are getting death threats or if it's just me. Maybe it's the fact that I have a weakness outside the agency that he can twist like a knife in my heart or the fact that I challenged him personally. Whatever the case, he hates F.O.U.N.D. and he hates me and now I'm paying the price.

I can't call Dave this late to make sure he's okay. I thought after the gala Orville would step off, but he knows as well as I do that F.O.U.N.D. will continue this case with or without me. He's capable of some impressive things. That makes him dangerous. It makes him unpredictable, uncontrollable. And if there's anything F.O.U.N.D. hates, it's not being able to control things.

Isaac is the first to wander into the office and find me half in tears. One of his arms wraps around my shoulders. I'm frozen, staring at the red-stained papers in my hands.

"What happened tonight?" Isaac's voice is soft. Low. Full of concern. He's trying to wrap his mind around this just as much as I am. He rubs at tired eyes and tugs at the white t-shirt hanging around his muscular frame. "What did you do to piss him off?"

"We didn't take any files. We didn't plant any bugs. I just talked to him. He hates F.O.U.N.D. He hates me."

"Are you sure there isn't anything you said that would anger him enough to send a few intruders into the mansion?"

"Not that I can—wait." I pause. When I blink, fresh tears trail down my cheeks. I swallow the lump in my throat. "I warned Ginger and Summer to get out. And I said I thought there was a mole in F.O.U.N.D. He probably caught it on camera and is trying to distract me. This isn't about Dave. This is about scaring me out of telling Sheila there's a double agent."

"That would probably piss him off."

"Yeah."

"Everything okay in here?" Dad looks inside. "Yikes."

"We need to unhook these computers before one of them starts a fire." Mom walks in and yanks the cords out of the wall. The flow of sparks comes to a stop. "Are you okay?"

"I am now. I have to call Sheila before going back to bed. Do you think she's still up?"

"The woman is nocturnal. It's probably safe to call her. Or at least Brian."

That's a good point. When we return to the living room, I notice that C.A.I.T.L.Y.N. has sent our home into lockdown mode. Thick metal sheets have slammed down over all of the windows and doors. The lights are dimmed to preserve power. The sirens have stopped, thankfully, but the living room is still a mess.

I fire up a video call with Sheila and she responds within a few rings. Dad is right. She's still wide-awake at her desk at Headquarters, *tap-tap-tap*ping away on her keyboard as if it was twelve in the afternoon instead of like three in the morning.

"Mia? What are you doing up so late?" She doesn't look away from her computer screen.

"I could ask you the same thing."

"I have three more debriefing reports to write up. Or have you forgotten you're not my only field team?" She takes a long sip of coffee from a *James Bond* mug. "Anyway, back to business. What's your problem?"

"We had an intruder. Blood on the floor, broken window, trashed office, the whole shebang."

"Is everyone alright?" Her attention snaps away from her keyboard and onto me in an instant.

"Yeah. Everyone is fine. I think Orville was trying to scare me into forgetting to tell you something important that I forgot in the mission debriefing."

"What?"

"I think there's a mole in F.O.U.N.D. Orville knew exactly who we were despite the disguises. He knew us by name. He must be getting his information somewhere."

"That would explain a lot. He always seems to anticipate our investigations. Someone on the inside just makes sense." Sheila's lips are pressed into a thin line. She knows what this means. Lots and lots of interrogations. And with the wave of new summer interns, that could take a while.

"That's all I have."

"Thank you, Mia. Get some rest, alright?"

"I'll try." A promise I hope to keep.

CHAPTER 28

I roll into Headquarters around noon the next day without stopping in the bakery beforehand. I was running way late due to the fact that I slept right through my alarm. I think once I explain myself, Greta will forgive me. She has a soft spot for Dave.

After grabbing the biggest travel mug I can find from the Headquarters café and filling it with the strongest coffee they have in stock, I head up to Sheila's office. Summer and Ginger are sitting on the couch around the coffee table. Elise is at her make-shift desk, and Sheila walks through the door just behind me. She's accompanied by Brian, who looks like he could drop at any second. His non-stop work schedule has not been kind to him.

He starts talking to Sheila one-on-one, so I break off and walk over to Elise's desk.

"How's your morning been, Elise?"

"Not so great. I just got out of questioning. They're trying to find the double agent, so all of the interns had to be checked. Oh my gosh, I've never been so scared in my life. That interrogator is so scary."

"That interrogator is my Aunt Leslie." Ginger grins. "And yeah, she's scary as hell."

"Sheila told us what happened last night. Are you alright?" Elise pushes her glasses further up her nose and tucks her hair behind her ears. At the mention of the attack, Ginger wraps an arm around my waist, followed quickly by Summer on the other side.

"I'm fine, yeah. We got lucky. By the time we got to the living room, the attacker was gone."

"I would have been terrified." Elise shakes her head. She wears a very mousy expression. Timid green eyes hide behind curtains of wavy red hair. "I could never imagine being a field agent. I'd rather be a manager or an administrator or something. Still here fighting the good fight, just behind the scenes where I belong."

"The field life isn't for everybody." Summer shrugs.

"Ladies," Sheila calls our attention, "Brian has prepared a presentation to bring us up to speed on Chemical Rebirth."

We take our seats on the couch, joined by Sheila and Elise. Brian uses a remote to fire up the holograms above the glass coffee table. Large colored syringes float through the air, rotating like pieces of a child's mobile. Deceivingly innocent, despite the danger that lies inside.

"Intel managed to decrypt more of the files the field department recovered. In the files, there was information about Chemical Rebirth, blah, blah, blah." Brian closes the file he's reading off of. "I know you don't care about the scientific specifics and terms. Basically, the chemical is used for illegal human experimentation. Orville believes he can bond these mixes to human DNA and invoke certain, uh...superior enhancements."

"Meaning what, exactly?"

"Strength, speed, regenerative healing, heightened senses, and—this one is the kicker—telekinetic abilities." Brian shakes his head. "In other words, he's trying to bring super heroes from science-fiction to science-fact. It's impossible, but he has tons of theories and formulas and the science isn't baseless. He knows what he's doing. On top of all of that, he seems to have the money, team, and resources to make it happen."

"So he's a power-crazed billionaire *and* a mad scientist." Ginger summarizes.

"Yes. That." Brian finishes off what I assume is at least his third coffee this morning given the way his hands won't stop shaking. "I admire him, but I also fear him."

"So what happens if he pulls it off?" Elise shifts uncomfortably in her seat.

"He'll have an army. I think that's the point. He's trying to make an army strong enough to overpower F.O.U.N.D." Brian's brown eyes flick from woman to woman.

I don't think any of us really know what to say. The Orville I spoke to was threatening, yes, but he was civil. Intelligent. He wasn't crazy like Brian is suggesting. Although I guess it would take someone crazy to send a handful of agents into a camp full of spies, to send an attacker to wreck the mansion of a family of them, to experiment on actual live human beings...

Maybe he's a better actor than he lets on.

"Good luck sleeping tonight, everyone." Ginger scratches her head, amber eyes wide as she inhales a breath. Her face has an expression of 'well, shit', and I guess I feel the same. I can't fight superheroes. I'm a spy, not Supergirl.

"So you're saying he could potentially have enhanced agents working in his agency and we'll have to fight them." Summer raises an eyebrow.

"Potentially, yes."

"Which is why I'm giving you a training day. No missions, just working on combat skills and weapons training." Sheila hands each of us a training pass. We say our goodbyes to Brian, Elise, and Sheila and change into our training clothes: sports bras, sweatpants, and comfy running shoes.

The three of us spend five or so hours in the training facility alternating between hand-to-hand combat and taking turns in the shooting range. It's a good distraction, though temporary, to keep me from thinking about Dave and Orville and the storm brewing on the horizon. Flurries of agents check in and out over the course of the day, but for the most part, it's a constant group of about a hundred agents working at the many, many stations.

After we finish up and shower and get changed into street clothes, we all head home. I pull into the garage just under an hour later.

As I enter the house, the last of the F.O.U.N.D. interior team leaves. You can barely tell anything ever happened. All of the papers have been cleaned up, the floors wiped of all the blood, and the walls touched up with a fresh coat of paint. All of the electronics in the office have been replaced. It's so abnormally normal. Shockingly so. Every scrap of evidence of the death threats are gone, as though they had never even existed.

"Oh sweetie, good, you're home!" Down the stairs comes Mom, lugging a large suitcase. "Your father and I got a call. We have to go to the London unit."

"What? Why?" What I want to ask is why *now*? Why couldn't someone else have gone, especially while we're facing the very real threat that is L.O.S.T.? Why are you abandoning Isaac and I? But I don't say any of that. I know my parents would never turn down a call.

"You know how these things go, M. We can't help it. You know that."

"I know."

"We'll be back two days from now," adds Dad, a duffle bag hanging from his shoulder. "I wish we didn't have to go, but it was a last minute thing. Given the circumstances, I wish it could be another way, but—"

"You know we wouldn't leave if we didn't have to."

"Right." I understand. They have a job to do for the greater good, F.O.U.N.D. couldn't function without field agents, blah, blah, blah. When we were younger, Mom and Dad used to send us off to Ginger's house or Summer's house, but now that we're older, we don't need a babysitter. We'll just be here alone for two days. "I know. It's fine. We'll be okay."

"We'll be more than okay, baby sis." Carrying five bags of groceries, Isaac steps into the kitchen. He sets the bags on the counter, drops his keys in the key bowl, and rests his shades on his forehead. "I got movies and snacks."

"That looks like a little more than snacks." I raise an eyebrow. Isaac has that look on his face, but I think Mom and Dad are too preoccupied with their mental checklists to notice.

"You can never be too prepared, baby sis." Uh-oh. Two 'baby sis's in one conversation. He's got a plan. And a sly wink to go along with it. Not looking good.

"All right. We're leaving." Dad sets his bag on the floor and wraps me in a tight hug. He presses a long kiss to my forehead.

Next, Mom does the same. When she pulls away, she looks at me for a long while, brushing the hairs out of my face. She tries to hide the tears welling in her eyes, but has no such luck.

"Be good, you two," she says, shaking her head. "Just be careful until we get back."

"We will, Mom." Isaac promises, hugging her after he hugs Dad.

"Your brother and sister and Ethan should be here tomorrow afternoon sometime."

"Good." I'll feel a little more at ease with our older siblings here. Not that I don't think Isaac would fight beside me, I'd just feel more secure with five agents here than two.

"And try to keep the house in one piece, would you?"

"We'll try."

Mom and Dad wave as they leave. When the door closes, Isaac looks at me with that mischievous gleam in his eyes.

"Are you thinking what I'm thinking?"

"Oh God. What are *you* thinking?"

"Two words: Spy. Party."

CHAPTER 29

"How fast do you think I can fill a kiddie pool with chocolate pudding?" Isaac has a half-inflated kiddie pool in one hand and an armful of pudding cups in the other.

"I have several questions."

"What?"

"We're throwing a party. Why do we need a kiddie pool full of chocolate pudding?"

"Why not?"

"Fair enough. Okay, but you know they sell larger amounts of pudding, right? Not just tiny little cups."

"They do? Shit. I'm going to the store."

"Okay. Have fun with that." I shake my head as he sets down his things in exchange for his car keys.

"Care to join?"

"I'm good. Gotta work on the guest list and the music." I pause. "I need my Taylor Swift CD."

"Right. I'll go get that."

The doorbell rings, and I spring from the table to answer it. Summer and Ginger have arrived. Ginger is wearing a cute orange tank top that says 'READY TO PARTAAAY' in bold white letters, a pair of pale jean short-shorts, and neon orange shutter shades.

A knee-length pink and white polka-dotted sundress hugs Summer's curves. Effortless blonde beach waves tumble down her shoulders. She's not as crazy-party-girl as Ginger, but she always looks hot. They both do, who am I kidding?

"Did someone order a party-planning committee?"

"Thank God you're here. Isaac left to get twenty gallons of chocolate pudding—don't ask—so there's a ton of stuff to do here."

"You're telling me." Ginger lifts the shutter shades onto her head, tucked into the cloud of wild natural curls, still fresh with hot pink streaks. "This place is *not* ready for a party. Do you have a guest list?"

"Working on it."

"A playlist?"

"Working on it."

"Well, we have our work cut out for us, don't we?"

Summer sets to work calling every agent we know and then some, spreading the word through texts and tweets. Almost every response is a yes. But despite inviting literally hundreds of agents to the manor, one invitation that never gets sent is Dave's. I just can't bring him into the chaos that is a field agent house party. I can't tell if I'm a terrible girlfriend for that or a great one.

It's almost an hour later that Isaac shows up with industrial-size containers of chocolate pudding, along with a mountain of gummy worms and a stack of Oreo boxes.

"What on earth—?"

"So, I was walking down the pudding aisle at the grocery store when I had an epiphany. I figured: what's better than a kiddie pool full of chocolate pudding? A kiddie pool full of chocolate mud."

"Oh my God." Summer, Ginger, and I reply to his sudden 'stroke of genius' by shaking our heads and offering mildly amused chuckles. "Fill your dumb pool and help us get everything ready, dork."

He winks. I just roll my eyes.

About three hours later, at 7:00 pm on the dot, the doorbell rings.

"No way. Brian Martin. At a party. Are you sick?" Ginger presses the back of her hand against his forehead. He laughs. I think this is the first time I've seen him outside Lab 32. It's definitely the first time he's been to my house. "You're not even wearing a lab coat!"

"I've just been really stressed lately, and I—"

"Whatever. You're early."

"The invitation said seven."

"Sweetie," Summer gives an empathetic look, "Everyone knows that you're supposed to show up at *least* ten minutes late. Must be a field agent thing."

"Is that the only t-shirt you own?" Ginger pokes him in the chest.

He looks down uncomfortably. "Um, yes."

"You don't need to keep it tucked in, you know." She grins as he hastily tugs the edge of his (of course) science-related shirt out of his khakis. One of her slender fingers taps against her lips, sparkly fingernails shimmering as she does so. I can practically see the wheels turning behind her amber eyes. "Hmm..."

"What?" I ask from the island in the kitchen.

"We'll be right back." Ginger grabs Brian's wrist and runs up the stairs.

Brian shoots us a look that begs us to save him from whatever Ginger's got planned. Summer and I only laugh. I have a feeling a very different version of our favorite nerd will stumble down the stairs a few minutes from now.

In the meantime, a flood of agents parades through the front door. Some carry drinks and food, others are here with nothing but their digital invitations and the need to blow off some L.O.S.T.-related steam. Ginger's famous party playlist blares from the speakers in the living room. People flock to the makeshift dancefloor in front of the fireplace.

You haven't seen dancing unless you've been to a field agent party. They're nuts. Some bob along to the music or sway or spin around like normal people. Others are doing backflips and front flips and breakdancing on my living room floor. There's one hanging from the chandelier. I'm pretty sure he's Canadian.

By the time Ginger and Brian venture back down the stairs, I barely recognize the red-haired teen trailing the wild child. His usually gelled hair is soft and tousled and free instead of professional and confined like it usually is. His khakis have been replaced by a pair of Isaac's ripped jeans, and his nice brown loafers were exchanged for a comfy pair of sneakers. He could be mistaken for an average high schooler instead of a brainy know-it-all with an IQ higher than most of the field agents can count (or so he claims).

He looks so normal that he blends right in with the others. No one so much as bats an eye at him, accepting him as if he's one of their own, offering him drinks or chips and dip. Maybe being with the field crowd isn't what he's always wanted, but it's what he's never had: a chance to have a social life instead of spending every waking hour in Lab 32 and pretending he doesn't have any friends. He does. About five of them, to be precise. And three of them are here. Maybe this is a good change.

"What did she *do* to you?" Summer marvels, hands settling on his shoulders. She turns him to face her, looking him over.

"It was all kind of a blur," Brian says. "And I mean that literally. She took my glasses and won't tell me where she put them."

"Ginger, no!"

"Ginger, yes." Ginger rubs her hands together. Her grin is absolutely mischievous. "Oh come on, Mia. The dork needs to unwind. And speaking of dorks—"

"Can we *not* talk about Dave?"

"Babe," Ginger sits on the other stool at the island as Summer and Brian are swept into the crowd of crazy, jumping partiers, "listen, I know how hard all of this shit has been on you, but can I be honest for a second?"

"When *aren't* you honest?"

"True." She takes my hand. "Girl, I love you. Okay? But, you can't let Orville get in your head. For once, you need to push everything out of your brain and just have fun. This is your party. I'm not gonna let you sit in the kitchen worrying yourself into a panic attack while everyone except you has a good time."

"But—"

"Nope." She tugs my wrist, dragging me out onto the dance floor. Though I'm reluctant at first, after a few seconds of standing among my dancing peers, my stress melts away. There is no Orville. There is no L.O.S.T. There aren't any double agents or death threats or oblivious boyfriends unaware of the vast spy agency that stands behind his girlfriend. There is nothing but music and fun and horrible dancing. On my part, that is. Everyone else is killing it.

The party is chaos. Absolute. Beautiful. Chaos. One of the agents from Toronto is still hanging upside down from the chandelier, swinging around wildly. I can't tell if he intentionally put himself there or if he somehow got stuck there, but he seems to be having a good time either way. Against all odds, Isaac's chocolate mud is a hit. The next time I walk past it, it's half-empty, which is impressive, even for a room full of hungry teenagers.

The living room is filled with the scent of heavy cologne and perfume mixed with sweat and spilled Cherry Pepsi. The beat of the music is so loud I physically feel the bass thumps pulsing through my body like a second heart. Strong. Steady. Loud as hell.

Of course, there's the inevitable game of Spin the Bottle unfolding around the coffee table. I steer clear, opting instead to join Ginger, who's deep in conversation with none other than

Archer Reynolds, who I didn't know was even invited or *here* until now. She shakes her head, laughing at something he's just said.

"No, bro. Sorry. I don't swing that way." Ginger takes a sip of her drink, still giggling a bit.

"Trying to flirt with Ginger, huh?"

"Trying. Trying is a good word," he agrees. "Where's your boyfriend? Didn't make it?"

"Wasn't invited. He's not an agent."

"He—what?" Archer looks taken aback. Everyone in the agency sort of assumes that everyone else in the agency only dates people from the agency. What I'm doing is kind of out of the ordinary. Not unheard of, but kind of frowned upon. Hard to maintain. "I thought agents who were born and raised into the agency..."

"Our Mia likes to live on the edge." Ginger playfully bumps my shoulder. I bump her back.

"Well anyway, I didn't know you were the party type, Crane."

"Sometimes, yeah. It just feels safer with all of this L.O.S.T. stuff, you know? I'd rather have an entire house full of spies than just me and my brother fending for ourselves."

"My mission partner John does the same when his parents leave. But they'd murder him if they ever found out."

The front door flings open, crashing against the wall loudly.

"WHAT THE FUCK DO YOU THINK YOU'RE DOING?!"

Oh shit.

Isaac, standing at the improvised DJ booth, abruptly stops the music and looks up like a deer in headlights. Someone somewhere else in the room hits the light switch. Three very angry-looking early-to-mid-twenty-year-olds stand in the doorway. Nikki, Jace, and Ethan, all of whom were supposed to get here tomorrow afternoon, are here right now.

Each of them has a suitcase in tow. Nikki and Ethan are still dressed in shorts, tank-tops, and shades, probably a bit cold in the absence of the constant Australian heat. Nikki's highlighted locks are pulled into a messy bun, while Ethan's tousled dark brown hair is a windswept mess. Jace, on the other hand, is wearing a snug cranberry knit sweater, black dress pants, and a pair of slick black dress shoes. His reading glasses hang from the collar of his undershirt. He looks slightly more awake than the other two, but not by much.

Nikki, whose shout stopped the chaotic party, looks around the room with fire in her eyes. The boy from the chandelier falls, plummeting to the couch below, and the rest of the party guests look at her in pure fear. It takes a lot to intimidate a room full of agents, but when you grow up with three little siblings, putting a stop to absolute chaos is what you call Tuesday.

For a few tense moments, it's absolutely silent. No one dares to make a move or utter a single word whilst getting the death glare from my eldest sibling. Jace looks on disapprovingly, and Ethan looks downright confused (but when isn't he confused, let's be real).

"Let me get this straight." Jace offers, stepping further into the house beside Nikki. "Mom and Dad go on a business trip, so you call every F.O.U.N.D. operative you know and throw a huge party. Yeah?"

"Well, the Hernandezes couldn't—"

"Isaac."

"Yeah, that's kinda what happened," he fesses up.

Jace's serious brown gaze locks into mine. "And you. You let him get away with this? I expected better of you."

"You know how it is, Jace." I shrug. He squints, obviously not amused by my effort. Or lack thereof. "It's not *that* bad. I mean, it's not like I invited Dave."

"I'm just..." Jace presses his hands together and exhales a long breath into his fingertips, trying to get a grasp. "I'm..."

"You kissed Mom and Dad goodbye, orchestrated an elaborate party, and planned to have it cleaned up before they come back."

"Yes."

A long, quiet pause. You could cut the tension with a knife.

"I've never been more proud." Nikki's badass exterior shatters like glass, a façade to mask how impressed she is with us for almost pulling it off without a hitch.

"Are you kidding me?" Isaac laughs.

The relief that floods the room is unbelievable. We thought they were here to bust us, but really they just want a piece of the action. I should have known. Nikki is even more of a party animal than Ginger is, and that's saying a hell of a lot.

"Not in the slightest." Jace rubs Isaac's hair playfully. "Do you know how many parties we threw when Mom and Dad sent you off to the Williams' house? You're just lucky I hacked out of C.A.I.T.L.Y.N.'s Party Watch feature remotely before Mom and Dad found out about your little scheme."

"C.A.I.T.L.Y.N.'s *what now?*"

"Something Mom and Dad installed when I was sixteen." Nikki explains. "After I threw my first party, they programmed her to monitor for loud music, an ungodly amount of people, too many snacks and pizzas being delivered, and so on. Jace figured out how to disable it when he threw *his* first party."

"Oh. So we're cool then?"

"Yes. We're cool."

"PARTY!!" bellows Ethan, who's been wordless for the entire exchange.

Instantly, the music resumes, lights flicking off as quickly as they were turned on. The dancing continues as if nothing had interrupted it. Nikki and Jace and Ethan all take turns hugging

Isaac and I. I haven't actually seen them in person since Christmas. Or, more accurately, F.O.U.N.D. Winter Evaluation.

"How are things? Is everything okay?" Jace asks, referring to Dave and L.O.S.T. and probably everything else.

"Things aren't ideal, but we're making it work." Or trying to, at least.

"Good." Jace's hand rubs my shoulder and he offers a small supportive smile. Summer and Ginger make their way over.

"Summer, if I knew you were here, I would've brought your sister by. She's probably back at your place by now." One of Nikki's mission partners is one of Summer's older sisters, Lizzie. The other sister, Brielle, works in the Berlin unit, and both of them are coming home for Summer's eighteenth birthday.

"I forgot to text her, but I figured she was flying in with you and Ethan and I didn't want to let it slip just yet."

"Smart girl." Nikki smirks. She then proceeds to show us, accompanied by Ethan, of course, what it means to truly party. And in that brief instant, I finally realize just how much I've missed having her around here.

The party starts to waver a few hours later, a steady trickle of agents leaving the mansion with dark bags beneath their eyes and sore muscles from all of the dancing and/or hanging upside down from chandeliers. Before we know it, it's just the Cranes and Ethan left cleaning up the mess.

Clusters of red solo cups are on every flat surface throughout the house. A few spills need to be soaked up, pudding smears have yet to be dealt with, and in general, it's just a mess. Nikki and I wipe down all of the tables and sweep the trash off of the floor while Jace, Isaac, and Ethan vacuum, move furniture back into place, and get things that are out of reach.

"There's a kid sleeping in the piano." Isaac cautiously pokes at him with the end of the vacuum's hose.

A pale, freckled arm lolls out of the grand wooden structure. I move to get a closer look. Being as tired as I am, I'm surprised to recognize Brian without his glasses on or his hair gelled back. He's not even wearing his signature lab coat.

"Brian." I grip his shoulders and give him a few shakes. "Brian!"

"Aah! W-where am I?" wide brown eyes scan the room.

"My house. Party, remember? You conked out inside the piano. Don't ask me how. I'm not exactly sure."

"Shit," he mumbles and rubs at his tired brown eyes. "Can you...help me...out of here?"

I grab ahold of him and pull him out with the help of Isaac. He tumbles onto the floor, scrambling to get to his feet.

"I wasn't drinking, was I? Everything is blurry."

"No glasses."

"*Ginger*," he hisses.

"Here." Jace offers Brian his reading glasses from the collar of his shirt. "They probably won't do much, but it might help a little until you can track her down."

"Thanks." Brian slides the thin metal frames up the bridge of his pale nose. "Could someone take me to Headquarters? I've uh...been boarding there for a while, so..."

"If you wanna stay here, you can." Nikki drops the last of the red solo cups into the trash can.

Ethan holds up the remains of the chocolate-filled kiddie pool with a quizzical expression. I dismiss it with the wave of a hand, silently promising I'll explain it later.

"The guest bedroom is wide open."

"I might have to take you up on that offer." Brian sways on his feet for a few seconds before passing out on the couch, snoring softly.

The genius kid might be used to nights and nights without sleep, but that's nothing compared to what he's survived tonight.

I scoop the nerdy little bundle into my arms and take him up the stairs. His head nuzzles into the crook of my neck, arm dangling freely. I kick open the door to the guest bedroom and drop him on the bed. I'm careful to take off his shoes and set Jace's glasses on the nightstand before tucking him into the covers.

"Night, dork." I rub his head.

He hums in content, snuggling deeper into the large bed. Just as I'm about to leave, he mumbles a soft thanks. A smirk tugs at my lips. I trudge halfway down the stairs while the others are coming up, so I turn around and go to my bedroom to get some sleep.

"C.A.I.T.L.Y.N.?" I whisper, laying sprawled out on my mountain of pillows.

"*Yes, Miss Crane?*"

"Sorry you got hacked. No hard feelings?"

"*None at all, Miss Crane.*"

"Good."

"*Miss Crane?*"

"Yes, C.A.I.T.L.Y.N.?"

"*Even teenagers deserve to have reckless fun every once in a while.*"

"Goodnight, C.A.I.T.L.Y.N."

"*Goodnight, Miss Crane.*"

CHAPTER 30

"'Check out the SSC complex,' Sheila said," Ginger grumbles, reading the scans from her glasses as we prowl through the dark empty soon-to-be Seavale Shopping Center. "'It'll be fun,' Sheila said."

"Just because we haven't found anything doesn't mean there's nothing to be found."

"Right," I agree. "The project is funded by Orville Enterprises. And it wasn't funded by them until last week when Louis picked up the project when it was about to go bankrupt."

"It looks pretty bankrupt to me. There's no one here. It's a ghost town." Ginger looks around. "Thermal scans all negative. It's empty. So much for that mission."

We continue the investigation anyway, planning to leave in a few minutes if nothing turns up. It's then that I see a glint of metal sticking out of a potted plant. I reach inside the very real, very moist dirt and uncover the offending object.

"What is it?" Summer kneels beside me and holds it in both hands. She shakes it. It sounds like a puzzle box, full of loose bits and pieces. After fumbling around with it for a few seconds, she manages to open it. There are plenty of switches and buttons and knobs set into a miniature control panel, meaning the jingling odds and ends must be the result of faulty wiring. What this thing does, I have no clue, but we're about to find out.

"Careful." Ginger warns, watching defensively as Summer hands the box to me. I look over the panel, eyes pausing at each knob and button before I dare to press anything. The label on a switch near the bottom left is nearly worn off. Promising.

At first, nothing happens. There's a faint buzzing and then silence. Ginger bolts upright.

"What did you do?"

"I don't know."

"I'm getting a bunch of readings. Holy shit. It must have been cancelling out my signals. There are people on the other side of that wall. A lot of people. They've got us outnumbered pretty badly. But," Ginger pauses, "there's also a shitload of Chemical Rebirth and an arsenal of weapons. This must be Orville's make-shift compound."

"Not for long." Summer states. "Should we wait for backup or take them on ourselves?"

"Sheila sent a message." Ginger reads from the monitor built into her glasses. "She wants pictures. Doesn't want us to go in or get caught, but she wants pictures to at least see how big the nest is and how many agents she'll need to send in later."

"What's the game plan then?"

"Mia, you're the smallest." Ginger points.

"So?"

"Take these, and we'll give you a boost up there." She presses her glasses into my hand and points to the air vent. "And watch out for anything else that's out of the ordinary."

"Great. Wonderful. Send little Mia into the nest of angry enemy agents. What a good idea," I grumble, sliding Ginger's high-tech glasses up the bridge of my nose. Ginger and Summer each lock their fingers together, making a step. We haven't made this formation since cheerleading season ended.

With their boost, I can reach the vent. Carefully, I undo the screws and pull off the metal grate, and then I climb inside the surprisingly wide passage.

I wiggle through the vent with difficulty, scanning the readings from Ginger's glasses every few seconds. It's never overly useful, though. Stuff like, *'passage: 3 feet wide'*, *'passage: 2 feet* tall', 'passage: made of reinforced steel', etc. Wearing these is the equivalent of wearing Brian Martin as a pair of glasses. Makes sense. He invented them.

Muffled voices echo through the metal tunnel. They don't seem too far off, so I keep army-crawling in that direction, listening for anyone else sliding through this claustrophobic nightmare. Luckily, there's nothing. Unfortunately, moving through the vent isn't as quiet as I'd like it to be. My leather jacket doesn't seem to help matters.

"*Anything?*" Summer transmits through my earpiece.

"Nope. No one's up here. I'm coming up on the vent to the other side."

"*Great.*"

"*Just keep moving you're almost there,*" Ginger says.

"*And please be careful,*" Summer adds as almost an afterthought. She's such a mom friend. I kind of love it, though. It leaves a warm feeling in my chest.

"Will do."

Three minutes later, I come up to the epicenter of activity. Through the grates of the air vent, I can't make out much, but the glasses indicate fifty-three people are in there, men and women with varying levels of muscle mass. Outnumbered is an understatement. These guys would have us swarmed. The room is very large, stark white walls and plain white floors are contrasted by the countless pitch black machine guns hanging on the weapons rack and men covered in black leather uniforms. They look like F.O.U.N.D. agents, almost identical besides one small detail: the badges across their right breasts. A different logo accompanied the four simple letters that have sent the agency of my employment into a frenzy. L.O.S.T.

I use Ginger's glasses to snap a few pictures before backing away from the grate.

My boots come in contact with something hard. A head. There's someone behind me.

Shit.

He inhales a breath, as if to yell and give away my location. One carefully placed kick knocks him out cold before he can do so. Now I have another problem on my hands: I have to get rid of this guy.

It's a tricky maneuver, but I'm strong enough to pull it off. I plant my feet in the center of his shoulders and push him out slowly. I don't want to make too much noise, and I don't want to crush his ribcage or something. This is the quietest option.

"*Mia, get out of there!*" Summer's voice is strained, sent into a panic by something on the other side of the conversation.

"What? Why?"

"*Group of attackers. Ginger and I can manage, but there might be more on the way.*"

"Got it. I'll be there as soon as possible. Ran into some, uh, trouble. I handled it though."

There isn't a response from the other two. I crouch, using my arms and the cold steel walls to turn myself around, facing the direction I came from. I push onwards with new desperation, ditching the armed guard in the nearest branch off of the path. I have never crawled so fast in my life. When I reach the open grate, I slip out and roll into position, ready to attack whoever is here. Ginger and Summer take out the last of them. The rest are lying across the floor. There's some bloodshed, but it's surprisingly clean.

Ginger wipes her forehead like this is normal. Like she's wiped out from a workout or cheer practice or an intense game of Wii Bowling, not from kicking the asses of about twenty agents of an illegal operation.

"Looks like you've got it handled, huh?"

"You could say that." Ginger smirks. "What trouble did you run into?"

"One of Mr. Orville's associates decided to pay me a visit. Knocked him out cold and left him in there." I return Ginger's glasses to her. "Now let's get out of here before the other fifty agents in the nest get wind of this."

"That is a beautiful plan." Summer leads the way to our escape vehicle, a F.O.U.N.D. van sitting in the parking lot. We so cleverly hid it beneath a giant sheet that says 'PROPERTY OF LOUIS ORVILLE. DO NOT MOVE.' in big bold letters. It seemed to work, meaning Louis probably isn't here at the moment.

Ginger slides into the driver's seat, gripping the steering wheel and checking herself out in the mirror. Her gold eyeliner is on point today, holy shit.

Focus, Mia.

Summer hops into the passenger seat, and I climb into the back just as Ginger takes off, speeding across the parking lot. The sheet blows off in the sudden rush of air, uncovering the front windshield.

Silence fills the car, but it's not awkward or uncomfortable. It's nice. We heave heavy breaths, leftover adrenaline still coursing through our veins. Ginger makes eye contact with me in the back seat every minute or so, as if to make sure I'm still here. Summer leans back against her headrest and stares at the roof of the car, blue eyes counting every fiber, every spec, every stray piece of fuzz.

"You okay?" I bump her seat with my foot.

She nods wordlessly, shoulders still rising and falling as she fills her lungs with fresh air.

"We had a close call." Ginger explains quietly. I can tell neither of them want to talk about it, so I don't push. Forty minutes later, the van is parked in the parking lot, we've been through debriefing, and we're out of uniform, ready to go home.

"I'm going home to take a nap." Summer whispers, pulling Ginger and I into a long, relieved hug. I nod, arms securing around her waist.

"Love you, girly." Ginger presses a meaningful kiss to her forehead. So do I.

After she escapes our embrace, the blonde makes her way down the hall towards the elevator. As soon as she's gone, a slow smirk returns to Ginger's lips. She's itching to lighten the mood, I can see it in her eyes.

"What's that look for, G?"

"We need to go to the mall to get Summer a birthday present. Or did you forget that the party is two days from now?"

"I forgot the party is two days from now."

"All right. Let's go, shall we?" We link arms, and in five minutes, we've gotten into Ginger's car, a cute little orange bug. The seats are covered in cheetah-print, and a pair of fuzzy purple dice hangs from the mirror. We toss our purses into the back seat.

Just as we start pulling out, Ginger's headlights shine on something plain and white, almost causing it to glow. A lab coat. Brian. She slams on the breaks, rolling down the window.

"Are you crazy?! This is the second time you've left the lab this week! What's wrong with you?!" Ginger leans out.

He jumps in shock, holding his frail little heart with the hand that's not clutching a small pink envelope. "Oh! I uh...How do you rent a F.O.U.N.D. vehicle?"

"Why?" I ask, leaning out the other window.

"Summer's not in there with you, is she?"

"No."

"Well, I, uh, she sent me an invitation to her birthday party, so—"

"Get in, loser!" Ginger motions back with her head.

Brian hesitates, but walks to the door and hops in the back seat, gently nudging our purses over with his foot.

She lowers her ridiculously large brown sunglasses down in front of her eyes before announcing with an unnecessary edge, "We're going shopping."

CHAPTER 31

Ginger's car practically vibrates with noise. Loud guitar riffs create tremors that resemble small earthquakes. Ginger jams out, bobbing her head to the beat.

"Keep your eyes on the road, Williams!" Brian looks terrified.

"Relax! I'm a great driver!" She laughs and cuts into the next lane. It's intentional, but she has no blinker to show for it.

"The turn signals are there for a reason!"

"Quit being a back seat driver! Sheesh, you science people are no fun!"

"You field agents are dangerous and reckless!" Brian shouts before sighing and sinking back into his seat. He's situated in the middle spot, all three seatbelts strapped across him in an attempt to keep him safe. Calling him paranoid would be an understatement, but I can't say I blame him.

The infamous orange bug rumbles to the sound of Ginger's driving playlist: heavy, loud, rock music packed with screaming electric guitars and pounding drums. It's basically her party playlist but slightly less danceable.

"Do you ever stop being intense and crazy?" Brian's voice is quiet compared to the music, but I manage to read his lips in the rearview mirror.

"No. She doesn't. Not really." I chuckle.

The poor scared nerd clings tighter to the seatbelts fastened around his lanky torso.

"You'll survive. I've made it this far, haven't I?"

"Should have taken the train..." he mutters.

Ginger parks in the parking lot nearest the mall's movie theater and steps out of the car.

"No lab coats allowed in the mall." Ginger tells Brian. He raises a skeptical eyebrow. "If you're hanging out with me, no nerds allowed. I've got a rep."

With a groan, he tugs off the pristine white sleeves of his lab coat and folds it neatly before setting it on the backseat and slamming the door.

We walk into the mall. As soon as we're through the front doors, Ginger makes a beeline for the entertainment store nestled between Hollister and the arcade. We rummage through the box of t-shirts in the back of the store for a few minutes to find something that stands out. Brian jots down notes on a pad of paper, pencil scribbling frantically.

"What're you doing, dork?" Ginger's fingers clutch the edges of a soft pink shirt with the *Star Wars* logo on it. Cute, but not Summer. She tosses it back into the box and searches for another one.

"I'm going to be honest with you. I don't know much about Summer. What do I get her?"

"She likes pink. A lot of pink." I manage to find a pink shirt with the One Ring on it, but again, it's not Summer. "But she's not much of a nerd. *Harry Potter* is the extent of her nerdiness. She's a Hufflepuff."

"I'm a Slytherin. In case you were wondering." Ginger winks.

"I wasn't." Brian tries not to smile, but his poker face is horrible.

We search through the box for about twenty more minutes before giving up and deciding to get her a cute stuffed turtle instead. I decide later I'll tie a pink ribbon around its neck or something.

After checking out, we head down the hall to the candy store, Sweet Tooth, where Ginger picks up twenty dollars-worth of Twizzlers.

"That's uh, that's a lot of candy." Brian stammers.

"Summer's loves sweets. Twizzlers are her favorite."

"I'm not much of a candy guy." he motions to the insulin pump strapped to the waist of his pants. I guess I never noticed. It's always hidden by his lab coat. From the pocket of his khakis, he fishes out a handful of wrapped hard candies. "I do, however, have a weakness for sugar-free butterscotches."

"I never knew you were diabetic."

"Not many people do." Brian shrugs. He and I stand a few feet behind Ginger as she loads her goods onto the counter. "Not that it's a secret or anything, I just...I never really talk to many people, I guess. The guys in Lab 32 are all so quiet."

"Well if you ever need like friends or anything, you know you have us, right? We're not just your coworkers."

"Thanks." He adjusts his glasses.

I bump his shoulder with mine, innocently glancing at a poster hanging on the wall. He bumps me back a little harder, and just as I'm about to bump him into next week, Ginger returns.

"I feel like I just missed something."

"Not really," Brian states, cutting off any further questions before leading us on to help him find a present for Summer. Our search takes us to one of the teen clothing stores. I don't shop here often, neither does Ginger, but Summer does, so that's all that matters.

"There's so much perfume." Brian coughs, blinking. "It's so dark in here."

"Summer comes in here all the time."

"I can't hear anything," Brian holds his hands over his ears.

"Join the club." I smirk.

Somehow, we manage to navigate the shadows and find the section of the store that is basically Summer incarnate. Pink, cute, with a splash of attitude, usually in the form of a dress.

"How's this one?" Brian tentatively takes a hanger off of the rack. Pink and black stripes stretch diagonally across this cute sweetheart-neckline knee-length sundress. A couple of large golden sequin hearts are sewn into the skirt. I've never seen anything quite like it, but Summer would wear this in a heartbeat, no questions asked.

"That. Is. Perfect." Ginger lets out a whistle. Her fingers travel over the skirt, feeling the fabric. "She is going to hug the living daylights out of you, dork."

"Really?" Brian's cheeks flush scarlet at the thought of it. "Why would she—?"

"She's just a huggy person, dude." Ginger shrugs, giving him a nudge towards the register. "Who knows? Might even get a kiss on the cheek?"

"Well, I—"

"Too cute." I laugh as he walks off, still stuck in a Summer-induced daze.

Eventually he snaps out of it and meets us outside the front entrance of the store. We make another stop in the cosmetic place next door to buy her some lotion, lip gloss, nail polish, and fuzzy socks, and then we head to the food court for soft pretzels and slushies.

"This place is nicer than I thought it would be." Brian takes a long sip from his Diet Coke, staring up at the skylights.

Decorative monarch butterflies hang from the ceiling and large-leafed tropical plants make the room feel like a rainforest. The summer decorations are nice, but I'm partial to the glittering snowflakes and thick green wreaths they put up around Christmas time.

"Maybe you should come here more often then, smarty pants." I give his foot a nudge under the table. He offers a grin, but doesn't kick me back. "You know, work normal hours like everyone else instead of sixteen hours a day, get a decent amount of sleep, try to have a social life..."

"I'll worry about a social life when we don't have to worry about..." he looks around, "you know..."

"Well, with any luck, we'll have that bastard behind bars by next week." Ginger leans back in her chair, her feet resting on my lap under the table. "And then we can return to our regularly scheduled lives. Well, except for you. I will help you make friends if it's the last thing I do, Brian Martin. Mark my words."

"You do that." He chuckles. "Maybe you could introduce me to your boyfriend, Mia. I hear he's a proud member of the Dork Society too."

"Oh, he is. A bigger one than you, even. Not smarter, I mean, just dorkier." I bite the end of my straw and take another large sip of the Pepsi flavored slushy. "He's a huge nerd. You should see his lair. It's a spectacle."

"I bet. How did you even meet him anyway? I mean, not to be rude, but usually the hot cheerleaders go for the big buff super-human football players, not the dorky little band nerds."

"I grew up surrounded by unintelligent lunkheads pretending to know what they're doing and acting like they're superior to everyone else. Pretty overrated, if you ask me. Plus, it's kind of taboo to date your assigned partners, so that's not really an option."

"Honey, if you weren't my BFF, I'd date you in a heartbeat." Ginger winks and blows a kiss. "But yeah, partners are kind of off-limits. Too risky."

"Wait, so you're—?"

"Dude, I'm as straight as a circle." Ginger laughs. "I thought you knew. I'm not exactly subtle."

"I swing both ways," I add. "Obviously."

"Wow. Good to know. And Summer is—"

"Gender doesn't really matter to her. She falls in love with a person. Not a gender."

"Okay." Brian nods. "The more you know, I guess."

"I do enjoy our little chats, Dr. Martin." Ginger presses her finger into the pale freckled skin of his cheek.

"Not a doctor yet, but I appreciate the title." He sighs, staring at the contents of his shopping bag. "I just really hope she'll like it."

"Believe me. She will. I promise."

CHAPTER 32

We arrive in the gardens of the Laurence's property on Saturday afternoon. Pink balloons and white streamers cling to every table and tent pole, turning the flower-filled garden into a Summer-centric wonderland. Dave's hand grips mine tight, his nervous blue eyes flitting across the crowd of Summer's friends and family. To him, this is a social battlefield, and the war has just begun.

In the week since the attack, Dave's recovery hasn't been easy, but he's doing fine. His black eye is almost completely healed and the stab on his leg is little more than a long scar. By now, he's just about back to normal.

"Okay there, babe?"

He nods, hand squeezing mine even tighter as his anxiety sets in. I slowly lead him onwards, towards the sea of people. I told him he didn't have to come, but he wanted to, so here we are. Immediately, I'm spotted by Summer's moms, Shelby and Jane. The two look more like sisters than wives, given their recent matching haircuts and blonde highlights. Their outfits are coordinated, each wearing flowery pastel sundresses and matching silver heart-shaped necklaces. They are literally couple goals.

"Mia! How's our girl?" In seconds, I'm trapped in a Mrs. and Mrs. Laurence sandwich. It's the best type of hug. Warm and soft and it smells faintly of rose-scented perfume.

"Doing fine at the moment." I motion to Dave. "This is—"

"Dave Bowen? The alleged boyfriend we've heard so much about?" asks Jane. She tucks a lock of blonde and red hair behind her ear and offers Dave her hand. He shakes it with a smile, shaking Shelby's hand right after.

"That's me, ma'am."

"Dave, meet Jane and Shelby Laurence. Summer's moms." I point over to the dance floor. "The one dancing with my sister is Summer's older sister Lizzie, and the oldest, Brielle, is around here somewhere."

"It's a woman-powered household." Shelby smiles pleasantly. She and Jane are radiating a perfect suburban mother vibe. Each of them is so much like Summer. It's almost as though she inherited all of their little ticks and habits. "Well, except for Benji. Our little beagle. The poor boy's outnumbered."

"MIA!!!" Summer literally tackles me in a hug, pinning me to the ground and pressing several kisses to my cheeks and forehead.

Dave laughs out loud, checking to make sure I'm not hurt.

"DIDYOUSEETHEDRESSBRIANGOTFORMEIT'SLITERAL-LYTHECUTESTOMG!!!"

"See it? I was there when he bought it. But for the record, he picked it out by himself. Ginger and I just gave it the best friend stamp of approval."

"He went to the mall? The actual physical mall?" Summer pulls out of her bear-hug and helps me up off of the ground. "When did this happen?"

"That boy has a serious crush on you. I thought he was gonna explode when we were talking about the possibility that you might hug him."

"Awwwww," Summer gushes. "What a sweetie. Speaking of sweeties, Dave, I'm so glad you could make it! How're you doing?"

"Better,"

"Good." She pulls him into a hug too. "I'm glad you're okay. Try not to scare us like that again, okay?"

"I'll try." Dave offers a small smile.

Summer pokes his cheek, kisses mine one more time, and then dashes off to entertain more of her guests. I take Dave's hand and wander over to the towering cake made by the one and only Greta Hertz and her amazing bakery crew. We've outdone ourselves, if I do say so.

The cake is vanilla, but the inside was dyed pink with food coloring. White frosting and fondant cover all three layers, and pretty little pink sugar flowers decorate every nook and cranny, crawling up the length of the massive structure like vines. A large 18 broadcasts Summer's newfound adulthood to everyone here.

"Is it weird to you that all of our friends are turning eighteen this year?" I ask, eyes fixed on the candle numbers.

"It's a bit crazy." He shakes his head. "I'm not ready to be an adult. I'm not even ready to be a senior."

"Neither am I."

"Contemplating the meaning of life, I see." Archer sneaks up behind us. Once again, it surprises me that he's here, but not too much. Summer (not so) secretly thinks he's really super hot. I don't blame her. He is. Just kind of an asshole and not my type. But still, hot nonetheless. "You see, if we were in England, she'd be able to legally drink, but you Americans and your stupid liquor laws..."

"Who are you?" Dave looks more than confused by the Brit's sudden appearance.

"Archer Reynolds. I'm a friend of your girlfriend's from across the pond." He gives Dave's hand a firm shake and a somewhat intimidating smirk. "It's Dave, isn't it?"

"That's me." Dave takes in the sight of the muscular British agent. It's not that he looks scared, just uncomfortable. Archer has about two inches and about forty pounds of muscle on him. I can see why he's a bit taken aback. "How do you two, uh, know each other?"

"Winter vacation. We always go to the islands with people from the company my parents work for." I reply with my rehearsed response. That's always the excuse we've used when it comes to the big International Winter Evaluation F.O.U.N.D. holds every year on one of their private islands. Just a company retreat is all. Totally not an Olympic-style competition to rank recruits from across the globe and compare their stats side-by-side.

Archer winks. "Crane goes on and on and on about you. You've really done a number on her." He glances across the tent. "Well, I'd love to stay and chat, but I have a birthday girl to sweep off her feet."

"Have fun with that," is all I can manage to say. I feel bad for Brian, but there's not much I can do. I'm an agent, not a miracle worker, and I'm not one to interfere in matters of love. Now, *Ginger* on the other hand...

Dave's eyes wander over to people dancing in the open space between the dessert table, the punchbowl, and the DJ booth. He offers his hand like Prince Charming, ready to return to the ball.

"Might I have this dance milady?"

"Why, of course."

Dave is not the greatest dancer that ever lived. Far from it. But he puts all of his heart into it, pouring his soul into his feet, and it's the sweetest thing I've ever seen, even if he happens to step on my toes once or twice. Dancing with Dave brings back memories of camp, the gazebo, the bliss of freedom from the spy world. Here we are, surrounded by people from the agency, entire families of agents, and yet it doesn't feel like there's anything here. The tent, the cake, the flowers, it feels more like a wedding than a birthday party.

Will Dave and I ever get that far? Married, I mean? Perhaps. He's my high school sweetheart. Maybe we're not meant to be soulmates. Maybe we'll break up over something dumb like the majority of our peers. Yet here and now, I could get lost in his eyes, in his smile, all afternoon without a single thought about anything else. I can't focus on anything but him and his warmth and the feeling of his hands in mine, of his lips against my skin, of his soft curls between my fingertips.

But illusions like this aren't meant to last, are they?

CHAPTER 33

The Fourth of July comes up fast, almost without any warning. As we usually do, the Cranes have a cookout with the Laurences and the Williamses and then go to the Seavale pier to enjoy the fair.

"Ginger! Ginger!" Ginger's twin brothers Gavin and Grant chant while grabbing at her hands and clinging to her legs and tugging on the hem of her American flag t-shirt. "Can we ride the Tilt-a-Whirl?!"

"You bet we can!" she shouts with an enthusiastic smile. Though she complains about getting stuck babysitting while she could be out partying (well, I mean, more than she already parties), we all know she secretly loves it. They're so cute. Super cute. Tiny taut curls bounce around their freckled faces, hazel eyes gleaming under the bright lights of the fair rides. Missing teeth only add to their childish innocence. "Come on, guys!"

Ginger runs off, leaving Summer with Archer, Dave, and I. Despite my valiant attempts to drag Brian out of the lab one more time this week, he said he really needs to put in some work on Chemical Rebirth and everything else the field department has recovered and the intel guys have attempted to decrypt. Keyword: attempted.

We stroll through the fair. Vendors' tents stand in rows upon rows, and beyond them are the beyond-rigged games that we have no chance in winning. Or at least, an average civilian would have no chance in winning. Three recruits of a top-secret defense agency and one very colorblind nerd might be able to turn the tables on these unsuspecting carnies.

And where do we land? The shooting game, of course.

I reach for the gun in the same second Archer does, our hands meeting. I tug it out of his grip and hold it up to my eye.

"Fancy a game, little lady?" asks the rather scrawny man with a beard to rival Dumbledore's.

"I sure do." I reach into my purse just as Dave puts a five on the counter, only offering a wink and a smirk. I realize he's never seen me shoot anything more than Nerf guns before.

"How many points for a goldfish?" Dave points to the small tank in the corner of the game tent.

"Like you need *another* one." I laugh. Last year, one of our first dates was to the fair. And I won him a goldfish, which he still has in a tank on his desk.

"Cosmo gets lonely."

"Alright, alright." I shake my head and look through the sights of the gun just as the little cardboard animals begin to move. The speed at which I get ten bullseyes startles even me. Soon enough, Dave is clutching a bag of water with a perfect little goldfish swimming around inside.

"And his name is...?"

"Midas."

"Midas?"

"The king that turned everything he touched to gold." Dave pushes his glasses further up his nose.

I can't help but crack a grin. What a dork. I give him a little shove. He shoves me back. Archer tries, but he can't replicate a round like mine. Once he's won an armful of teddy bears, we move on.

After walking around for a bit, the four of us decide to ride the Ferris Wheel. Dave and I board it first, sliding into the seat. My bare thighs kiss the cold metal, sending a chill up my spine. Dave's arm wraps around my shoulders and pulls me tight against him. Warm lips brush against my temple as the swinging car lifts into the chilly night air. I take a few of the silent moments to count the glimmering stars before looking down at the groups of people down below.

It's then that I spot the L.O.S.T. agent.

I feel as though I'm trapped in the world's most dangerous game of *Where's Waldo?* He's leaned up against the corndog stand, arms crossed, staring me dead in the eyes. I break eye contact and turn my head into the crook of Dave's neck. My heart starts to race. The thought of Orville shattering everything I've worked so hard to protect is all too real and the reality of it is staring me in the face, here and close and relevant. I feel a growing knot twisting deep in my stomach. Everything changes now.

"You okay?"

No.

"I'm fine. It's just cold out here." My voice comes out as a hoarse whisper. I have to force the words out. Another lie. After a year full of lies, of withheld truths, isn't now the time to be honest? Now, when it matters more than ever? His arms wrap around me tighter, trying to shield me from the cold. I wish his cozy red sweatshirt could shield me from reality instead. "I love you, Dave."

Goodbye.

"I love you too."

I press a lingering kiss to his soft lips. Large hands support my back and waist, pulling me closer. I melt into his touch, trying to make this moment last as long as possible.

I want him to remember *this* Mia before he sees the other one again. The one with steel in her eyes and fire in her heart. The one who's killed too many people to count so she could protect the greater good. The one who would give her life to protect him. And now, that terrifying Mia won't be a flickering image that goes away with some sleeping meds. She'll be real. Permanent. Irreversible.

The ride ends. The car stops. We get out. Summer and Archer are in the car behind us, but before they can get out, something cold and hard digs into the back of my head, a strong hand twisting my 'dominant' arm behind my back. What this asshole doesn't know is that I'm ambidextrous. I disarm him in a quick movement and grab the handgun from his loosened grip.

BANG!

I shoot him in the foot, grabbing a very dazed Dave's wrist and running as fast as I can into the nearest attraction: the fun house.

"Did you just shoot that guy?!"

"We don't have time. They're coming."

"Mia!" Dave's eyes are wide and blue. He tries to pull his hand from my iron grip, but I don't let go. "What the hell is happening?! What the hell *are* you?!"

"Do you trust me?"

Heavy breaths slip from his lips. The look in his eyes, the fear, it pulls the knot in my stomach tighter. There's a long moment of tense silence before he finally answers.

And despite it all, he doesn't hesitate.

"Yes."

"Follow me. I promise you, I will explain everything after we lose these guys." I squeeze his hand and pull him deeper into the reflective maze. It's tricky to navigate. I try to use the reflections to my advantage, but we crash head-on into a pane of glass.

I look to the entrance. Three large, heavily armored guards saunter in. Their guns are held in front of them, each aimed at a reflection of me. One quick tug pulls Dave out of the deadly ring and into another hallway of distorted images of us. Twisted, altered versions of reality run alongside us in our sprint to freedom.

No matter how far or how fast we run, we cannot return to the way things were. There is no going back.

We reach the end, stepping through the rotating tunnel with careful steps. A trip-up now could be the difference between freedom and capture.

BOOM! BANG! BOOM!

Fireworks erupt overhead, filling the sky with dazzling exploding displays of red, white, and blue. Orville knows what he's doing. In a crowd like this on the Fourth of July, screams of terror will be mistaken for celebration. Gunshots will be written off as fireworks. No one will question it. No one will come to help.

I pull Dave into a photo booth for cover, pulling the curtains shut behind us. He looks at me as though I'm a bomb, like I'll explode any second. I hold his face and press a long kiss to his lips, my final goodbye if something goes wrong, but he doesn't kiss me back. He stands there, unmoving. I pull away. His eyes search me with sadness, regret, guilt. He doesn't look at me like he ever has before. It's unsettling.

I feel like a monster.

The curtains rustle and I pull Dave on, out of the booth, as fast as I possibly can. We dart through the fair-goers gazing up at the fireworks in the sky. Every explosion makes me shudder at the possibility that it could be a gunshot.

Our feet pound against the wood of the pier, hearts racing, hands becoming slick with sweat, but I still grip his hand and run. I push all thoughts out of my head, all of the doubts, the worries, the fears, and I just run.

But it's not enough.

Out of nowhere, two gigantic men with biceps the size of bowling balls seize us. Strong arms snake around my waist and my feet leave the ground. I punch, kick, thrash around, but the guard is unmoved, unaffected, unforgiving.

The gun in my grip, my only defense, crashes to the wood of the dock and skitters off of it, landing in the water with a final splash. Dave struggles, but he's nowhere near as strong as I am, nor is he as strong as the guard holding him.

The man holding Dave pulls a gun from the holster on his belt, pushing the barrel to Dave's head. His blue eyes meet mine, filled with terror.

"[*Quit struggling, little mouse.*]" He hisses at me in fluent Russian. His accent is thick, and the only feature uncovered by his black mask is a pair of dark eyes. "[*Or your love will die.*]"

My limbs hang limp as soon as he says it. There's still fire in my gaze. Anger, fear, regret. Guilt. Dave swallows, staring up at the sky.

"[*You do not need to do this.*]" I reply. "[*You want me. Leave him. He means nothing to you.*]"

"[*You do not understand, Miss Crane. You are useless. Worthless. We came for him.*]"

I don't have the time to ask him what he means before I take a hard blow to the head.

And then there's darkness.

CHAPTER 34

Strong hands compress my ribcage over and over, quick and harsh. A warm pair of lips forces a breath of air into my lungs as someone's fingers pinch my nose shut and another hand tilts my head back. My eyes pop open. I sit up and cough the contents of my lungs onto the pier, a splattering of sea water.

As my vision slowly comes together, I expect to find my boyfriend beside me. Instead, it's Archer.

One of his hands rests on my shoulder. Piercing green eyes are filled with concern. My throat feels raw, my body numb and cold and soaking wet. Drenched clothes cling to my skin and strings of wet hair fall in front of my eyes. I don't exactly remember what happened, but I try to piece together the events as best as I can despite my muddled mind and the pounding headache developing where I was hit.

Archer's lips move, but I don't hear any noise. I shake my head and raise an eyebrow. His large hands cup my face, long fingers gingerly removing my hearing aids. The tiniest bit of noise filters through my eardrums. Faint, almost a whisper.

"*Are you okay?*" Summer, who's kneeling beside me now, asks.

I nod before signing: 'Where's Dave?'

Her expression is blank, grim. She blinks a few times and swallows thickly. One of her hands slips into mine. Her lack of an answer is answer enough.

Dave is not here. They didn't make it in time.

I take a few breaths, long and deep and beginning to falter. There are a few silent moments before my shoulders slump. My stomach drops. I swallow the lump in my throat.

I can't look at anyone. I can't form words. I can only cry. I was weak. Useless. Just like the L.O.S.T. agent said. I wasn't able to protect Dave when it mattered most. Every effort I've made to hide him from my grim reality was only delaying the inevitable.

They took him. And there's nothing I can do to change it.

PART 3

CHAPTER 35

Despite the call to the agency the next afternoon, I'm tempted to stay inside my fort of blankets and tissues. I'd rather stay home than deal with the newest addition to the complications of being a teenage spy: captured civilian boyfriends. Ginger and Summer push past the mass of sweat and sadness and drag me out into the cold, cruel reality that stole my Dave.

The ride to Headquarters is a muddled blur. My eyelids are heavy, tears threatening to escape down my cheeks, but I don't let them. Holding it in hurts, but letting it out makes it real. I'm not sure which pain I'd rather suffer.

Everything feels like a dream. Every statement, every condolence, every saddened gaze turned my way feels fuzzy, not quite there. I feel like I'm in a little boat, drifting further and further from shore. The world is out of focus, throbbing in time with the pounding in my head. The morning continues like this until Brian speaks in Sheila's office, clipboard in hand and holographic PowerPoint prepared.

"I know who took Dave, and I know where this guy is."

"You what?" My eyes snap up to his, and immediately I regain my focus, heart racing. The dizzy feeling has left my head, leaving me alert and on edge, fresh with adrenaline.

"It wasn't all that hard." Brian clicks through the first few slides of his presentation. "Despite the fact that there are quite a few hired hands in Orville's index, only a handful of them are Russian males, and only one of those has dark eyes, as you described."

The slide changes, showing the full face of the man that held a gun to Dave's head. Rugged scruff covers his chiseled jawline, and broad shoulders are matched with large tattooed muscles. A long black tattoo reads in Russian: 'The weak will perish at the hands of the strong." A chill runs up my spine as my eyes meet his tired, darker ones. There's something in his gaze, something wicked. Anger. Or something worse. Revenge.

"Viktor Ivanov, 24 years old, 6 feet, 4 inches tall. Born and raised in Russia but moved to America with his younger sister Natalia when he was fifteen. He's flipped from job to job, but most recently, he's been working for Orville. It's rumored that he and his sister are some of Orville's experimental Enhanced, but that's not confirmed yet."

"So where does this asshole like to hang out?" Ginger crosses her arms, resting the heels of her boots on the coffee table.

"We have reason to believe his nest is a place on the docks called Louie's Buoy." The rusted old warehouse on Seavale's coastline flashes on the screen. A large painted sign hangs over the door, broadcasting the name along with a cartoon seagull. "It makes sense. According to witnesses, no one saw the men that attacked the two of you last night. They got away to somewhere close before transferring Dave to a more secure location."

"So when are we going?" I sit up, ready to get this show on the road. The sooner we can head out, the better. We don't have time to lose. If we wait too long, Dave will become Orville's newest lab rat.

"Mia, did you hear a word I just said?" Brian asks incredulously. He pushes his glasses further up the bridge of his nose. "The guy is 6'4" with biceps the size of your head. Plus, he's Enhanced. Probably. Going in there alone...It's suicide."

"He took Dave. If going to pay this lug-head a visit to get information is what it takes to get him back, so be it."

188

"There will be two hits in that fight, Crane. Him hitting you and you hitting the ground."

"I'm not saying we have to fight."

"And she doesn't have to go alone." Summer speaks up. "It's not like we'd let her leave without us anyway."

"Three against one." Ginger adds.

Brian shakes his head. "No. That's dumb. Even with three of you, h-he's stronger and taller and—"

"This is not the ideal way to get information for the case." Sheila looks up from her mountain of paperwork. "But, given the circumstances and the timeframe we have to work on this...I don't think we have much of a choice. If there's a lead, we damn well better chase it before it goes cold."

"B-but Administrator Dormer, you can't possibly be considering this. I mean—"

"I know, Brian. But we're running out of options. Anything else will take too much time. Time we don't have."

"We'll get suited up." I stand up from the couch, with Ginger and Summer right behind me. We take our assignment slips from Sheila before walking out of the office. After changing into uniform and getting our bikes from the garage, we ride down to the docks, parking in the lot outside Louie's Buoy.

The warehouse stands tall with two majestic flags, one American and one Russian, waving above the doorway. The thick stench of fish and saltwater hangs in the air, perhaps to cover the scent of chemicals and gunpowder, but one can never be too sure. Sticky black-red smears of what appears to be blood are caked around the metal doorway and on the concrete below us. I shudder at the realization that this could be Dave's, or any of the countless others that have been kidnapped by Orville's hitters.

A long moment of grim silence passes before I take the first few strides toward the entrance. Summer and Ginger stand outside the door, agreeing to wait as backup and preserve the element of surprise. Each of them gives a silent goodbye in the form of a nod or a small smile.

The moment I step through the doors, all eyes turn on me. At least fifteen bulky mercenaries are roaming through the tall steel building. Some carry crates, others operate cranes, but all of them stop to stare at the fresh meat. It only takes a minute to find Viktor in the crowd, a gleam of familiarity in his stark eyes. The grey tank-top hugging his toned body does nothing to hide neither the bulging biceps nor the tattoos that cover them, a threat to those who threaten him. And though I wouldn't consider myself weak, per say, compared to him, my arms look like toothpicks. Twigs. The man could snap me in half.

"[Leave!]" He barks, but not to me. The others in the room scatter through the back door. One agent, a girl, Natalia I presume, lingers in the doorway before leaving, but soon she's gone with the others, leaving Viktor and I alone in the cavernous space.

He takes large, confident strides towards me. The closer he gets, the more evident our height difference becomes. The only noise in the tense silence is the steady *drip, drip, drip* into the metal bucket sitting in the corner.

"What brings you here, little mouse?" his thick accent is matched with a smirk. The soft echo of his voice rings against the walls. "Looking for a job? Or something more..."

"You know what I'm here for." I don't let my intimidation show, pushing away the ever-growing urge to run for the hills. "Where is he?"

"I'm afraid you'll have to be more specific." He crosses his arms, causing his thick veins to pop. I swallow the lump in my throat. One of his large hands strokes the dark stubble on his chin. "You see, we are sent to pick up tiny weaklings on a regular basis."

"David Bowen. Seventeen years old. About yea high," I hold my hand a few inches above my head, "blue eyes, curly brown hair. Ringing any bells?"

"Perhaps..." He tilts his head, looking down on me from the new angle. "The scrawny one with glasses that wept like a child when we threw you into the ocean, Agent Crane?"

Tears sting my eyes, but I don't give in to them. My jaw clenches and I nod, not daring to respond verbally.

"I'm not sure where he is. But I could find out for you. If."

"If *what*?"

"L.O.S.T. has positions for those as skilled as you and your partners, Miss Crane. Orville doesn't wish to fight you any longer. Why struggle against us when you can join us?" He steps closer, dipping down his head so our eyes are almost level. From this close, I can smell his thick musk and his forest-scented cologne. Warm breaths ghost across my cheeks. He's so close. Too close. I don't move a muscle in fear of showing him any weakness, any vulnerability that he can use to take me down.

"Over my dead body," I hiss, glaring up at him. He only smirks.

"I thought you might say that. Well, no harm in asking." He takes a step away. The heat of the tense moment dissipates, replaced by a sudden chill.

My fingers drift to the gun on my holster, brushing over the cold metal.

"But you should know one thing right now." His voice drops down to a whisper, and he begins signing. 'Without my help, you will never find him.'

His expression isn't menacing. Not threatening. It's more of a warning. A silent message that won't be picked up on any of the cameras and microphones Orville might have stashed around here. It's a message for me and me alone.

Without another word, I leave the warehouse.

CHAPTER 36

"Girls, there's something I feel I should tell you before this situation becomes any more dire." Sheila sits us down before the three of us head home for the night after our debriefing.

Headquarters is a very different place after dark. Most of the interns are gone, the halls are deserted, a few stray janitors clean up the ghost-town of a building, and armed guards stand posted at every hall.

None of us speak, but she has our attention. Slender fingers sweep down the length of her black pencil skirt, straightening out the creases. Her tired eyes show hours of fatigue, and something else: tears. Red, splotchy skin has been covered up by nearly meticulous foundation, but the longer I look, the easier it is to make out mascara smears.

"Are you okay?" My words are swallowed by hers.

"Since this case opened, I've faced you with a heavy heart. I'm afraid I haven't been entirely honest with you. Even though what I'm about to tell you is classified, it's something you should have been told from the beginning." Sheila swallows thickly, silent tears trailing down her fair cheeks. "Louis Orville's wife, Bethany...she was so much more than the beautiful trophy wife of a billionaire."

"What do you mean?" Summer's voice is quiet.

Ginger doesn't speak, but looks on warily. Concerned anticipation glints in her amber eyes and a slight frown tugs at her lips.

"Bethany Orville was an agent of F.O.U.N.D."

My stomach drops and my pulse quickens, eyes searching for something to rest on as I put the pieces together. If Bethany was an agent, why does Orville hate everything we are?

"What?"

"She was placed in the theater the day they met." Sheila starts. There's a long pause before she continues. "I was there too. The mission was to use Louis as a way to get closer to his father, Louis Orville Sr., who was in charge of a corrupt weapon production company among other things. Because she was the better actress, Bethany got the role of Juliet, while I played the Nurse. Louis was cast as Romeo. He thought they were star-crossed lovers, meant to be, but all she ever saw him as was her mission."

"So she didn't love him." Ginger states. "Like at all."

"No. She didn't. But I loved her." A long pause and a shaky breath. "And she loved me." Sheila continues, pulling a tissue from the box resting on the coffee table. "I watched her snuggle up close to him, going on dates and kissing up to his parents, all to get a glance or two in his father's office, steal files from his cabinet. She and I would whisper our I-love-yous in private whenever we could get away, careful not to be seen by anyone who would tell him about us. We were more than mission partners, but no one ever knew."

"But they got married. She married him and she didn't even love him."

"Louis' father got into the darker side of the industry. She needed to stay in close. There is nothing closer than marriage. By the time the kids came around, it was too late. She drifted further from the agency, barely able to send and receive updates, her busy schedule hardly allowed rendezvouses. She had been sucked into the Orville vacuum. There was no escape. Not until it was too late."

"Damn."

"There are not many things I regret about Bethany. But I do regret losing her, and I do regret letting her slip away from me." Sheila wipes away the stray tears, squeezing the ball of damp tissues in her hand. "He hates F.O.U.N.D. not only because his daughter was killed in the crossfire, but because he was fed nothing but lies for years."

"And he thinks I'm doing the same thing to Dave because he works for a business owned by Orville Enterprises."

"Exactly." Sheila tosses the wad into the trash. A shaky sigh escapes her "There's no way to stop his reign of vengeance. The only way to stop him is to kill him before this gets any worse than it already is. That's all. Go home. Get some rest."

I know what she says is right, but I doubt after anything she's said tonight that I could get a wink of sleep.

When I get home, Jace, Nikki, Isaac, and Ethan are waiting on the couch with a mountain of movies and an endless supply of popcorn. I snuggle into the nest of siblings, immediately trapped in Nikki's bear hug with fresh sister kisses all over my cheeks. Her coconut-scented perfume is comforting. I smile through the welling tears I've been holding in all day, snuggling into the crook of her neck.

"It's okay, baby sis." Isaac's fingers comb through my messy chocolate brown locks. I feel Jace's arms wrap around all of us, and soon Ethan does the same from the other side.

"You all right, littlest Crane?" Ethan's thick accent carries concern. I nod, but I don't have any words. I've never felt more loved than I do right now, in the arms of my family. The last twenty-four hours have been rough, but I guess at least for now, I'll be okay. I have to be okay.

After a few movies, I wander down the hall. I tell the others I'm going to the bathroom, but if we're being honest, I have no clue where I'm headed. My feet seem to be conspiring against me, but I follow them anyway, down the hall, down the stairs, and into the brightly lit trophy room.

Of course. Of course I would end up here.

On these walls are the names of those who came before us. The Crane legacy. Four generations, from my great-grandparents to my grandparents to Mom and Dad to my siblings to me. I trace the letters carved in wood and metal with my fingertips. If they could see me, what I am, what I've become, what would they say? Would they have faith that I can get myself out of this mess, or would they be ashamed I couldn't save him. I couldn't save him from Orville's revenge trip. I failed to protect him.

"You okay?"

Jace leans against the doorframe. He looks very cozy in his navy blue sweater. Reading glasses rest on his forehead and a book dangles from his hand. I forgot. This is his reading spot. But since he left for England, it's kind of become my getaway destination, a thinking place to escape to when things get to be too much.

Looking at these pictures, the medals and plaques, it helps me remember everything I'm supposed to be. These people have stopped assassinations of world leaders and taken down corrupt nations, they've eliminated attempts of chemical warfare and stopped nuclear bombs from leveling cities. They're legends, inspirations, and I'm...well, I'm just me.

"Oh, uh, yeah I guess. I just come here sometimes..."

"Kind of intimidating, huh?" Jace offers a knowing smile as he takes a seat on the bench beside me. "All of them are field agents except for me. Well, me and Grandpa Wayne, I guess. Actually, I think I was sitting right here when I realized all of my years of field training were for nothing."

"Yeah?"

"Yeah. I don't know what I was reading, but I do know how scared I was to face Mom and Dad. And I know it's nothing compared to what you're going through, but I know it will get better."

"Maybe. I don't know. It's just...I knew dating Dave was a bad idea the moment I met him. I knew it would come with a price because everything always does, but I didn't listen to the voice in my head. I went against the rules and now I'm paying for it."

"I promise you, things will work out. Maybe not the way you want, but they will." He puts a hand on my shoulder. I look up and meet his eyes. "You're strong, Mia. Stronger than me. Stronger than anyone I know. And if anyone can do it, it's you."

"I'm not so sure about that."

"I am." He pauses. "Plus, the 36-hour veil of secrecy goes up tomorrow."

"Meaning?"

"F.O.U.N.D. has to inform the family of the situation. All of it." My jaw drops. "Agency rules."

"I forgot about that. Oh my God, someone has to tell Dave's mom."

"You could ask Sheila if you could go. Might help her to have a familiar face break the news to her. Might help both of you to talk about it." Jace's hand rests on my back.

"You're right." I snuggle under his arm and into his soft knitted sweater. My voice is muffled in his shoulder. "Thank you so much. I needed this. I love you, Jace."

"I love you too. We're all going to help you through this. I promise."

CHAPTER 37

Two cars are sitting in the Bowens' driveway when we pull in the afternoon of the next day. One I recognize as Mrs. Bowen's minivan, and the other is Dave's. My heart sinks a little at the thought of his name, at the thought of his empty car that he's not driving because he's gone. This might be harder than I thought.

Walking up to the front door, I imagine the late-night visit Mrs. Bowen got the night it happened. Her face flashes in my mind, shock and horror registering as tears form in her eyes. I blink the thought away, shuddering. Sheila knocks on the front door.

"Hello?" Mrs. Bowen warily peeks out through a crack. One green eye looks around before she opens the door any wider. Her voice is thick, and her eyes seem glossed over, as though she's been crying recently. I don't blame her. So have I. "Mia? What are you doing here?"

"Mrs. Bowen, this is Sheila Dormer, an administrator from F.O.U.N.D. We're here to talk about Dave."

"What does my son have to do with...that?" Concern laces her voice. I can hear her heart breaking. She thinks he's been lying to her about that. About being an agent. *He* hasn't been lying. Just me.

"Nothing." Sheila reassures her. "Your son has nothing to do with our organization, but—"

"I do." Both of them fall silent. I feel their gazes lock on me as my eyes find the ground. "He was taken because of me. It'd be easier to explain, but it'll take a while."

"Well, I don't exactly have much to do until tonight." She's not dressed in her scrubs, which means she must have the night shift, as she often does. "Come inside. Take a seat."

So we do, albeit awkwardly. I take a seat on the couch that Dave and I have cuddled on countless times. The ghost of his warmth is still there, and his grey sweatshirt is draped over the back of it. My eyes wander anywhere but to Mrs. Bowen's. I can't look her in the eye. This entire time, her son's girlfriend has been an operative of F.O.U.N.D. and she had no clue. Granted, neither did Dave. I betrayed them both, and he paid the price for it.

"What exactly happened?" Mrs. Bowen speaks slowly, a short pause between each word.

I take a shaky breath, struggling to compose my thoughts. I rehearsed my speech at least sixteen times on the way here, and yet the words still get caught in my throat. It's as if even my very thoughts have abandoned me when I need them most.

"Dave was taken by enemies of the agency. Russian mercenaries that work for Louis Orville's corrupt agency, the League of Science and Technology, or L.O.S.T." Sheila reads from a thick file of papers, detailing the capture and the agents involved. "The police weren't given all of the details, but since it's been 36 hours since the incident, we're allowed to disclose classified information to family of those involved."

"Where do you fit into all of this, Mia?"

"I..." I take a large breath, gathering enough courage to meet her emerald gaze. "I've been an agent since birth, Mrs. Bowen. Born and raised like my parents and grandparents before me. I fell in love with Dave despite agency regulations, knowing full well that I would get attached emotionally and that it would compromise my mental state and possibly put him in jeopardy. It's my fault that he was taken. Orville thinks that I'm leading your son on, that he's my mission because of...something that happened to Orville in the past. A betrayal."

"And is he?"

"What?"

"Is Dave your mission?"

"No. Absolutely not. He's my boyfriend. We met outside of agency circumstances, simply by coincidence. Everything about our relationship is real, not a fabrication of F.O.U.N.D. or anything else." I pause, tears welling in my eyes. A lump forms in my throat. This is definitely a harder bridge to cross than I had anticipated. "I promise you, I miss him as much as you do. I-I let him down. I was there when they took him and I couldn't protect him. It's all my fau—"

"Amelia Crane, it is not your fault." Mrs. Bowen takes a long stride forward and wraps me up in a tight Mom-hug, letting me bury my face in her lilac sweater and soft brown curls. "You did everything you could. These...these men that took my David, I know that they won't be out there for long."

"Why?"

"Because I believe in you and your agency. And I know that you'll do whatever it takes to bring him home."

"I promise I will." There's a long silence. "Mrs. Bowen, do you mind if I look in Dave's room while Sheila talks to you about agency things?"

"Go ahead." She offers an understanding, but sad smile. "Going in there might help. I know it helps me, just to look at his things, do a little tidying up."

"Thanks." I give her another brief hug before heading up the stairs to Dave's bedroom.

The entire space is so him. Unlike the nerd cave in the basement, Dave's room is much more organized. It's way cleaner than it was the last time I was in here. All of his belongings are grouped into boxes or stacks or shelves. Each of his t-shirts is folded, and he tried to arrange them by color, but they ended up a jumbled mess due to his colorblindness.

Green covers are spread over his bed, pushed up against the wall. They complement the pale green paint that I helped do in the winter. I lost a perfectly good shirt that day to the Great Paint War of Late 2015. We were a mess, but at the end of the day, the walls looked nice, and that was all that mattered.

On the wall beside his bed, Dave has several Polaroid snapshots taped up in perfect rows of five. Most of them are older, at least from last year. Others are newer, from camp and the rest of this summer. The first is from the beach, of our *Star Wars* rings and intertwined fingers. I'd do anything to go back to that day, or the picture beside it, of the bonfire at Secret Falls, or the one next to that one, of the gazebo in the middle of the woods.

A picture is worth a thousand words, as they say. I would do anything to tell him even three: I love you. Or three more: I'll find you. Or just two: I promise.

My fingers trace over the pictures, around each white edge with care. Some are labeled, others aren't. There's a picture of the back of my head on a sunny spring day. A flower is stuck behind my ear, tucked into the mess of brown waves. I faintly remember this day. A trip to the beach, or maybe the park. On the bottom of the picture, there's Dave's scrawl in blue ink: May 5th, 2016.

I had a mission that day, just after that, actually. I remember a picnic filled with fresh strawberries and sweet lemonade that stained Dave's blue polo and a very vengeful bee that just wouldn't leave him alone. I remember his large hand around mine and his soft lips against my own.

Another is labeled December 12th, 2015: a picture of the frosty winter woods. Warm feelings of Dave's cozy blue winter jacket and his long grey and red striped scarf come to the surface. He was wearing a soft crimson knitted hat and black mittens. Stray snowflakes caught in my hair as Dave's hands cupped my cold and rosy cheeks. It was a night of fogged-up breath and a starry sky. A night of boot prints in the fresh snow and frost-covered pine trees standing high above us, of spontaneous snow-angels and matching mugs of hot cocoa with extra chocolate syrup, of our first kiss.

March 18th, 2016. Two days after Dave's seventeenth birthday. Two mugs, one with Spider-Man on it, and the other painted with Spider-Gwen. We were sitting at the island in my kitchen after my cheer practice and Dave's last-minute marching band rehearsal for the upcoming St. Patrick's Day parade. Despite being beyond wiped, we still managed to have our weekly date night, even if it was just watching a movie and having a warm drink together. To an introvert like Dave, a quiet night in is way better than anything else we could have done that night anyway.

April 4th, 2016. A bright red umbrella and ladybug rain boots on a soggy afternoon. Intertwined fingers and a warm comic book shop to hide in from the storm. Kissing in the rain before leaving him behind to foil the assassination of a visiting world leader.

July 4th, 2015. Fireworks and grilling burgers. The colorful flashing lights of the fair rides. Sparklers spelling words against the dark night sky. The pier. Attackers. L.O.S.T. F.O.U.N.D. Failure. The new memories mix with the old in a toxic blend and I'm forced to shift my gaze, trying to blink away the flashes of a gun against my head, drowning, of Archer's desperate lips on mine, forcing air into my lungs.

This is too much. I thought I was ready, but I'm not. I might never be.

CHAPTER 38

When I get called to Headquarters later in the afternoon, I expect good news. I need good news. I need something to believe in, a lead to chase. Well, a lead besides Viktor Ivanov's attempt to recruit me. Needless to say, the news I receive is less than pleasing.

Elise sits at her desk in Sheila's office, shuffling through files about potential L.O.S.T. bases. Since the 4th of July, the base at the mall construction site has been deserted, and shortly after my visit to Louie's Buoy, the docks were cleared out too. They seem to be withdrawing, but they aren't gone. Something tells me this retreat is temporary. When they come back, it'll be with force.

This is like finding a spider in the house; the worst part of finding the spider is not finding the spider. It's losing the spider. We can only hope to find our spider and kill it before it's too late. Before this web gets any more complicated than it already is.

I take a seat on the couch, messing with the sleeve of my uniform jacket until the hologram projector starts. The video buffer symbol spins a few times before being replaced by a white arrow. Sheila doesn't say anything when she walks into the room. She only sits on the couch and takes my hand before starting the video.

Dave, dressed in only a hospital gown and a pair of grey boxers, is sitting strapped to a chair. There's something off about him. He's not injured or hurt. He looks healthy, even. He just seems different. Maybe the fact that I can't pinpoint the problem scares me the most. Dave swallows thickly, his blue eyes swimming behind his thick glasses. Bright lights shine in his face, as though he's in a lab being examined like an animal.

My heart races as I try to prepare for whatever is yet to come. Before anything else happens, Sheila gives my hand a squeeze. Elise has stopped working, and her eyes are glued to the screen along with ours.

"M-Mia," Dave squeaks, his eyes locked onto a spot slightly above the camera lens. A chill runs up my spine as soon as I hear his voice. "As you can see, I'm unharmed. If y-you want me to stay that way, stay away from..." Dave's voice breaks, fear in his eyes. A loud click sounds in the background of the audio. He takes a shaky breath, shoulders heaving. "S-stay away from L.O.S.T. Let them do their work or...or..."

There's a long silence. He trembles.

"MIA YOU HAVE TO STOP THEM OR EVERYONE WILL DIE!"

BANG!

A fresh bullet wound tears open Dave's stomach, causing him to contort and writhe in pain, screaming all the while. I gasp and slap my hands over my mouth. Hot tears run down my cheeks. There's nothing I can do to hold back the sobs that rack my body, shaking me like a ragdoll.

"I LOVE Y—" The feed cuts out.

Another long silence. Well, it's not silent. The sounds of my crying occupy the large office. Sheila and Elise don't offer any words. There aren't any words for what I've just witnessed.

"How." I state through the tears that stream down my cheeks.

"The intel department hacked it from Orville's system. He tried to delete it, but not before we found it." Her lips are pressed into a thin line. "Mia, despite the dangers to himself and the other dozen teenagers that have gone missing since he has, Dave wants you to fight. He needs you to fight."

"I know." Something snaps deep within me. Fire burns behind my eyes. "I just need a place and a time and I'm there."

"Most of the bases are deserted, Agent Crane. When we find one, you'll be the first to know."

"I better be." I get up and leave before I break anything in my anger. I'm beyond grieving and self-pity. Now the only thing left is rage, and I plan to act on it.

The next two weeks fly by. I fall into a routine; the same thing every day, like clockwork. My days are filled with chasing cold leads to empty warehouses and abandoned sheds. My nights consist of hours and hours of training, too much caffeine, and not nearly enough sleep. I take out my anger on the punching bag in the basement, but I would give anything to swap it for Orville's face. Isaac amends this by taping a picture of the billionaire there. For motivation, he claims.

Summer and Ginger come to the house almost every day to train, but really it's just blowing off steam until we get the lead we've been waiting for.

More intel pours in, but nothing that will help us at the moment. Dave and another dozen kids were taken to be tested on. They've been dubbed "Orville's Unlucky Thirteen" by the intel department. Seven girls, six boys, according to the hacked files. Jace has been working on it overtime. He's the best hacker in the department, so he's been a great help to Great City Headquarters, given that we're at the nucleus of the L.O.S.T. problem.

Even with all the extra help and more of the international agents coming to lend a hand, progress is slow.

One of the monotonous afternoons, I get an email from Lucia Hernandez:

Mia,

Heard about Dave and the others. We're doing our part here, but we don't have a clue where they're keeping the patients. Good luck with everything. I know this must be so hard on you. Harder than it is on us. Just know that we're here for you, and if anything comes to the surface, we've got your back.

-Lucia

"You all right in here, M?" Jace is standing in the doorway of the office, a concerned brotherly look on his face.

I nod, closing my laptop. "I'm good. Just an email from Lucia. She said they'd help if we need it."

"Good to know. Um, Ethan and Nikki are waiting for you in the training room."

"Thanks."

When I get to the training room, Nikki and Ethan are not alone. Standing in a semi-circle on the mat is Isaac, Ginger, Summer, and Archer, the last of whom I haven't seen since he saved my life on the pier. A memory flashes in my head. I push it away just as quickly as it came, desperate to rid myself of that night until everything is back to normal. Or, whatever we find the new normal to be after L.O.S.T. is wiped off of the face of the earth.

"What's this? An intervention?" I look around.

"Of sorts." A smirk tugs at Isaac's lips. He crosses his arms. "We need to train. The old fashioned way. Your busywork is nothing but that: busywork. You need to focus. In the wise, wise words of Troy Bolton: Get your head in the game."

"Meaning?" I cut him off before he can break into song.

"It means we train, Crane. One on one." Archer tilts his head. "May the best agent win."

"You are so on, British." A slow smirk spreads across my lips.

However, despite my challenge, the first to approach isn't Archer, but Ginger instead. I take a step back to dodge one of her fists straight to the face. The others all pair up, starting fighting sessions of their own. In moments, I'm in the zone, instincts kicking in and adrenaline pumping through my veins. Ginger is no longer Ginger. Instead, she's an agent of L.O.S.T., an enemy of F.O.U.N.D., and it's my job to take her down.

She pounces, but I side-step, and she tucks and rolls gracefully, recovering immediately. I watch her movements, preparing for her next attack. Punch, punch, punch, block, block, punch. Quick, powerful jabs that I manage to catch and dodge, interjecting them with a few hits of my own.

A few minutes pass and I feel my hands become slick with sweat. My heart is racing and my breathing is heavy, but so is hers. I do a back handspring and use the wall to spring forward. My fist becomes locked in her hand, so I dive beneath her, between her legs and take her arm down with me, essentially folding her in half. She flops onto her back, groaning.

"Shit." She mutters, scrambling to her feet.

I watch her for a few seconds, silently blinking a few times before she launches forward out of nowhere. Our fight becomes a power struggle, each of us pushing to tackle the other to the ground, and just when I think I have the upper hand, I hit the mat. Hard. Ginger's fingers cuff my wrists and I'm pinned by her body, unable to get up. A slow smile finds her lips.

"Got ya."

"Yes. You did."

Her lips peck my cheek before she crawls off of me and helps me to my feet.

"Need some help there, Crane?" Archer smirks.

"I'm all right. Want me to kick your ass next?"

"If that's what you call arse-kicking, you might need a reevaluation."

"Oh really? Have you been training since you were five years old? I think not."

"Maybe you should put your money where your mouth is." He challenges. I open my mouth to reply, but the lights flash and the screen by the door activates.

"*Call from Headquarters. New mission dispatch for Amelia Crane, Summer Laurence, Ginger Williams, Archer Reynolds and John Jacobi.*" C.A.I.T.L.Y.N.'s monotonous voice rings through the large room. We stop in our tracks.

"Who's John Jacobi?"

"My mission partner. He's back at Headquarters." Archer explains, hands on his hips. We all look to each other, waiting for someone to make the first move. "Right then. Let's get a move on, shall we? Haven't got all day."

If only I knew then that everything was about to change.

CHAPTER 39

"**W**hat's the deal? Talk to me, Martin." We walk briskly into Sheila's office and plop onto the couch for our briefing. John has been waiting for us for an undetermined amount of time. His face says it's been a while.

As soon as we got the news, we tried to get here as fast as possible, but traffic has never worked in my favor before and today was no different. If this is about what I think it is, I know our allotted time is very short. We have to move before they do. And by 'they' I mean L.O.S.T. Obviously.

"Two-hour window. Our hackers found an active L.O.S.T. base that we believe is housing Orville's Unlucky Thirteen," Brian explains.

"Where?" Summer leans against her knees, adjusting the zippers and straps on her complicated leather boots. We're suited up. All we need is a vehicle and a plan. A location would be helpful too, though.

"A vacant ice rink called Snow Daze. It's owned by a branch of Orville Enterprises called Local Mind, the branch that owns Lucky's, along with a few other local businesses: coffee shops and whatnot. Business is usually booming in the summer, so we knew something was up when they announced a three-week maintenance shut-out. One hack of the cameras and—"

"Okay, okay, we get it. Now what's the bloody plan, mate?" Archer urges Brian on.

John nods silently, his arms crossing his muscular chest. His tousled brown hair is slicked back neatly, much like Brian's, and the sleeves of his uniform jacket tightly hug his biceps. He's incredibly built, even for a field agent. John's bulk rivals that of Viktor Ivanov, and that's saying a hell of a lot.

"According to the hacked footage, Orville is keeping his 'patients' there. All thirteen, as far as we can tell. However, they don't seem to be in the best shape. Many of them are sick physically...and some mentally. Psychological breakdowns are as common as the waves of nausea. It's not pretty. Also, they started packing up a few hours ago. You have a very short window to work with before they pack up the prisoners."

"How much time are we talking?"

"Two hours, minus a fifteen-minute ride there and an approximate five-minute break-in."

"So an hour-forty."

"Yes." He sets five pairs of custom-made boots on the table, each stamped with our agent codes. He sure whipped these up awfully fast. That's quick even for him. "You'll need these. They look like standard-issue F.O.U.N.D. combat boots, but if you flip the switch on the heel—" *Shink!* Sharp metal skates slide out of the bottom of them, instantly transforming them into something worthy of the wintery battlefield.

"Agents," Sheila speaks up, "you'll need to pull out all of the stops. If you don't bring them home now, we don't bring them home period. Orville will have them shipped off to God-knows-where and we might very well never be able to find them."

"All or nothing."

Sheila nods, her eyes locking into mine. I feel like she's gazing into my soul. "Good luck. Hopefully you won't need it."

We're dismissed without another word, earpieces activated and weapons loaded. They dispatch us in a van. Large, black, with room for thirteen passengers in the back, plus two agents driving and three sitting at the windows in case of gunfire.

Summer takes the wheel with John riding in the passenger seat. He doesn't speak nearly as much as Archer, despite being just as good-looking as his fellow Brit. Archer, Ginger, and I take our seats in the back, manning the windows like hawks. If anyone attacks, they'll regret it.

"Are you scared, Crane?" Archer asks. There's no smirk on his face. No sarcasm in his voice. He means it.

"Yeah. A little."

"We'll be fine." Ginger attempts to lighten the mood. "We always are. Orville doesn't know who he picked a fight with. He's underestimated us before."

"Has he? He always seems one step ahead." Fireworks erupt in my mind, reminders of that night, of drowning and twisted reflections and captured boyfriends. I shiver and snap back to reality. Now is not the time. "It seems like we always take one step forward and two steps back."

"I'm just saying...maybe we haven't been on our top game, but we are now. We're the agency's best, aren't we?"

I don't respond. No one does. We're not the best, we're just what they have to work with at the moment, what with the sudden double-agent screenings and countless agents dropping like flies at the hands of Orville's other recruits worldwide. The L.O.S.T. problem is much bigger than F.O.U.N.D. is letting on, and if we don't do something fast, it'll only get worse.

Summer parks the car beside the back entrance. All of us but John file out. He's deemed himself the getaway driver, and he certainly has the firepower to defend himself if need be.

After picking the lock and hacking the security system, we creep inside, sticking to the shadows. L.O.S.T. recruits hustle and bustle every which way, carting huge crates of what I can only assume is Chemical Rebirth and whatever else Orville's cooked up in his mad science lab. I shudder at the thought of anything manufactured here coursing through Dave's veins, but after two weeks of being here and there and everywhere, it's more than likely.

I sign that we should split up. Archer follows me along one wall while Summer and Ginger creep down the other. There are guards posted, but they're too busy monitoring the hired hands to notice us. With our black uniforms, we almost blend in. If you didn't look closely, you would never be able to tell the difference.

We reach a door labeled: "Patients' Wing. AUTHORIZED PERSONNEL ONLY." Convenient.

The lock is automated, only unlockable with Orville's fingerprint. I lean forward, stretching my fingers as I reach for my tool kit. Before I so much as touch the lock, the door swings open. Thirteen men cart out thirteen patients, straight-jacketed and strapped to dollies on wheels. Some are knocked out, others are writhing weakly as the meds begin to kick in. The third one in the line is Dave, sweat causing his thick brown curls to stick to his slick forehead. New bruises are beginning to form on his face and there are dark bags around his eyes. He's paler than usual: physically, emotionally, and psychologically drained.

I take a large stride forward, but instead of confronting the man taking Dave away as I had planned to do, I come face-to-face with Viktor Ivanov and his sister Natalia.

"I see you've returned for more, little mouse. It is not wise of you to pick fights you cannot win." Victor cocks his head to the side, an intimidating air surrounding him. And though I'm hesitant to approach, I do. I don't really have a choice.

"Just turn over Dave and the others and no one gets hurt."

"Oh please, Crane girl." Natalia's accent is even thicker than her brother's. A dangerous gleam in her eyes leaves me feeling uneasy. Something is coming. Something dark. "The only one getting hurt today is *you*."

She barely even touches me, but sends me flying across the ice. I skid into the wall, hitting the edge hard. It hurts, but I push myself to my feet. I charge to make a rebound just as Archer takes a hit from Natalia equally as strong as the one I just took and finds himself on the other side of the rink. Brian was right. Viktor is enhanced, and so is his sister. I have a feeling I don't want to know what Viktor is capable of.

My skates slide into place, allowing me to move across the ice with ease, rather than slipping and stumbling my way across the glassy surface on ordinary boots. I kick up a flurry of snow, digging the heels of my skates into the smooth ice. Viktor bats it away. He raises his hands as though it's a warning, but before he can do anything, Ginger slams into his side, knocking him over.

"Brian, you were right. The Ivanovs are Enhan—" Another blow from Natalia, this time to the stomach. I double over, clutching my abdomen and cursing loudly. Summer has found her way over to the eye of the storm. A knot of L.O.S.T. agents forms around us. Natalia and Viktor are somewhere in the mix. I try to get a glimpse of the Unlucky Thirteen, but I'm not tall enough to see over the towering guards all around us.

"John, watch out for the Thirteen. They should be leaving the building any second."

"*Will do.*" He replies, but there's no reply from Brian.

"Mia, our very short window just got a whole lot shorter." Ginger knocks out an agent by slamming him over the head with a briefcase she must have found. Judging by the loud clang, I'd say it's empty, but even so, it's done its job. "They're leaving. Now. There's no time."

"We have to do something." I step on the closest agent's toes, slicing them with my skates, and then immediately force his head onto my knee. Summer fires a few shots, but does so carefully to avoid shooting the patients, wherever they wound up.

"Mia, Archer, you two go find the Thirteen. Ginger and I can handle this."

"Are you—" My throat closes up without any warning. No one is close enough to choke me, but that doesn't seem to matter. My windpipe has been forced shut and I can't breathe. My mouth moves, but no words come out. I cough, but there's nothing there. I reach to my throat expecting to find fingers, but I only find skin: my own.

I start to get dizzier as my feet leave the ice, legs dangling in the air uselessly. Viktor's hand is outstretched, fingers cupped as if...as if he were force-choking me Darth Vader-style. I feel like a bomb just dropped. Telekinetic powers aren't just in comic books anymore. They're right here, and I'm dying because of them.

I fail to call for help, unable to make a sound. Dark spots cloud my vision. I blink a few times and my body weakly shakes before I go limp. Summer clocks Viktor in the face from out of nowhere. I fall ten feet to the ice below, sputtering and coughing as though I had been drowned all over again, making this the second time now that Viktor Ivanov has literally taken my breath away.

Archer's large hands pull me off of the ground and drag me on after him and Ginger with Summer not far behind us. As soon as we're off the ice we retract our skates, transforming them to boots once again.

"Get back to the van! They're getting away!" John shouts into the transmitters.

"On the way, mate!" Archer replies. We're out the door in a matter of seconds. The stark sunlight is blinding compared to the dimly lit ice rink. The sliding doors of the van are wide open. We jump inside, dragging them shut as John takes off out of the parking lot and down the road, onto the highway, wheels squealing as we launch into action.

"Where are they?" I lean over John's shoulder. He points to a large black truck ahead. I nod, taking my seat at the gun resting by the back window. My eyes peer through the sight, and I ignore the pounding pinching pain in my head as I take aim at the back right tire. The bullets bounce off, ricocheting as if they were made of plastic, children's toys instead of deadly weapons. This means that the windows are probably bulletproof too.

"John, can you get any closer?" I glance up at the escape hatch on top of the van. Summer's eyes meet mine in wide-eyed realization.

"Mia, you can't."

"Watch me." I unbuckle my seatbelt and stand up, pulling down the ladder and popping open the hatch. Slowly but surely, John creeps closer to the back of the truck. It's gonna be a longshot, but I think I can make it.

"Mia! Unnecessary risks! Remember?!" Summer shouts again.

"Don't get yourself bloody killed, Crane! I don't want to scrape you off the pavement!"

"MY BOYFRIEND IS IN THE BACK OF THAT TRUCK PROBABLY BEING TORTURED! I THINK I CAN HANDLE MYSELF, THANKS!" I holler as I get a foot on the ladder, then another and another until my head clears the top.

"Take out the driver! We've got your back!" Ginger squints through the sight of her gun, ready to shoot if need be.

I suck in a huge breath as I swing my leg up onto the roof of the van. The wind nearly knocks me off of my feet, and my head pounds with the start of a concussion, probably from one of the many blows I took in the rink. Crouching, I find my center of gravity and take slow baby steps closer to the front of the van. The top of the truck's trailer towers seven feet above me. I couldn't reach if my life depended on it, and I left my grappling hook at home, unfortunately.

I hop back into the van, closing the hatch behind me.

"Too high. John, I need you to get as close to the front of the truck as you can."

"I'm trying," He switches lanes, swerving to the right. His fingers grip the steering wheel until his knuckles turn white, face knit in concentration. "Hold on tight!" I grab one of the handles on the roof for balance. Everyone tilts to the left until we're straightened out again. Summer and Archer move away from the left door, aiming their guns there in preparation. We inch closer and closer to the front of the truck. My heart races—*thump-thump, thump-thump, thump-thump, thump-thump*—so loud and fast that it's all I can focus on. I swallow thickly as we finally close the distance and the doors slide open.

This is it.

In one bounding leap, I latch onto the passenger door of the big black truck, my hand gripping the handle and feet firmly planted on the platform. The window opens, the cold barrel of a handgun brushing against my skin. Before the passenger can fire any shots, Ginger shoots him instead. Blood pours from a hole on his neck and he slumps forward, limp and unmoving. I climb through the open window over him and whack the driver in the head with the base of my gun. He's out.

It doesn't take long to take control of the truck, sitting on the lap of the unconscious driver. I watch in the side-mirror as Ginger pulls the van doors shut.

"Vehicle clear. Patients secure. Taking the next exit." A wave of unbelievable relief washes over me as I steer the truck into the nearest exit. We pull over into the parking lot of an off-the-highway store that exclusively sells fireworks, or used to until they went out of business. As I park, the only thought I can manage is how relieved I am that after two long hard weeks, I'll finally see Dave. I'll finally be able to hold him in my arms and tell him everything is going to be okay.

I climb over the conked-out driver and wipe the blood off of my leg before hopping out of the truck. My boots kick up dirt from the bare parking lot, creating a dirty fog. It thickens as the

F.O.U.N.D. van pulls up beside me. No one says much as they wait for me to pick the padlock hanging from the thick chain on the back of the truck. I work with shaky hands, nervous, but excited to see Dave again. To really see him.

Summer, Archer, Ginger, and John all point their weapons at the door in anticipation of guards that could be waiting inside the truck. Finally, the lock pops open. I slip the chains off and open the doors wide.

It's dark inside, but more importantly: it's empty.

My heart sinks, my hopes of seeing Dave again plummeting like rain from the heavens. Then, large, wet drops fall from the clouds, washing the blood off of my leather uniform. I shake my head. Words don't form in my mouth. They just sit in the back of my brain, a jumbled mess of broken thoughts and hollow feelings.

He's not here.

None of them are.

L.O.S.T. still has them.

"Oi, there's something way in the back." John snaps twice and then points, a hand over his eyes to see into the dark truck. I see it too. Red numbers.

3...2...1...0...

We hit the deck as fast as possible, taking shelter behind our bulletproof vests and praying it will be enough.

BOOM!

CHAPTER 40

There are 438 glow-in-the-dark stars on my ceiling. I just finished counting for the third time. It seems like a lot, but it's not so hard from my spot on the floor. After all, pretty much the entirety of my time is free time now. The problem is out of our hands and we are "not allowed to do anything that could further endanger the Unlucky Thirteen until F.O.U.N.D. has assessed the situation and the international council has met to discuss moving forward."

If that's not a huge red flag waving to tell me that everything is not okay at all, I don't know what is. My boyfriend has gone from an innocent civilian unknowingly breaking the agency's third rule to an unwilling accomplice of a mastermind's revenge plot.

All of my energy was building up to that mission. Everything was leading up to that one moment. The moment where everything would be better again. Everything would be fixed in an instant, years of secrets forgotten, and problems concerning L.O.S.T. ignored for the moment. For a moment. One perfect moment.

But life is not a fairytale and wishes like that aren't meant to be granted, especially not *my* wishes. Not with all of the blood on my hands. These stains will never go away. There is no wiping the slate clean.

I've been lying here for hours, thinking over everything Sheila told us when we got back to Headquarters after a very long and very quiet ride. We blew our chance. The Thirteen are gone, and no matter where Orville took them, we can't do anything about it now. Not without committing an act of treason, at least.

Sheila said we were lucky the explosion wasn't very big. Orville was probably counting on us being inside the back of the truck. It's a good thing we weren't, or we'd all be dead and Dave would have a much larger problem on his hands.

Finally, a voice drags me back to reality.

"Blimey, you alright in here?" Archer. I don't respond or move or even blink. I just continue to lie on the carpet of my bedroom that needs to be vacuumed and stare at the unforgiving green stars on my ceiling. "I'll take that as a 'no' then."

"He's gone."

"No. He was transferred to an undetermined location. He was moved with the others. He's not...not that we know of, I mean. And I'm sure if Orville had killed him we would know. He would be itching to gloat."

"He's the only reason I'm fighting. The job would have been— *should* have been—handed off to I don't know...better agents."

"Better agents? Do you hear yourself, Crane?"

Again, I don't reply.

"They chose you and Ginger and Summer for the job for a reason. They sent you for a reason."

"Because there was no one better available in the very short window we were given to work with."

"Perhaps. Or rather, because they believed in you?"

"Look where that got them. You heard what Administrator Dormer said before we left. 'If you don't bring them home now, we don't bring them home period'." I sigh. "It's over."

"You're from a long line of agents, Crane."

"Stop."

"No. You're from a long line of agents. You are a legacy. A legend."

"I SAID STOP IT!" I yell. My heart races. I squeeze my eyes shut and take a few deep breaths. After a long pause, I finally manage to mumble a reply. "I don't feel like a legend."

"Maybe not." He pauses, sitting cross-legged on the floor beside me. "But someday when you and that bloke of yours have kids, won't you want to tell them about the time their mother stole a plane and traveled halfway across the country to save his arse?"

I raise an eyebrow and sit up, leaning back on my arms. "What are you saying?"

"Your genius mate, Bryce or whatever his name is—"

"*Brian*, continue."

"And your older brother, they hacked into footage from Orville's private airport. Thirteen patients wheeled into one of his very large planes, headed towards the west coast."

"So we stowaway?"

"Too late. Already took off."

"Damn."

"But they have a plan. They explain it better than I do."

"Lead the way."

Forty-seven minutes later, Ginger, Summer, Archer, Nikki, Ethan, and I ride the train to Headquarters together.

We walk through the lobby as normal, checking in with our IDs and claiming we're on our way up to see Sheila. We are not, however, on our way to see Sheila.

We are going to steal a plane.

Large jackets conceal our overnight bags, sunglasses hide our eyes, and large sunhats and visors are our solace from the many cameras scattered through the plane hangar.

"*Are you almost there?*" Brian whispers into the earpiece stuck in my hearing aid. It was easy to conceal without question, a simple fix, and suddenly I had camouflaged communication. Why he didn't think of something like this sooner is beyond me.

"Yep," I reply. "Which plane did you guys hack into?"

"*Ummmmm...*" Jace trails off. I imagine he and Brian are sitting at the desk in the office together while Isaac sits there uselessly, bringing them water of coffee or Doritos or whatever they need to keep hacking and programming. "*You're looking for Plane 403. It looks like a standard airliner on the outside, but inside, you've got all the gadgets you need.*"

"Thanks." I turn to the others. "403. Look for 403."

"There it—no. Over there—no. I think it's that—never mind." Ethan looks around.

"There," Nikki directs his pointing finger slightly to the left. "That one."

"Found it. Moving in now. You sure no one's using it soon?"

"*There's nothing on 403's schedule for the next three weeks. You guys should be back in under forty-eight hours, so it won't be a problem.*" Brian states. The *click-click-clack* of their fingers flying across their keyboards accompanies the sound of his voice. "*Summer, I'm going to need you to hack a tiny bit of code into the plane's mainframe. Do you think you can do that?*"

"She doesn't have an earpiece, doofus."

"Ask her then."

"Summer, Brian needs you to hack something into the main computer of the plane manually." Why Brian didn't ask Ginger or I to do it is another question for another day, but I'd say it has a fair bit to do with the fact that he definitely has a huge nerd-crush on her. That and he doesn't want her to spend any more time than necessary with the incredibly attractive British agent to my right.

"I've got it. No problem."

"She's good."

"*Good. Be careful. All of you. I mean it. Mom and Dad are gonna be beyond pissed when you get home.*"

"It'll be worth it, though." I can barely hear Jace's reply before providing a silent one of my own.

I hope so.

Something tugs at me a little as we walk up the stairs and into the plane. It feels strange, like I'm stepping outside a bubble. Once we take off, we'll no longer be at Headquarters, the building I grew up in. Once we leave, we don't have any protection. We are defying direct agency orders. And yet, as I break the first and arguably most important field agent rule and soar into the cloudy skies, I have never felt so free.

It's time to right my wrongs, to get my life back on track, and if I have to raise a little hell and break a few rules to get there, so be it. Orville deserves everything that's coming to him.

CHAPTER 41

The plane ride is long. Almost seven hours long. If nothing else, I try to sleep. But no matter how exhausted I am, I can't get my eyes to close without bringing the images of the fireworks and drowning at the docks and suffocating at the ice rink and the exploding truck that could have killed us. I've had nightmares before, but nothing like this.

Never anything like this.

Once I give up on sleeping, I leave my bunk and instead sit on the couch in the main compartment of the large plane. While it looks standard on the outside, the inside is full of high-tech screens and cozy couches. No use sending a spy into another country without the comforts of Headquarters, right? It feels more like a house than a plane, what with the painted walls and the carpeted floors. You wouldn't even notice the six or seven surveillance cameras unless you were told to look for them.

Of course, Jace hacked into them so the agency can't see what we're up to, but that's beside the point.

I can hear Ethan's snores from here, and if you think that didn't contribute to my sleep deprivation, you're wrong. I love the guy, but I need my rest, and his constant chainsaw impression is not helping matters.

For a while, I think everyone is asleep except me, but I find Nikki camping out in the cockpit, watching the auto-pilot do its thing. Jace and Brian are taking turns managing it from home, making sure we're not in the path of the authorized planes in the area. We aren't...that I know of anyway. Coffee steam wafts from the red mug between her hands. Her black-manicured nails drum against the ceramic, a quick, steady rhythm.

"Hey."

"Hey."

"Ethan?"

"Yeah." I take a seat in the co-pilot's chair.

"Are you okay?"

"Yeah." It's a lie.

"*Mia*." Dammit.

"No. No I'm not."

"I didn't think so." She offers a sad smile, taking my hand in hers and rubbing my knuckles with her thumb. "You've been burying everything for so long, hiding so many things from him...I think we all knew it was going to come out sooner or later, but...no one knew it would happen like this. No one wanted it to happen like this..."

"Yeah."

"This is harder for you than it has ever been for me, but love isn't easy. If it was, everyone would have it."

"Yeah. And I mean, I get that what Bethany did to Louis—pretending to love him and marrying him and having two kids with him only to get closer to his father—it was messed up. Really messed up. If I were him, I would feel the same way. I might not go about it this way, what with the kidnapping teenagers, bioengineering a chemical capable of generating super-humans, and trying to exterminate an entire worldwide agency of protection filled with people who have families and lives, but..."

"She broke his heart and died. And to make matters worse, she took their daughter with her." Nikki pauses, staring out the window into the darkening sky. "I wonder what happened to the other one. The one that lived. Charlotte, I think. That's what the file said anyway."

"That sounds about right," I say. "I don't know. She's probably off in college. Or fresh out of college. She'd be what, like your age?"

"Yeah, around there. I wonder if she knows what her dad's up to these days."

"I wouldn't doubt it." I chuckle. "Maybe they're both evil."

"Probably."

"Hey Nikki?"

"Hmm?"

"Do you think Dave's still alive?"

"Yeah." She nods. "I don't think they'd kill him without reason. Not when he's one of Orville's lab rats." Her words leave an unsettling feeling in my stomach. Lab rat. Dave being tested on. Being...changed. The thought of it makes me feel sick, but there's nothing I can do about it on this plane. As soon as we land, Orville better be ready.

I end up going back to my bunk to catch a few more hours of sleep before we get to Caillte City, Washington, the location of Orville's biggest and most secure building. Appropriately enough, Caillte City, Washington lies at the end of the Caillte River, which was followed by a group of Irish explorers who happened to get terribly lost while seeking out California. Therefore, they named the river, and the city, for that matter: lost. Orville's largest base is located in Lost City. Coincidence? I think not.

Whatever's coming will not be good.

Before we can even think about those problems, we have a bigger, more immediate problem to deal with: we are about to land in a F.O.U.N.D. Headquarters that is not our own, disembark from a plane we have stolen, and explain to the administrators that are not ours that we are justified for committing what is basically agency suicide.

We could all die for this. Or worse: get fired.

Brian and Jace call us as soon as the plane lands inside Caillte City Headquarters.

"Okay, so there's good news and bad news." Brian doesn't even bother offering a greeting before addressing the immediate problems with our current situation.

"Bad news first." Ginger crosses her arms.

"Well, um. All of you have been put on the F.O.U.N.D. Rogue Watch for diverging from the orders you were given and stealing a plane. As soon as you get out of the plane they're going to arrest you, probably." Jace's face tells us we're screwed.

"Oh yeah? And then what?"

"There's good news. Be patient."

"What's the good news?"

"Well, Administrator Dormer has the papers for your clearance in her hands as we speak. More bad news: she's not thrilled that you defied her orders without asking." Brian adds, his fingers leaving the keyboard in front of him for a brief second to readjust his glasses. "And until Isaac and John, who is very upset you guys left without him by the way, can convince her to sign them and call the Caillte City administrators to tell them you're not traitorous L.O.S.T. agents who hijacked a plane and flew halfway across the country to L.O.S.T.'s largest base..."

"Basically, you have to stall." Jace adds.

"Great. Wonderful." Summer looks out the nearest window. "We're surrounded."

"Yeah. Um. Well, good luck with that."

CHAPTER 42

Seconds after we step foot out of the plane, we're surrounded by guards with large guns, and the rest is history. There was no stand-off, no heroic resistance. We just took it silently without so much as a struggle. God, these handcuffs are cold. Usually I'm the one arresting people, not the one being arrested.

They move us to a waiting room. Bland walls surround us, remnants of ugly floral wallpaper still managing to hang on after the years since they tried to paint over it. Keyword: tried. While the rest of F.O.U.N.D. is perfectly kept down to the very last detail, the waiting room is only ever seen by those who are passing through, a limbo for those whose fates have yet to be decided.

The guard at the door stares us down, eyes examining our cuffs every few minutes, as if to make sure we haven't managed to pick them despite our lack of movement or energy at the moment. Still, you would have to be stupid to try to escape while unarmed and handcuffed when the guard at the door basically has an arsenal in his hands. What they lack in wall décor, they certainly make up for in firearms. Damn.

The woman who's been watching us since the moment we stepped through the door, tries to make cheery small talk. She knows who we are, that we're probably going to go on trial for treason or stealing a plane or something, but she still hangs onto every word that slips out of our mouths, every incredible tale of bravery. She has our files in front of her. If she has any doubts, all she needs to do is look down.

A few begrudgingly-long hours later, a call comes through her phone: a call from the head administrator of the Great City

Headquarters. This is why it took so long; Sheila had to call her boss. I'll bet you anything she was not thrilled about that. We'll hear about it when we get home, I'm sure. That is, if Sheila doesn't kill us first.

After the call comes through, so do our boarding papers and a new mission statement from our very frustrated administrator:

You six are despicable. I cannot believe you managed to steal an agency plane and run across the continent to take on Orville. You are devious, dangerous rogues that F.O.U.N.D. may come to fear someday.

I could not be more proud.

Be careful, and please, please bring them home.

-Sheila Dormer, F.O.U.N.D. Administrator

Great City, NY Headquarters

We also receive an email from our parents:

Amelia Elizabeth Crane, you are grounded. Nicole Eliana Crane, we are ashamed you let her get away with this. Ethan Ezekiel Shipp, we expected better of you.

That said, you have done everything we raised you to do. You are not mindless drones conditioned to follow the orders no matter how unfair. You think for yourselves and do what is right, no matter the risk. That's all we could ever ask of you.

And yes, despite the previous point, you are still grounded.

-Mom and Dad

P.S. Summer and Ginger are grounded too.

P.P.S. Archer is probably also grounded. Though we have yet to hear from his Administrator. Or his parents for that matter.

We spend another three hours filling out extensive amounts of paperwork, which I guess is a fitting punishment for our deeds (although no one should have to suffer these paper cuts, but that's an argument for another day. Preferably one that doesn't involve stealing a plane.) It turns out, there's a lot more involved in this process than we thought there would be. I mean, it's not like we're transferring here permanently or anything.

It occurs to me when it starts getting dark out that I've never spent a night in another Headquarters before. Changing into my assigned gray uniform pajamas and brushing my teeth with a toothbrush that doesn't belong to me and getting into the bed of our shared dorm room feels so weird. It's bizarre. We've entered the Twilight Zone.

Agency at night is different than agency during the day. The lights are dimmer. The only activity is the occasional stray scientist or intern wandering the hall, or a custodian mopping the floors. It's so bare, especially on the boarding levels. There aren't any pictures on the walls or holographic diagrams and maps with helpful spy tips. There aren't any field agents in their full leather uniforms, stomping through the halls in their heavy boots. There are only a handful of very sleepy agents in plain, drab pajamas, void of all makeup and all energy, and filled instead with the unshakeable dread that comes along with what we will face tomorrow.

Orville's building is no doubt filled with unspeakable horrors. Who knows what his Unlucky Thirteen have faced in the twenty-four hours since we've seen them last? What if Orville's procedures are irreversible? What if they're deadly?

We won't know until tomorrow.

We sit in the cream-colored hall between our dorms. I rest my chin on my knees, arms hugging my legs as tight as I can. I wish I could curl into a little ball and disappear. Maybe we all do. The others don't say much, so neither do I.

Part of me, Adventurous Mia, Brave Mia, F.O.U.N.D. Field Department Poster Girl Mia wants to leave immediately-right-now to get this done and over with, rip it off like a Band-Aid. The other part of me, Scared Teenage Soon-to-be-Senior Mia doesn't know what she wants. She sure as hell doesn't want to run head-first into a mess bigger than anything she's ever faced in her entire life, but she also loves Dave. Both of the Mias do. They would do anything for him. *I* would do anything for him, even if it means dying to try to protect him. That's what scares me the most.

Without a conversation or anything besides meaningful eye contact and supportive expressions, we get up and retreat to our rooms: Archer with Ethan, Ginger with Summer, and Nikki with me. We call Brian, Jace, Isaac, Mom, Dad, and Sheila before bed, but we hear the same message over and over again: good luck, bring them home, don't die.

Good luck. Bring them home. Don't die.

I make no promises.

CHAPTER 43

Breakfast the next morning is silent. Training after breakfast is silent. Our briefing for the mission is silent. No one dares to speak. There are no reassurances. No words of comfort or congratulations. This is our last chance. For real this time. There is nothing left if we fail. If we fail, they die. If we fail, *we* die.

Our temporary Caillte City administrator, Jacob Jacobson, sends us to the weapons department with three other field agents from this Headquarters. We stock up on handguns, grenades, smoke bombs, tasers, and syringes full of the same sleeping meds Isaac used to knock Dave out at camp. I clip them to my belt, making sure everything is in order before hopping into a laundry cart filled with towels.

Archer piles more towels on top of me, carefully tucking them into every empty spot. He's the first one of us to speak.

"You alright down there, Crane?"

"Yeah."

"No you're not. But at least you're covered up." Archer's lips tug into a soft smile.

"Scooch, babe. I'm in with you." Ginger hunkers down into the sea of linens with me, covering herself up to her shoulders. The other agents pile more on until we're invisible. Summer, Nikki, Ethan, and Archer all adorn pastel-colored scrubs and turtlenecks over their uniforms and medical masks to cover their faces. Two of the Caillte City recruits get into the other cart, and the third is our assigned field techie. It's not a thing we do back in Great City, but I see the value in it. Having an engineer/medical specialist waiting for us in our escape vehicle is make or break in this situation, especially when we have to load up to thirteen potentially physically and mentally unstable patients onto our bus.

Ginger grips my hand tight beneath the towels while Nikki and Summer push our cart. Finally, we board the bus, wheels squeaking up the ramp and into the large interior. Once we're safely inside and on the road, there's some small-talk. It's the standard pre-mission jitters times one-thousand. The theater and the rink and everything we faced before...they were nothing compared to this.

We are walking straight into a hive of angry bees. I can only pray we don't get stung.

The ride to Orville Enterprises seems to take forever. Our techie parks the bus in the bottom layer of the parking garage adjacent to the building with the huge glaring blue and white OE logo. Ginger and I duck beneath the mountain of white, only able to listen as Summer and Nikki are stopped at the door. They hand over their fake OE IDs. Large hands move the towels aside, uncovering Ginger and I. We play dead, eyes closed, bodies gone limp.

"Well done. You know where to take them." A gruff voice instructs. To them, we are nothing more than new patients, new additions to the Thirteen. Replacements if needed. Experiments if wanted.

He covers us up again. No one dares speak until we get into the elevator, followed by the boys and the other agents. As soon as the doors close behind us, I release a slow, relieved sigh. Ginger's amber eye, the only part of her I can see, winks—or blinks, I can't tell—at me as her fingers intertwine with my own, holding on tight.

We are inside Orville Enterprises. Inside the building that is housing my boyfriend, the building that is the creation of a dangerous, vengeance-driven man as a part of his vengeance-driven plot to rule the world and bring my agency to its knees.

The only noises I can hear are that of my heartbeat and the buzzing of the elevator. A ding sounds as we reach each floor and my stomach drops as we inch closer and closer to where they're keeping the other patients: The top floor, floor 62. I count each story silently. My breaths come out harsh and heavy, chest shaking. I feel numb. Finally, the doors open and the cart lurches forward again.

With my left hand, I cling to Ginger. The other arm reaches for the gun holstered to my belt, fingers fastening around the cold metal. Ginger traces a message onto my arm.

R-e-a-d-y?

I reply.

Y-e-s.

"Down the hall. Third door on the left." A kind woman's voice tells them. I imagine a receptionist's desk with a cheery secretary like Cathy sitting there, working day-to-day for a company that tortures teenagers. Of course, this woman probably doesn't know the horrors that happen behind closed doors. She doesn't know the tragedies that take place in this very hall. She only knows the paycheck she gets at the end of the month.

The cart shifts as we turn the corner into the hall. The air is colder here. Even under a mountain of towels, I can tell that much. It smells of spray paint and hospital floor-cleaner. My stomach grinds in an agonizing knot. I swallow thickly, trying to ignore the pinching pain between my eyes.

Two loud thuds sound, and then some footsteps, a few gunshots, and two more thuds.

"Coast's clear." Summer whispers. Ginger and I claw our way out of the towels just in time to see Archer hop down from the security camera, screwdriver in hand. The busted camera crashes to the floor, pieces of the lens scattering at his feet beside the unconscious guards.

"If I were a Dave, where would I hide?" Ethan mumbles quietly, peering in the windows of the thirteen heavy steel-enforced doors. "Ah. That's strange."

"What is, babe?" Nikki takes a few steps toward her fiancé.

"There's no one in there."

"What?" Archer looks for himself, through the window of another door. "Nah, he's right. Nothing in there, neither."

"Where is everybody?" asks one of the Caillte City agents, a sixteen-year-old redhead named Paige.

"Not here. That's for damn sure." The other, a brunette Irish boy named Finn, adds.

"*Attention all staff: intruders have been found on Floor 62. Eliminate them at all costs.*" Orville's voice speaks calmly over the intercom as though this is an everyday occurrence. At first I think the doors behind us, the ones we came through, will open with a supply of new guards sent to take us out.

But then something much worse happens.

The doors all around us swing open mechanically. What once appeared to be empty rooms (due to tricks of the light or mirrors or some other bullshit) are the very rooms that house Orville's Unlucky Thirteen, strapped to their tables. All thirteen bolt upright simultaneously, restraints popping off. They take forced steps towards us like zombies. The steps drag, but become more natural with each movement. More warlike; a march.

Each of the patients is marked with their initials and a number, gleaming bright on their stark white uniforms. It's a blinding contrast to the black of the F.O.U.N.D. uniforms I've grown up surrounded by. It's clean, pristine, and it only reinforces the 'lab rat' sentiment I've come to dread.

The first to take a swing at me is a girl with long black hair labeled: JW09. Her eyes are dark and menacing, a wicked gleam hidden deep in her brown gaze. Thin eyebrows are knit together in concentration. She leaves a dent in the steel wall where my head would have been had I not ducked to avoid her powerful fist.

I take a step back, not willing to use my gun or any of the weapons on my belt (except for the knock-out drug) against these innocent teens-turned-weapons. I'm 99 percent sure they're under some kind of brainwash or mind control, and they are definitely Enhanced.

The next to attack me is a tall girl with straight dirty-blonde hair: WM04. Her hands thrust forward, and a wave of telekinetic energy blasts me to the wall with a loud boom. I groan, peeling myself off of the floor in time to avoid another wave. She lunges, making an attempt to punch or tackle me or something, but she's not nearly as strong as the other girl was.

"We have to get out of here." Summer dodges the fist of a tall blond boy and trips him with her foot. "They're too strong. There are eight of us and thirteen of them."

Archer dives out of the way, towards the door to the stairwell and pulls it open. Ethan and Nikki are the first to duck through, then Paige and Finn, and finally Ginger, Summer, and I, though they have to drag me by the wrist. As soon as I slip through the doorway, they slam it shut, trying to hold it with the combined weight of their bodies, but we all know it won't hold. Not when they have super-strength and telekinetic powers and God-knows-what else.

"Come on, Mia!" Archer drags me up the stairs. I try not to budge, fire in my eyes. I grit my teeth and stand my ground.

"DAVE IS OUT THERE! I CAN'T LEAVE HIM!"

"DAVE AND HIS NEW FRIENDS ARE TRYING TO MURDER US WITH THEIR NEW SUPERPOWERS, MIA! WE DON'T

HAVE A BLOODY CHOICE!" Archer's voice is sharp and loud, echoing through the stairwell. I hear footsteps below us. As the bangs on the door get louder and more powerful, I know we don't have much time to make a decision.

Before I can do anything, Archer throws me over his shoulder, carrying me (despite my loud and frequent protests) without much effort. He takes the stairs two at a time. When we reach the first landing above us, the others dash up, releasing the door to the flood of Enhanced patients.

"HQ, we're gonna need a chopper. And fast." Finn transmits into his earpiece in a panic. He's not wrong. There's no way we could possibly make it back down to the bus like this. While he's at it, Finn tells the techie to get out. As far as we know, he does.

Moments later, we make it to the roof where Orville is waiting. We fall into formation, backs facing each other in as tight a circle as we can manage. I reluctantly draw my weapon, clicking off the safety and holding the barrel towards the brainwashed teens. Orville snaps three times, causing his new pets to form a perfect ring around us.

"I see you've met my new recruits." Orville walks around the outer circle casually. His steps are slow, gloating, and his face bears a look of unadulterated pride. He stops behind the agent directly in front of me.

Dave.

I almost don't recognize him. He's bigger, thick and muscled and at least five inches taller. The large agent in front of me is a far cry from the scrawny pale nerd I saw only a few weeks ago. He clenches his jaw, blue eyes glaring at me with something I have never seen in his gaze until now: pure seething rage. His shoulders rise and fall with each heaving breath. Tears form in my unbelieving eyes. Though I can't fathom the changes that have taken place, his label doesn't lie.

DB03.

My boyfriend has become a number. A code. Nothing more than the label on his jacket. A monster with murder in his eyes.

"They're amazing, aren't they? State of the art in every way. Scientifically groundbreaking." Louis' hands come to rest on Dave's broader, more muscular frame. He has to stand on his toes to peer over my boyfriend's shoulder. I don't say anything. "If you think Viktor Ivanov is powerful, you should see the force behind this one. He's my personal favorite."

"What did you do to him?" My words are forced through clenched teeth.

"I'll show you." Orville whispers something in Dave's ear. A command.

He raises his hand, causing my feet to leave the ground. Instead of lifting me by the neck, I feel all the pressure around my abdomen.

"Dave, please." I plead desperately as fresh tears trickle down my cheeks. He's unresponsive, eyes narrowing. The pressure tightens. Tingles shoot through my legs and it gets harder to breathe as my ribcage becomes compressed. "Dave." My voice is a whisper now. Weak. Vulnerable. Broken. *"Please..."*

The other F.O.U.N.D. agents warily aim their weapons at the rest of the enhanced in fear that the others might do the same. A short jolt of power shoots through me. Static shock times twenty. My gun clatters against the gravel. Two fateful words leave Orville's lips before he slips through the door and back into the building.

"Finish them."

The others delve into an intense battle, but the only one attacking me is Dave. It's personal, intimate. What a better way to die than at the hands of my boyfriend?

"Dave, I need you to listen to me. Look at me. David. Dave. Babe. I love you, okay? I know you're probably mad at me for everything—" My voice cracks in time with my ribs. I let out a yell, heat flushing my tear-stained cheeks. "I love you so much. It's my fault this happened to you. I-I couldn't protect you. I'm sorry. If you kill me, so be it. It's not your fault. This isn't you. This is the thing he's turned you into. It's—it's okay. I forgive you."

Something softens behind his eyes, even if only for a moment. He drops me and falls to his knees as my body hits the pavement. I cough, my entire being shaking with every breath as I struggle to compose myself. It's hard to get to my feet, but I manage, stumbling towards him. His face is knit with uncertainty, with fear. He looks at his hands. Tears slip down his cheeks as he stares at his palms. His gaze turns up to me. I kneel in front of him.

"M-Mia?" he chokes out between sobs.

I nod, smiling through tears of my own. "It's me. I'm here. I found you."

"I'm so sorry." He sobs into my shoulder, wrapping me up in his bigger, stronger arms and pulling me to his broader, more muscular chest. "I'm so sorry. I'm so sorry. I'm so—"

"It's okay," I whisper in response. My lips press to his cheeks and nose and forehead and lips over and over again between words of comfort and reassurance. "It's okay, I promise. It's okay."

Before another word slips from my mouth, all of the patients slump over, eyes closed. Orville must have shut them down. I support Dave's weight, holding onto him tightly despite the pain. He's much heavier now than he was before, but I manage. I don't know how, but we have to get them all out of here and fast.

Then, like a guardian angel, the shiny black F.O.U.N.D. copter touches down on the roof.

CHAPTER 44

The plane ride back to Great City HQ is quiet. Caillte Head-quarters loaned us a bigger jet with more bunks for the recovered patients to sleep in. Although we could leave them there and not take the risks involved in bringing them back home, leaving them in Caillte City would be leaving them too close to Orville.

Dave is fast asleep with his head on my lap, the rest of his body sprawled over the two seats to my right. He's so big now. I take several minutes to look him over, trying to adjust to the sudden change. Something like this doesn't just happen overnight. It's unnatural and sort of unsettling. If Orville is capable of doing something like this, who's to stop him from creating a real-life version of the Incredible Hulk? Or an army of super-soldiers?

We're safe, as far as I know. It took a while to track him down, but we managed to save them. We saved them all. Now we can bring them home to their families and help them get their lives back on track. Cure them if possible. Help them if needed. According to the handful of primary scans and tests, they didn't have any trackers on them, and their condition is stable. For now.

All thirteen are hopped up on sleeping meds that will hopefully keep them asleep until we land. A telekinetic meltdown on the plane would be catastrophic. Basically, we would all die.

Dave's breaths are heavy, his face drawn into a sleeping scowl. He shivers. I pull the blanket further around his shoulders and press a gentle kiss to his forehead. My fingers lace through his thick mess of hair. As superficial as this sounds, I'm really glad Orville didn't touch his curls. I wouldn't have even recognized him if they had been buzzed off on top of all of the other physical changes.

Ginger and Summer are passed out in another trio of seats, a heap of tangled limbs. Archer leans against the wall near me and looks down at my miracle of a boyfriend.

"That's him, eh?"

"Yeah." My fingers graze Dave's soft cheek. "Hard to believe, but...it's him."

"You sure?"

"The bloodwork matched. His face, his eyes...the body might not be his, but everything else is. It's going to be hard to get used to, but I've pulled through worse." Dave lets out a little snore, adjusting himself in his sleep. My fingers trail down his back, rubbing small circles here and there. I lean back against my seat. Against my better judgement, I let my straining eyes drift shut for just a moment. I can already feel myself slipping. "We did it, Archer. It's over."

"We'll see about that." He chuckles.

A few moments later, I feel a pair of warm lips against my forehead. I feel safe under his gaze. I know he wouldn't let anything happen to me or the rest of us. For once, I can get a nice, deep sleep. I can be at peace without worrying about Dave being killed. He's safe in my arms. We are safe.

When we land at Headquarters hours later, people from the medical staff take away the Thirteen for further testing and recovery. Their physical condition is questionable and their mental condition is less than ideal. There is no doubt it'll take them a while to heal from this experience on all levels. But I'll be there for Dave every step of the way, no matter what it takes.

It's dark out. Night time. Despite my nap on the flight home, I am beyond exhausted, as are the others. With nothing better to do and no immediate responsibilities at—I check my watch—1 a.m., I head to the cafeteria to pick up some coffee and wait for further news. Ginger and Summer leave to get some much-needed rest. I should, but I can't. Not with Dave here, at least not until I'm sure he's okay.

Elise is sitting at a table alone, sipping coffee from a Darth Vader mug and reading something on her agency-issued tablet. I take the seat across from her. My muscles ache. I definitely dislocated something, but my injuries are the least of everyone's worries at the moment.

"You guys are back already? How did it go?" She practically slams her tablet shut, eager to listen to my field agent tales of wonder and whimsy. They're like pirate stories. People from my division spend their time comparing battle scars and arguing over which of our dangerous missions was most dangerous.

"We found them. They're here. Not in perfect condition, not as we last saw them, but they're here. And they're safe. And that's all that matters right now. I'm sure we'll get the rest figured out."

"So no one died?"

"We got lucky."

Elise takes my hand across the table, a soft smile tugging at her lips. "I'm so glad everything worked out. I was worried something would go wrong. Orville is just so scary, you know?" She shudders. "He's crazy. I didn't know my job would be caught in the thick of things, but basically every administrator, agent, and techie in this place is tied up on him."

"He's the greatest threat right now. Hopefully, it'll pass sooner than later and then we can focus on whatever comes next. This is always what happens. Eliminate the greatest threat first, then work on the rest."

"What happens to the other problems?"

"What do you mean?"

"Orville can't be the world's only problem. There have to be other drug dealers and terrorists and corrupted organizations. Right?"

"I guess. It's just not my assignment. I've been a bit too busy to read up on my local events, you know?"

"Oh. Right." She tilts back her mug, finishing it off. "Well, I'm here way too late. My roommate is gonna freak out if she hasn't already. I'll see you tomorrow—er, later today, I guess."

"See you then."

I'm left alone for almost three hours before Brian makes his way through the cafeteria doors.

"Hey, uh the med staff wanted me to tell you that you can visit Dave now. They got all of his paperwork sorted out and he's awake, but he won't be for very long, so if you want to have an actual conversation with him it has to be soon."

"Thanks," I grab my coffee and walk with him to the elevator, riding up to the medical wing. Brian must notice my slouching or the odd limp in my walk.

"Did you dislocate something?"

"Yeah, probably."

"You should ask them to pop it back into place while you're down here."

"I'm fine. I've handled worse."

"I don't know how you field agents do it. You're crazy. If I get a paper cut from my files, I whine about it all day, but you walk around in this condition like it's nothing. I can't comprehend that."

"For the record, I whine about paper cuts all day too. But when it comes to things like this, I just don't think about it. Not when something else matters more."

"Huh." He tilts his head. "I guess I hadn't thought about it like that. Maybe when you're jumping off of buildings and dodging bullets and disarming time bombs, a pain like—what is it, your shoulder?"

"Yeah. Hip too, probably. Maybe a broken rib."

"Something like that doesn't bug you? Insane."

"I've got better things to worry about."

The elevator doors glide open and we walk briskly down the hall to where they keep the critical patients. They're grouped up in a few rooms with two or three in each, arranged in the order they were IDed. Dave is in the first room along with patients JN01 and LE02. He's awake, sitting in the bed closest to the back of the room. The curtains are drawn around each of his roommates' beds. Dim white lights shine, not quite distracting me from the heavy scent of floor cleaner.

But there. There he is.

He's leaning up against his mountain of pillows, eyes half-closed as he struggles to keep his clear blue gaze focused on me.

"Are you too tired? I can come back later, if you want."

"Stay," he mumbles, one of his longer muscled arms reaching out for my hand. We touch, and it's like fireworks. The good kind. I missed this. I missed holding his hands and kissing his warm lips.

As soon as I pull away, I notice the trashcan beside his bed is full of tissues covered in bright red splotches. He smiles weakly and leans back again.

"How are you doing, babe?"

"I'm okay."

Silence.

"I'm glad you're okay. Really, really glad."

"Me too."

More silence.

"Are you sure you're all right? You seem fazed."

"I might be a little. I'm just really tired and..." He lets out a great sigh. "I drained like four water bottles a minute ago. I don't think I've ever been this thirsty. Is that normal?"

"I'm not really sure what normal means anymore." My voice isn't more than a whisper. It's true. Nothing is normal. Not anymore. Normal people can't move things with their minds or punch dents in solid steel walls. But then again, normal people aren't trained assassins that can speak nine languages either. Maybe nothing is normal. Well, nothing in *my* life anyway. "I'm not sure there ever was a normal for me."

"You're amazing." He breathes, tired blue eyes meeting mine. His hand squeezes tighter. "I mean it."

"Are you...are you mad?"

"About what? About you being James Bond? About you saving the world? Nah. I'm not mad. I don't think I could ever be mad at you for that." He pauses, his voice wavering the slightest bit as he continues. "But we're real, aren't we? This...us...I'm not your mission. R-right? You're still Mia?"

"David Thomas Bowen, I love you more than I have ever loved anyone. You and I are as real as it gets. As for who I am, my job is the only thing you didn't know. Probably. Probably also the fact that I can speak nine languages."

"So if you don't work at a bakery, where do the cupcakes come from?"

"I *do* work at Sugar & Spice."

"You what?"

"It's my cover, my agency-assigned job, but I actually bake and frost cupcakes and stuff. It's a functioning bakery, just full of spies."

"Will I get a cover?" His question sparks a million thoughts in my mind. Will he get a cover? Why on earth would he ever— Oh.

Oh.

He wants to be a spy. And now, with his rippling muscles and biceps that rival my brother's, not to mention all of his crazy new powers, there's nothing stopping him.

"We'll see." My reply is short. I try not to show the pain hidden behind my words, but he catches on quickly.

"Are you...is that not a good idea?"

"You've seen what my job means, Dave. The danger involved. The dark side. You've been to hell and back because of me. Because I looked into things I shouldn't have. Because I was— because I *am*—a threat. A weapon. I don't want you to end up like me."

"You're still alive."

"Not without paying for it." I tuck the hair behind one of my ears, a black hearing aid standing out against my tan skin. His eyes widen.

"You weren't—but I thought you—I thought you were *born* hard of hearing."

"No. That's—" I sigh, taking a moment to compose myself. "Long story short, I was nine years old training in Russia and I got a little too close to a hand grenade. It uh, took out one of my trainers. I'm lucky to be alive at all. The hearing aids Brian designed give me most of my hearing back, but it's not perfect. It'll never be perfect. I mean, right now I have a dislocated *something* and more bruises than I can—"

"Wait, did *I* do that?" His hand slips out of mine as though I'm made of glass. As though touching me for one more instant would shatter me to pieces.

Silence.

"Mia, *please*."

"It wasn't you." The words feel as heavy as lead when they leave my lips. "You weren't in control. It's not your f—"

"I hurt you." Tears take form in his sad blue eyes. "I...Oh my God. I thought—I thought maybe you were okay, that I had dreamed some of it, but..."

"It's okay, Dave." I grab his hand quickly, squeezing it tight so he can't pull away. I can feel him trembling in my touch. "Everything is gonna be fine. It's okay. I'm okay."

"But it's not okay. He changed me there. He molded me into some weapon. Some...monster." A big wet tear splatters onto the back of my hand.

I get out of my chair and sit on his bed instead, pulling him into a tight hug. My arms wrap around his torso and my head finds a spot beneath his. Dave's body racks with sobs, causing me to pull him closer yet, his warmth enveloping me.

"You are not a monster."

"I c-could have k-killed you—"

"This was not your fault."

"W-what if I lose control again? W-what if Orville's training comes back? W-what if—"

"Dave, look at me." He doesn't. I try again, softer this time. "*Look at me.*"

Reluctantly, he brings himself to meet my gaze. His breathing gradually comes down to normal speed and he rests his head on top of mine.

"I'm sorry." I can barely make out the words he mumbles.

"I'm sorry too. For not being able to find you faster. Maybe if I had..."

"Shhhh," he presses a long kiss to my forehead, "let's just...maybe we should talk about this tomorrow. My head is spinning."

"Okay." I kiss his lips one last time before standing up.

Once he thinks I'm out of earshot, his sobbing resumes. As much as I want to comfort him, I know he needs to let it out on his own. I can only help him if he wants it, and right now, I'm the last person he needs to see.

Seeing no other option as to where to take a nap for a few hours, I wander down to the lab floor and check myself into the Crash Room.

So things didn't go perfectly with Dave. I didn't expect them to. Honestly, I'm just glad things weren't worse.

We are both broken, smashed to bits by cruel circumstances and vengeful twists of fate. Now I have to pick up the pieces.

CHAPTER 45

Large hands shake me awake under two hours later. A smattering of footsteps trails down the hall.

"Get up, woman!"

"What? What's happening?" I shake myself out of the sleepy haze, blinking and rubbing at my eyes as someone helps me to my feet and drags me down the hall.

"They're dropping like flies!"

"Who?"

"The Unlucky Thirteen, that's who!" I recognize Archer's very anxious and very British tone.

"What do you mean?!"

"No one knows! The med staff is baffled! They just started dying out of the blue! Four of them are dead!"

"Is Dave—"

"COME ON!" he roars. We don't even bother waiting for the elevator. Floods of people are dashing through the door to the stairwells. We follow the stream, getting stuck in the sea of people jamming the door. "MOVE! GIRLFRIEND OF NUMBER 03 COMING THROUGH!" Archer tears past people, pushing and shoving and doing whatever he can to get me to Dave's room.

I have never seen so many people crammed into a space so small. Medics watch the heart monitor like hawks, watching the pulse line jump and dip at a rapid rate. One of Dave's roommates is already gone, and the other is in the same condition as him.

Dave's eyes are shut tight, his body trembling, ribs convulsing as he struggles to stay alive. Sweat beads on the forehead of his clammy red face. His expression is one of pain, suffering. He groans, his back arching away from the pillows behind him before slamming back against them repeatedly. I can hardly watch.

I don't dare speak. I don't dare move. I just stay, forced to do nothing, to sit idly as he slips away.

Dave's roommate dies four minutes before he does. They tried to bring them back. They tried to bring all of them back, but to no avail. They couldn't shock life back into their hopeless bodies.

I've been sobbing so hard I can barely breathe. My limbs feel numb, my heart hollow, and I can hardly see anything through the tears that cloud my vision. They're large and frequent and I fear that if I don't stop soon, I'll drown in them.

Archer has his strong arms wound tight around my shaking frame as he talks into my ear, but I don't hear a single word that comes out of his mouth. Everything is a blur. Nurses and doctors rush past us, flitting from room to room as they struggle to figure out what went wrong enough to kill thirteen teens in twenty minutes.

The entire infirmary is shaken to its core. Grieving parents of the newly-found teens trail the hallways, surrounded by knots of agents, comforting them while trying to fill out paperwork.

I force myself out of Dave's room. I can't look at his lifeless body one more time. I can't comprehend what this means now. I can't even wrap my mind around life without the curly-haired dork that stole my heart.

Life is not worth living if Dave is not in it.

My *Star Wars* ring sits idle around my finger, almost taunting me. I will never hear him utter those words again.

I love you.

A wave of silence sweeps over the crowd as something sounds that none of them expected to hear.

A heart monitor.

I walk into the room just in time to see Patient SL07, a seventeen-year-old boy named Samuel Lewis bolts upright in his bed, sweating profusely and sucking in every breath as though it's his last. As far as he knows, it could be. His dark brown eyes dart around the room, eyeing the nurses warily.

"What happened?" His voice wavers. "W-where am I?"

"I'm Mia. Mia Crane." In the absence of voices, I am the only one to speak. No one moves a muscle. Tears stream down my cheeks, but my tone is calm, steady. Slowly, I take steps forward. I'm not sure what his Enhancement is and I don't want to set him off on accident. "You're at F.O.U.N.D., in the infirmary. You...you died. All of you did, but somehow—"

"We've got a heartbeat!"

In the next room over, Patient LH12, a girl named Lily Hamada springs to life. After her, Patient RC10, Raphael Cataldo, makes a return. These are miracles among devastation. Hope where there is none. It makes me believe for a moment, for just a single moment, that Dave could come back too.

But no matter how long we wait, or how hard we hope, or how fiercely we pray, Dave and the others don't move a muscle. There is no life in their cold bodies. They're all gone.

CHAPTER 46

The funeral is the next day. As much as I wish it would rain, there's not a single cloud in the clear blue sky. Instead, sun shines down on the polished mahogany casket, a perfect summer afternoon to mourn the death of a loved one.

Mrs. Bowen doesn't say much to me before the service. The look on her face says enough. She's alone now. No husband, no son, no hope of grandchildren. Her flood of tears is a stark contrast to my lack of them. It's not that I'm not sad. I'm devastated. But all of my tears have already been shed, leaving me instead with an emptiness, a hollow lack of emotion, a calm face to mask the pain.

We had him. We found him. He was safe. And then he died. It feels like all of this running around, all of this chasing L.O.S.T. and Orville and trying to find the Thirteen, was for nothing. Ten of them are dead.

Mark, Nick, and Toby approach me before the service as soon as they find me. I'm standing in a ring of spies, and yet despite the leather and the sunglasses, they don't hesitate to come over and wrap their arms around me, each of them taking a long moment to hug me and tell me it's going to be okay. They've only met me once, and they still care enough to make sure I'm alright after everything that's happened.

I can't bring myself to tell them it's my fault.

I sit through the funeral as a shell of my former self. It feels as though Amelia Crane is no more, as though the only thing that ever made her real is the very person inside that casket. The cold, lifeless body that belonged to him. Everything that made him funny, happy, sweet, nerdy, is nothing more than a dormant brain. He is a corpse.

A ghost.

Instead of a suit, they decided to honor his wishes and lay him to rest in his *Star Wars* hoodie. If it weren't a few sizes too large, it wouldn't have fit him at all. Not after all of his...enhancements.

He flashes in my mind, the Dave I knew. The one that came to camp with me. The one that didn't yet know that the moment he met me had sealed him into a deadly fate.

"Just make sure I have a nice funeral, okay? Lots of flowers and a good organist and for the love of God, don't let them bury me in a suit. I'd prefer my Star Wars hoodie. The one with the lightsabers, not the—"

I shake it away, fighting the tears threatening to spill over my cheeks. He was joking. It was supposed to be a *joke*. And yet here we are.

His *I know* ring is still wrapped around his finger like a wedding band. An unfinished vow. A lonely half of a broken promise. Mine is dangling from a chain around my neck.

I watch with empty eyes as they lower him into the ground.

Orville has taken away the one thing I care about. He has stripped ten families of their children. And he will pay for it.

Once everyone leaves the cemetery, even Mrs. Bowen, I take some time alone at Dave's grave. The headstone has yet to arrive. Linda wants to get it engraved with a quote from a super hero movie or something. Instead, I stare into the hole. The man with the truck full of dirt waits in his seat for me to leave.

Carefully, I kneel down in the grass. At this point, I don't care about the green stains I'm sure I'll end up with on my nude tights. I close my eyes, take a deep breath, and for a long moment, I swear I can feel him standing behind me.

I imagine him there. A hand on my shoulder, looking down at himself, looking down at me as a few silent tears trail down my cheeks. I wish he was here to wipe them away, to make all of this harsh reality nothing but a bad dream. But he's not. And he never will be.

"I let you down." My words drift away on the summer breeze. "This is on me. Everywhere I go, death follows, but I never imagined it'd be yours. I hope you can forgive me. Someday."

I look up into the sky, which shines as bright and blue as his eyes. A shaky breath escapes me, accompanied by another wave of tears.

"I won't let him get away with this. I promise you. Orville will pay. No one else will have to suffer like you did. No one else will die at his hands."

My next words come out so quietly I can barely even hear them.

"*Not if I kill him first.*"

PART 4

CHAPTER 47

Every minute that passes seems to trudge by, settling into an agonizing drag. I shut myself in my room, taking solace in the warmth of my blankets and sweatpants. Anger has wedged itself deep inside my grieving heart and I feel like everything inside me has shut down. Nothing is working. And no matter how hard I push, the furthest I move for almost an entire week is only down to the kitchen to grab snacks and water bottles after everyone else has gone to bed.

Eventually, Ginger and Summer come by and force me into the shower. The warm water helps, but it still hurts. I can't think about him. I can't think about anything. No matter where I go or what I do, something always reminds me of him. No matter how hard I try to forget, I can't.

David Thomas Bowen is etched into my brain like a tattoo and there's nothing I can do about it.

Another week stumbles by only slightly quicker than the last. Jace, Isaac, Nikki, Mom, Dad, and even Ethan all visit my room frequently, bringing me food and movies and trying to distract me from the Daveless world waiting for me beyond these walls.

And yet, as time moves on, the nightmares only get worse. Just when I think I might have a good day, fireworks and funerals plague my sleeping world, and every time I wake up from one of them, the wound feels as fresh as it did the day I lost him. It's like losing him all over again.

Three weeks after the funeral, the agency still hasn't reached out to me. In my unstable state, I don't blame them. However, the anger building up inside me needs to be released. So, while everyone in the house (except for Jace, who's been taking his work home so he can keep an eye on me) is at the Facility, I sneak down to the training room and stand in front of the punching bag.

While my hits start out as pathetic as I feel, soon they're something to fear, lethal weapons of my long-untapped rage. I throw punch after punch until I feel numb. I don't even notice the pain or the tears running down my cheeks until the training door opens and Archer runs to me.

"What are you doing, Crane?"

"I—"

"You're bleeding!"

"I just—" Now that he's mentioned it, I finally notice the crimson smears on the leather bag. I look at my fists. Raw, bloody knuckles glare up at me angrily and my fingers twitch. I collapse to my knees. In seconds, Archer is there with the first-aid kit. He wraps my hands.

"I needed to." My voice is quiet. He doesn't reply. He only nods. I inhale a shaky breath. "*I'm sorry.*"

"You don't have to be sorry."

"Why are you here?"

"Thought you might need me." He closes the case with a click and brushes the tears from one of my cheeks with his large fingers. "How are you?"

"*He's gone, Archer.*" Fresh tears accompany a burst of sobs, and instantly, his arms are around me, tight and close and warm.

It helps.

From that moment on, Archer hardly leaves my side. I think it's partially because he's afraid to leave me alone. I already had one babysitter, but now it feels like I have two. I don't mind it all that much. I like the company.

After a few days, he stops going back to the agency every night and starts sleeping in one of the guest rooms. Now, when I wake up screaming, he's always there in under a minute to make sure I'm okay.

"You alright, Crane?" His voice is husky with sleep as he walks into the room. I click on the lamp, and he squints at the sudden light. All he's wearing is one of my brothers' borrowed shirts and a pair of boxers. I wipe the sweat off of my forehead and nod.

"F-fine." There's a hitch in my voice. He hands me the water bottle sitting on my nightstand and presses his palm to my forehead. The bed dips under his weight, and then his hands find their way around one of mine.

"Do you want to talk about it?"

"Not really."

"Is there anything I can do to help?"

I'm quiet for a long moment before replying, a crack in my fragile whisper. *"Just hold me."*

"Okay." He's quick to pull me against his chest, into his strong arms.

It helps.

I sit silently in the kitchen the next morning, eating a bowl of cereal and watching the screen of the TV with guarded eyes. F.O.U.N.D.'s news logo flashes across the screen, as C.A.I.T.L.Y.N. overrides everything else with an important message from Headquarters.

My phone rings, but I don't pick it up, eyes glued to the screen, listening intently for the next bit of news. Something. Anything. I have to dig my claws into something to get rid of the intense emotional fog that's been hanging over me since Dave died. The anger. The hate. The need to make things better. The craving for vengeance is unshakable. The only way to get rid of it is to give in.

Jace got called in this morning, and Archer went out to get ice cream at the grocery store. For the first time in almost an entire month, no one is home except me. Everyone, my parents, my siblings, my friends, are all at Headquarters, working overtime in the agency's scramble to bring Louis Orville to justice and bring an end to L.O.S.T. once and for all. Or at least, before it gets any worse.

Just as I get up from the table to clean my dish before finally heading to work to help the others, an emergency notice flashes across the screen: EXPLOSION AT SUGAR & SPICE BAKERY. 4 DEAD, 15 INJURED.

My heart drops into my stomach and I glance over at my phone as it rings for the third time. Mom.

"Please tell me you're not at the bakery yet."

"I'm not at the bakery." I swallow thickly. My heart starts running a marathon "I was just about to leave, but it's all over the F.O.U.N.D. Channel. What happened?"

"A bomb went off inside. They have reason to believe it was a L.O.S.T. operative undercover. All available agents are going in now to help clean the wreckage and find survivors. Every other entrance to the agency and the tunnels have gone into lockdown, afraid that any of them could be the next target. Headquarters is in chaos."

"Where are you? Are the others okay?"

"I'm trying to find Sheila to tell her I got ahold of you. Your father and Jace are fine here at Headquarters, and I think Isaac and Nikki are on their way to the bakery to help them remove survivors and victims from the scene."

"Okay. I'm on my way."

"Mia, this attack was most likely meant to target you and your loved ones. Something to draw you out of hiding. The final nail in the coffin. You can't just come out here. You're in danger. A target. There are people ready to kill you on sight. You're only safe at home. I know you want to fight, but honey, maybe it'd be best to sit this one out."

"I know." I sigh, a long, thoughtful sigh. "But I can't just sit here and do nothing. I'll be careful, I promise. I love you, Mom."

"Amelia Elizabeth Crane! You can't just—!" Click.

I mute my phone. The explosion is my fault. I have to make sure my friends are okay no matter the risk. I already lost Dave. I'm not losing anyone else.

After leaving a note for Archer, I take the stairs two at a time, running into my room and tugging on my uniform as fast as I can. My fingers swiftly lace up my heavy black boots, zip up my uniform zippers, and pull my hair into a tight bun at the back of my head. It doesn't take long to find a red wig in my closet full of disguises. I pull it over my hair along with a ridiculously large pair of black sunglasses that hide basically my entire face. I am almost unrecognizable, a completely different person.

I am no longer Mia Crane. I am simply a grieving F.O.U.N.D. agent setting out to get revenge.

"C.A.I.T.L.Y.N., send my family and Ethan messages that tell them I love them, and whatever happens today, I appreciate everything they've done for me, but this is something I have to do."

"*Will do, Miss Crane.*" There's a long pause while she computes. "*Miss Crane, no matter what happens to you, I will have been grateful to know you. Or as Isaac would put it, as grateful as an AI without human emotions can be.*"

I chuckle at her words. I didn't know she was capable of humor, but I guess she is when it matters most. I get a little choked up looking around my room. There is no going back. If I set out to infiltrate L.O.S.T. today, which I have no choice of after I leave the mansion, this could be the last time I set foot in here. The last time I talk to C.A.I.T.L.Y.N.

I walk to the garage with this knowledge in mind. That if I go, I might not come back. This is a choice I make every day, but today it has a new weight. People have already died. Ten of them. Four more at the bakery and potentially countless more if I do nothing. My one life in exchange for many is a price I'm willing to pay. And if all else fails, at least I'll get to see Dave again.

By the time I get to the bakery, five people are dead and twenty have minor to major injuries. Fortunately, I don't know many of the dead. Sure, I've seen them around Sugar & Spice, but most of our exchanges were just in passing. No major conversations or life-changing moments. Unfortunately, I can't find Summer or Ginger or Greta, all of whom were signed in at the time of the explosion. I ask around a bit, not disclosing my identity to anybody, but asking if Agents Williams, Laurence, and Hertz have been recovered yet. They haven't.

The place of my assigned cover since I graduated to field agency is no more than piles of scorched brick and smashed tile. I've been inside this building almost every day since I turned fifteen. Everything that made it unique is gone. And the people that worked in it are strapped to stretchers and zipped inside body bags.

I help the survivors of the blast get out of the wreckage. The faces are a blur, blended together. Women and men that I've known for the better part of three years limp out with sprained and broken limbs, burns and bruises and scrapes.

It's about an hour before I spot Ginger getting checked by a paramedic. He shines a flashlight in her eyes, nodding before walking away. I run over, nearly tackling her in a hug.

"Who the hell do you think—?!"

"Ginger, it's me," I say. Her anger fades to confusion and then to relief. "Where's Summer?"

"They took her to Headquarters with the last bus of survivors. She's fine. So am I. A little fazed, but I avoided the initial explosion, which really helped my case. Some of the others weren't so lucky though. Greta is in critical condition."

"Oh my God."

"They helicoptered her to the hospital for treatment, but they don't know how much they can do for her." She looks at me for a long time, gauging my reaction. I feel numb. I've been numb since I lost Dave. "You know what we have to do, don't you?"

"I know what we have to do. We have to kill Orville. We have to end his operation before anyone else gets hurt. Preferably before he finishes his super-human army."

"Sheila's never going to let us. You know that. She's lost too much already."

"We don't have a choice. The agency is cowering in fear. They're not fighting back. They're hiding. We can't. Not when it's this important. We have to strike, and we have to strike now, before it's too late."

There's barely even a pause before she replies.

"Alright. I'm in. What's the plan?"

We leave the crater that used to be Sugar & Spice right as the cops show up and start blocking things off. Ginger clings to me, riding through the city on the back of my motorcycle. When we get to Headquarters, there's basically a mob in the lobby, trying and failing to get through security. I whip off my wig and shades and scan my ID, pulling Ginger behind me before anyone questions us.

I shoot Summer a text from the locker room while Ginger changes into a less-scorched uniform. She says she just checked out of the infirmary, and a few minutes later, she shows up in the girls' room. She's got a black eye and a bandage over a cut on her forehead. Besides that, everything looks normal. She looks fine. And even with her injuries, she still looks gorgeous and more than ready to kick some ass.

"Archer and John are outside waiting for us. They heard the news and came running. Brian and Jace made their way into one of the hacking centers to help us through, and Isaac is trying to find Nikki and Ethan. We need all the help we can get."

"Thanks." I hug her tight, holding her closer and longer than I have in a very, very long time. I could have lost her today. I could have lost both of them today. I'm glad I didn't, but the day is still young and we still have a lot to accomplish before I would declare any of us safe. "Meanwhile, I managed to get word out to Mateo and Lucia Hernandez. They're on their way, but they can't come to HQ because of the lockdown, so we'll have to meet them at a rendezvous point."

"Sounds like a plan."

Summer changes into a fresh uniform while I wait by the door. We paint on blood red lipstick and mascara as dark as the night. War paint for soldiers going to fight the good fight. For a moment, I feel like Wonder Woman. Invincible. And then, I see the vulnerable teenager hiding behind my brown irises. I look away.

We walk out into the hall, where the others are waiting. Isaac's quest appears to be fruitful, as Nikki and Ethan are waiting there with the others.

"Alright. Let's go. We have a very slim window as is."

Ethan takes the lead and Nikki passes out earpieces to the others while holding her fiancé's hand.

"Thanks, you guys. I mean it. You're all risking everything. I don't know what I'd do without you."

"No thanks needed, sis. As strong as you are, you can't do it alone." Isaac ruffles my hair. "And we all know you would do the same for us if any of us went crazy and decided to go Rogue not once, but twice."

We make our way to the garage, where Jace and Brian have worked their magic once again and found us a van that isn't booked for today. A daunting task today of all days to say the least. We load our gear, packing as much as we can possibly fit inside: guns, grenades, smoke bombs, tasers, stun guns; the works. Ginger is equipped with her glasses as usual and we all have Brian and Jace (who have barricaded themselves inside a broadcast center) speaking in our ears and listening to all of our conversations.

Just before we get into the van and pull away, out of F.O.U.N.D.'s reach, Sheila comes into the parking garage, tears streaming down her cheeks.

"Are you here to stop us?" I ask after a long silence. "Because I'm sorry, but we can't let you do that. This is too important."

"I can't lose you too, Mia! I lost Bethany all of those years ago! I'm losing Greta right now!" Her shoulders shudder as she sucks in a huge breath. "I can't lose my agents. Not after all of this. Just stay here. Please. We'll figure it out together."

"We all know we don't have that kind of time on our hands." Summer looks at her through a swollen eye. "But for the record, you're the best administrator a girl could ask for. And we love you more than you could ever know...But you said it yourself. We're not your only agents. You have to worry about them. The others. They need you too, just as much as we do. But we need you here. And we need your support."

"If you see our parents, tell them we're sorry, but if they won't do anything, we sure as hell won't sit around and watch Orville destroy the agency that's given us everything."

There's a long silence. Everyone except Summer, Ginger, and I are loaded up and ready to go. John is sitting at the wheel with Archer in the passenger seat.

"We don't have all day, ladies!" His very impatient British accent calls through the van.

"Shut up!" We all shout at him.

"Sheila, you have given us so much. You have done so much for us. You practically raised us. All we can ask you to do now is give us a chance. If all of us die trying to protect everybody, so be it. Dave died because of Orville, and I won't let him die for nothing. Not without at least trying to avenge him."

Another long pause. Sheila's eyes meet each of ours for a long moment, silent tears streaming down her face. She nods.

"Go. Go now. Security is coming. You don't have much time."

"Thank you." Ginger and Summer hop into the van. With one foot in the door and my hand gripping Ethan's, I look to her gratefully. "You won't regret it."

"As someone who has lost someone I loved to Louis, I hope you're right." She gives a proud smile. "Now give him hell. I'll hold off the guards."

Sheila walks back through the door she came from and seals it off electronically.

"*John, drive to the theater. The Ivanovs were seen entering there not too long ago with what appears to be Orville's latest batch of lab rats.*" Jace instructs.

"Time to rain on their parade." John drops a pair of sunglasses down in front of his eyes. "Hold onto your hats everyone, this might be a bumpy ride."

CHAPTER 48

We arrive at the theater mere minutes later, thanks to John's maniac driving. No one is complaining though. I pick the lock of the back door, and we're in without too much trouble.

Beyond the door, our next task is finding Natalia and Viktor and putting a stop to whatever the hell they're doing. Jace said 'new lab rats' meaning a bunch of unconscious teenagers probably on wheels for easy transport. It just makes sense when we find a gurney. But what we find on it is not a teenager, nor is it a dead body, thankfully.

"It's a dummy." Nikki concludes, feeling its skin. Rubbery and limp and filled with stuffing. She's right. It's a dummy. And not a very realistic one at that.

"What the hell...?" I look down the hall for any sight of the Russian siblings. The only sign of activity is the stage. Lights and sound and theatrical music. Promising. But it could also be a trap.

"This way." Archer motions for us to follow after him. We do, single-file onto the stage, where Viktor and Natalia are waiting.

Their arms are crossed and they wear stern expressions. Though they're trying to appear intimidating, Natalia's puffy eyes deceive her. She's been crying recently. As to why, your guess is as good as mine, but I'm sure it has something to do with a betrayal of Louis Orville proportions. The dummies were fake, a way to lure us in. And now that they've got us here...

"It is about time you arrived, Crane. How was the funeral? I heard the weather was very nice." His words are a stab in the heart, salt in the wound, but they also seem very rehearsed. An actor's lines. Part of their little show.

"You're outnumbered." Ginger looks between the two of them. "Turn yourselves in now and we won't have to kill you."

"We are outnumbered?" Natalia's eyes skim over the group of us. From the wings of the stage, a line of men and women walk into the spotlight and surround us in a deadly ring. They're here for a fight. I plan to give them one. But the Ivanovs and all of these guards up front means one thing. Orville isn't here. We're in the wrong place, and now he knows we're coming.

The fight ignites, guns a' blazing. We take cover behind whatever we can find, but the wooden set pieces don't offer much protection, given that they're all made of, well, wood. The crate I'm hiding behind explodes, spilling metal briefcases across the stage floor. I grab one, using it as a shield Captain America style. Dave would be proud.

As soon as I'm close enough to one of the enemy agents, I whap him in the face with the briefcase, causing him to stumble back while holding his nose. Ginger and Summer take on Natalia. They're careful to dodge her super-powered punches. Archer and John take on Viktor, but not very effectively, as John is currently dangling in the air, gasping for a breath that's never going to come. Until Archer shoots Viktor in the leg, that is.

The rest of us focus on taking out the twenty-some L.O.S.T. agents. The difference between our training and theirs becomes very obvious very quickly. We are more brutal, more ruthless, our fighting is outside the box. These agents are very by the book, which means something pretty important: Orville might be good at making super humans, but he is a terrible fighter. That's where we'll get him. We have found a foothold, and we will climb the mountain he's built and burn it to the ground.

We whittle the group down to two: the Ivanovs. But with their powers, even with eight of us, we're still at a disadvantage.

"It doesn't have to be this way." My eyes lock onto Natalia's. We can't beat them in a physical fight. There is no maybe. There is no hope. Not physically. Emotionally, however..."I don't know what Orville did to you two. What he's put you through, but I know what he's capable of. He killed Dave because I crossed him. He was afraid of me and my friends and everything we've done, so he took it out on a weak link."

"Are you calling us weak, Crane girl?" Viktor tilts his head and walks closer. He puts on an air of confidence, a bluff, but I see right through it. He can't fool me. Not when his sister looks like she'll shatter into a million pieces at any second.

The pain in her eyes is unimaginable. She looks horrified. Her hands shake and she falls to her knees. Viktor looks to her with concern, kneeling down beside her. "Natalia, please. It is okay. Be strong. We are strong. *We have to be strong.*"

"Natalia," I approach slowly, my voice low and my gun holstered, "it's okay. We'll help you. You don't have to be afraid of us. We're the good guys."

"That is what they all say!" Natalia wails, tears finally spilling from her eyes.

Viktor wraps his long, muscled arms around her smaller form, trying to comfort her, but it doesn't seem to be working.

"That is what he said. 'F.O.U.N.D. is twisted. F.O.U.N.D. is bad. F.O.U.N.D. will make you regret everything you stand for.' But you are not the ones—" Her voice breaks. Viktor shakes his head with wide eyes in an attempt to get her to stop talking. She continues. "You are not the ones with bombs strapped to your chests."

"What the—?!" Ginger takes a step back. "Are you serious? His own agents?!"

"Just the..." Viktor speaks up now, unzipping the front of his uniform. A mess of wires and flashing metal shines under the spotlights. "Ones who do not cooperate. Hard to when he forces you through deadly medical procedures against your will."

"Alright, that's about enough of that, eh?" John pulls out his gun.

"Bloody hell! What are you doing mate?! Are you mental?!" Archer shouts, taking a step away from him.

A second later, the tall brunette shoots Archer in the stomach.

I pull my gun. All of us do, aiming them at John as Archer hits the floor, gripping his wound. John shot him in the gap between two layers of bulletproof armor. A double agent inside our very crew. Isaac kneels beside the fallen Brit, but the rest of us focus on his partner gone Rogue.

"So you're one of them. It all makes sense now." I step closer to John when no one else dares to and slowly piece together the puzzle.

An arrogant grin creeps across his face, eyebrow lifting as he watches the wheels turn in my head. Amusement is evident on his features. Pride, even. It's disgusting.

"You followed the wrong truck away from the rink. You suggested I go inside and check out what you knew was a bomb. You were angry we didn't take you to Caillte. You...you've been trying to get rid of us all along!"

"You American agents are so dense. I can't believe you didn't put it together sooner. You fight the great fight, and you can't even sniff out a mole in your midst. And you, Archer. Recruited for your *skills*, mate? You're the most pitiful of all. Couldn't even tell your bloody partner was working with the enemy. Disgraceful. Where have the Facility's standards gone?"

"Thanks, mate. Means a lot." He winces as Isaac tries to keep pressure on his wound. "Crane, just kick his arse already, would you? I'm dying over here—"

"I'm going to put you all down. Put you out of your misery." John points his gun at my head, directly between my eyes. "Starting with you."

"If you shoot her, you're going to have six new holes in your head." Summer cocks her weapon, eyes narrowed at John. "And the first one will be from me."

"No need for that." Viktor lets go of his sister, standing behind John instead. All of his fear, all of his worry has melted away. Instead, the Ivanov is left only with rage. Well, that and telekinetic prowess. "Orville can blow us to hell for all I care. If you are with him, you must die too." He looks at me, peering into my soul with his dark eyes before he makes a move. "Can you help us if we help you?"

"Tell them we can. Headquarters is kind of a mess, but I think we can figure out the bombs if you can get them inside." Brian transmits after a very long silence on their end. I hear him typing rapidly, and I hear Sheila's voice inside their makeshift fortress. *"Do it. Sheila said she can get them in. Take care of John and send the Ivanovs here with Archer."*

"They can help you. I promise." His eyes don't leave mine. Viktor raises his shaking hands in the air, John lifts away from the floor, helpless. As much as I want to shoot him, I don't. Instead, I pull a syringe full of sleeping meds off of my belt and jab it into his neck.

"Sweet dreams, asshole." He tries to resist it, but to no avail. His eyes flicker a few times before drifting shut.

"…regret this…" he mumbles. I assume he's talking about us, but maybe he's had a change of heart. Probably not.

"I'll take the Ivanovs. And Archer." Isaac volunteers. "Ethan, want to come with? Grab that traitorous bastard?"

"Yeah. Let's do it." After a moment of thought, Ethan grabs John out of the air, motioning for the Ivanovs to follow him.

"Thank you, Agent Crane." A very shaky Natalia hugs me. I'm cautious. She's done so much to us. So many bad things. And yet, I smile at her embrace, holding onto her just as tight as she holds me for the brief moment before she follows my sister's fiancé to safety.

"I love you, Nik. I'll see you soon, yeah?"

"Be careful, E." She kisses him quickly, combing her slender fingers through his dark brown locks. "I love you too."

Isaac carries Archer carefully. He lets out a yelp of pain. Crimson soaks his uniform, thick and sticky and red. He points to me with a weak finger. Isaac carries him closer.

"Give him hell for me, yeah?" His voice is no more than a hoarse whisper, but the fire in his eyes couldn't be any more powerful. Archer's shaking bloody index finger pokes me in the chest, right over my heart. "Give him hell for *Dave*."

There's a moment where our eyes just meet, and I fear it might be the last time I see him. I don't know if it'll be him that dies or me. What I do next is caused by a flurry of emotion and desperation.

I kiss him.

In this instant, facing my death, I forget about Dave. I forget about L.O.S.T. and Orville and everything. I get sucked into the heat of the moment. And I kiss him.

Archer's lips are soft and warm, moving in reaction to mine. He groans, but I'm not sure if it's in surprise, pleasure, or pain. Perhaps all three. I almost forget that Isaac is present at all until he clears his throat, obviously annoyed or in a rush. Both. I linger just a moment too long, turning what was meant to be an innocent I-might-die-today-goodbye kiss into a this-could-be-something-I-never-noticed-before-but-kind-of-like-and-it-scares-me kiss.

After losing Dave, I thought I would never be happy again. Orville broke me, shattered me to pieces. Maybe Archer will be the one to put me back together.

"Believe me," I smirk, pulling away from him after a long, passionate moment. His eyes are locked on mine, fire still ablaze in his sharp green gaze. "That's the plan."

CHAPTER 49

After Isaac, Archer, John, Ethan, and the Ivanovs take the van back to Headquarters, we're stuck waiting for a ride. The black van that pulls up to the curb is an answered prayer carrying two people we need very much right now: Lucia and Mateo Hernandez. After losing four of our heaviest hitters, my cousins' help is much appreciated.

"Hey there, primas. Need a ride?" Mateo leans out of the passenger window. One press of a button on the van's high-tech console opens the sliding door to let us in. We have as many weapons as we could take out of the other van without looking too suspicious as we waited here for someone to pick us up. "Where's your brother?"

"With Archer and the others in the first van."

"Ah."

"You okay?" Lucia glances back over her shoulder from the driver's seat. Everyone piles into the van. I slam the door shut behind us and Lucia takes off. I assume she's talking about Dave.

"I'm all right. I just...this is something we have to do."

"Stop Orville or kill him?" Mateo asks. "There's a fine line between getting even and going insane, prima. Be careful that you don't mix them up."

"Do what you have to." Lucia adds to her brother's unexpected words of wisdom. "He killed Curly and God knows how many others. Killing a killer doesn't make you a killer. Not when you're preventing more death in the process."

"Where are we going, Lucia?" Summer asks.

These two have met a few times at yearly Winter Evaluation. I think everyone is acquainted, given that all of the boys except for Mateo went in the other van. It's just Ginger, Summer, Nikki, the Hernandezes and I now. Six agents to take down a legion. It's going to be tight, but if we use all of our resources and don't pull our punches, we should be able to make it. It'll be difficult, sure, but working for F.O.U.N.D. isn't supposed to be easy.

"*Lucia and Mateo are going to take you all to the factory where Orville is mass-producing Chemical Rebirth kits that are set to ship to all of his facilities worldwide.*" A helpful tidbit of information from Mr. Brian Martin. "*Our signal is spotty at best. You can't depend on us for much after you leave city limits. We probably won't be of much help.*"

"That's fine." Ginger replies. "Did the van get there?"

"*Just pulled in. Archer's going to be fine. Jace and I are working on the bombs now with the rest of the tech department.*"

The signal goes static for a few seconds before becoming clear again.

"*Summer, Ginger, Mia, it's been a pleasure to be your assigned science nerd.*"

"The pleasure's ours, Doc. You're gonna go places, I swear. Nerd Martin will be a household name, just you wait." Ginger smiles.

"*Not if I blow up in this lab. Sorry! Sorry, I didn't mean—you're not going to explode, Viktor, calm down. Alright, Sheila's going to monitor you as best as she can until we get these vests figured out, but—*"

Static. The signal is gone as soon as we enter one of the tunnels exiting Great City. We're alone now.

We spend a few minutes once we get to the factory to count our remaining weapons. I have a thought.

"How many bombs do we have?"

"What are you...?" The wheels turn behind Nikki's seafoam eyes and she slowly nods. "Bomb the place to smithereens. Make them come out to play and get rid of Chemical Rebirth in the process."

"Exactly."

Ginger and Summer empty their bombs onto the floor of the van, counting them as Nikki and I add ours and Lucia and Mateo hand over what they have. They handle the bombs carefully, as bombs should be handled, counting each with care.

"Twenty-seven." Summer's eyes skim over them again, but she sticks with her conclusion. "We have twenty-seven to work with. What's the plan?"

"Lucia and I will take Nikki and bomb the place. You three wait outside for the cowards to come crawling out and then finish the job." Mateo's plan is what I had in mind, but he's drawn the lines I was afraid to, separating us into groups. I know it has to be done. If we all go in, he'll be able to escape. Someone has to be ready to catch him.

So we wait in the van while Nikki, Lucia, and Mateo dash inside the door on the side of the large brown building, each of them laden with more bombs than they can carry. The means with which to cripple a kingdom.

Tense minutes pass in silence with no more than the static in our ears to keep us company. We wait and wait, listening for the first explosion. The first of many. There are gunshots. Faint shouts. And then—

BOOM!

It begins.

The large metal and brick structure rumbles. Smoke billows from the shattering windows, filling the sky with angry black clouds. We hop out of the van, invigorated. Here it comes.

An inferno rages inside the large structure standing before us, and out spill the agents. Not ours, no, *theirs*, coughing heavily and very disoriented. Ginger and Summer initiate the battle, keeping them away from me so I can take out Louis as soon as he rears his ugly head.

And believe me, it doesn't take long.

After the first wave of them pour out of the blazing building, Orville is just after them. His stormy grey eyes lock on mine as he walks closer. He has a gun, but so do I, and he knows as well as I do that I will win that battle.

I stand tall, confident, with my gun poised and aimed at his forehead, finger hovering over the trigger. Graceful, strong, even in the face of the task at hand. We stand in the eye of the storm, surrounded by battling L.O.S.T. agents getting annihilated by my best friends in the entire world.

"Are you really going to do this, Miss Crane? Make me a martyr for my cause? I'm not the only one, you know. There are others. They will come for you, and they will not be as kind to you as I have."

"You murdered David Bowen in cold blood. You dangled him over my head like a piece of meat, a treat for a cooperative little dog. Well you know what, Louis? *I'm not your bitch.*"

"I didn't take you for a murderer, Agent Crane."

"You of all people have no right to call me that." I seethe with rage. "It's your fault he's dead, Louis! You killed ten innocent teenagers to spite me and my agency! Killing you will keep people safe! And it's my duty as an agent to keep people safe."

"Then do it, Mia. If you're so noble and brave, do it. Strike me down. Pull your trigger. Or are you too scared to live up to your legacy?" He challenges. "Mia Crane, the smallest of the Crane line. You've got awfully big shoes to fill, don't you? Descendant of Margaret Everheart, of Walter Wayne. Groundbreaking people. Trailblazers. And well...you're you. So tell me, Miss Crane. What makes you worthy of their blood?"

"I'm not. You're right. I am just me." I take a step forward. "But I've already lost too much because of you. I won't let anyone lose anything else at your hands."

I stare at him for a long time. Silent. Lips pressed into a thin line. Jaw set. Eyes narrowed. Waiting.

"You're all bark and no bite. Too scared to kill me, even after all of your training. All of your years in that cold, heartless Facility. You are a disgrace. A waste of talent. My wife Bethany would have struck me down if I hadn't killed her first, and yet here you are, too afraid to do the same."

"You killed your wife?" I put the pieces together. The fire. The fire that claimed her life and the life of their daughter. The fire he hides behind, that he broadcasts as his one tragedy, his one defining moment. The fire that took almost everything from him. And he started it. "Your daughter?"

"I did what had to be done. I killed a killer. If that makes me a murderer, so be it. I killed your boyfriend, so why not kill me? Avenge him. Be one of the heroes he worshipped so fondly, one of the super-spies he fawned over. But don't come crying to me when you finally realize that you're nothing but a—"

BANG!

Monster.

Blood splatters against the pavement of the parking lot, bright and red. My heart races. There are no fights around me. There is no one. I am an island. I am alone in what I've just done. And though my stomach sinks in dread, there's something satisfying about killing this man that has done so much harm, a man that has hurt so many. He's gone. It's over.

Or so I thought.

The door of the factory whips open one last time, and along with another wave of sputtering L.O.S.T. agents, my cousins, and my older sister, comes a familiar face: Elise. Sheila's intern.

"Dad!" She dashes across the pavement in a uniform that is not anything an intern would wear. This is a field uniform. Armor. She's here to fight, and it won't be on our side.

Dad. The word rings through my mind as she looks down on the mangled corpse of her father. This woman isn't Elise Ellivro as she claimed to be.

And then it hits me. The letters rearrange themselves in my mind, flipping around to reveal something I should have known from the moment I met her.

Ellivro is Orville spelled backwards.

This is Charlotte Orville. The twin that survived. The double agent. She hid in plain sight, working with F.O.U.N.D., working inside it as one of us, a lowly intern. And despite it all, I believed her when she said she hoped everything would turn out alright. She had already known they wouldn't.

"*You.*" I hiss. Ginger and Summer turn their attention on the traitor.

"Elise?"

"What are you doing here?"

"She's not Elise." I take cautious steps towards her, gun raised. "She's Charlotte Orville. We were wrong. There wasn't one double agent. There were two of them."

"Well." She looks up from her spot crouching on the pavement. Tears stream down her face. "At least there's a brain in that heartless shell of yours."

"Heartless? Me? The one who lost her boyfriend because your father decided to use him as a lab rat? I'm heartless? Not you, the daughter of that monster, who aided and abetted his killing sprees like a little saint? Try again."

"Your agency is the reason my mother is dead. The reason I grew up without my twin sister." Her cold words tell me her father never told her his little secret. "I lost my best friend. I lost my mom. And now, I've lost my dad too. I have nothing. And you... you have everything. Sure, you lost that dork you thought was your *true love*. But you're a beautiful girl, Amelia. You'll move on." A wicked smile stretches across her red lips. "If I let you live that long."

Ginger fires two bullets, but instead of another splatter of blood and another dead body, the bullets freeze in mid-air before clattering to the ground uselessly. A telekinetic. This might be harder than I anticipated.

Mateo signs that he and Lucia and Nikki will take on the remaining guards while Summer, Ginger, and I try to solve our Charlotte problem. She hoists Ginger and Summer into the air with each of her hands, suspending them upright, stiff as boards.

"Which of your friends should I kill first, Mia? Blondie or the rebel? Take your pick. The other will die soon enough."

"How about neither?" I charge at her, driving my fist into her face with a satisfying crack. She stumbles backwards, clutching her now-bleeding nose. Ginger and Summer drop to the pavement and get back to their feet, ready to fight her.

"That was a nice move. How about I show you one of mine?" Charlotte smashes her fist into the ground, causing it to crack and tremble at her touch and when she looks up at us, her nose straightens, the blood fading to nothing. Strength and healing, too. Charlotte is a Swiss Army Knife of super powers. Who knows if this is even all she has? Maybe there's more.

God, I hope not.

We work our asses off to dodge her punches, both physical and invisible, tucking and rolling and trying to get some hits in, but there's not much we can do. She's invincible. Well, she *seems* invincible. But I can see it in her face, in her eyes. She's tired. Charlotte may have powers, but she isn't a fighter. Not like we are. Her training doesn't hold a candle to ours. We just have to hold out long enough for her to show her vulnerability. I have a feeling that won't take much longer.

She puts on a brave face, using other L.O.S.T. agents as telekinetic projectiles, but we evade the attacks. Using her mental powers seems to drain her the most, and with her regenerative healing, there's only one way to take her out: a headshot.

Ginger takes a few steps towards me. So does Summer. The cloud of leather-covered agents surging around us seems to dwindle. A legion brought to its knees by a small group of advanced combatants. F.O.U.N.D.'s best and bravest indeed.

Charlotte's moves are calculated. I watch the wheels turn behind her bright green irises, watching us like a panther ready to pounce. Her fingers stretch as she reaches, pulling whatever power she has left from the depths of her. The way her eyes roll back into her head, the way every inch of her shakes uncontrollably, betrays her mask of confidence. She's scared. And she should be.

From behind, Lucia and Mateo latch onto the redhead's wrists, pulling her back no matter how hard she struggles. I take long strides to where they're holding her. Our eyes lock. Her jaw clenches, and rage seethes from her small body. A lamb in wolf's clothing. A girl inside a weapon, but a danger no less.

I raise my gun to her head, pressing the cold metal against her soft skin. The gun that killed her father. The gun that has killed so many before her. The gun that will kill more after her.

"Do it." She challenges, barely even struggling against Mateo and Lucia anymore. Her body goes limp. "End my pain. My suffering. Let me be with my family again." Her mascara runs down her cheeks in watery streaks. "I'll just keep fighting. I'll just keep killing. I'm a monster, Mia. *He turned me into a monster...*"

My finger tightens around the trigger, but I never finish the job. Instead, I let the gun clatter to the pavement, already red with blood.

"No. I won't."

"Then let me do it." She wrestles herself from Lucia and Mateo's grasp and picks up the gun. I don't even have time to react.

BANG!

Her limp body sprawls across the parking lot beside her father. I can hardly bear to look at the horrifying display. Two twisted, corrupted minds blown all over the cement. Both of them are gone. Like Dave and the rest of the ten. They're gone and they'll never come back.

All six of us stare at the heap of bodies in stony silence. Our transmitter signal still isn't worth shit, but the static seems to perfectly capture the mood. Ginger takes my hand. I look to her as I take Summer's hand.

It's over. It's finally over. We won. What's left of the factory burns behind us, all of the people that worked inside it are sprawled around us in a deadly array. We are not unscathed, bearing holes from bullets and cuts from knives, bruises, black eyes, sprained and swollen limbs, and faces caked in blood. But from the ashes, we will rise.

CHAPTER 50

The graveyard is sunny when I visit Dave the day of the "Goodbye L.O.S.T." party that I have to make an appearance at. It doesn't feel right without coming here first. To say goodbye to him before I say goodbye to the very thing that caused his death: the virus that we eradicated, the murderer that we killed.

I'm a different woman, now. The David Bowen buried beneath this earth wouldn't recognize me. I have the eyes of a stranger. Hollow. Broken. Someone who has lost too much and found too little.

My hair is pulled up into a sort of rolled bun, pinned tightly to the back of my head. Blood red lipstick is painted across my lips, and my black dress barely hides the wounds from the battles I've fought. I look like I'm dressed up for a funeral rather than a party. But in a way, I guess I am.

His grave is still unmarked, waiting for the headstone. Then it will be final. Literally set in stone. Until then, the raw dirt sits there like an unfinished poem, a reminder of the fresh wound.

I swallow thickly, turning two roses in my hands. I stare at the silver band around my ring finger. The words on it mock me. Three words I will never tell him again. His lips will never utter them. He died believing he was a monster who deserved his fate, and I wasn't able to convince him otherwise before I lost him. That's on me.

I pull the ring off of my finger and instead slide it up the stems of the pair of red roses.

"*I love you.*"

A tear slips down my cheek. A single tear. I wipe it away as fast as it appeared, stooping down to set the crimson flowers on his eternal resting place. A final goodbye. I hope somewhere he sees me.

Wherever he is now, I want him to know that I cared. That I loved him more than he could ever know. That he wasn't a monster. That he never was. That he never could be.

I want him to know that I'm okay.

Later, I attend the party at Headquarters. It's in the training room, a high-ceilinged make-shift ballroom at the moment. Everyone from the interns to the administrators attend. Everything has been dropped to celebrate the elimination of F.O.U.N.D.'s greatest threat yet. After cutting off the head of the snake, the other bases worldwide fizzled, and every base of operations self-destructed to protect their information, their identities. They're gone. F.O.U.N.D. doesn't care how. But should they come back, we'll be ready.

My night is full of empty conversations with people I barely know, celebratory hugs and handshakes and slaps on the back from my parents' friends and friends of the friends and friends of the friends' friends. I've never felt so popular in my life. But I don't know that I like it.

They know what I did. The blood on my hands. The man I killed and the woman that took her life to be with him.

They know what I've lost too, so if they see the sadness in my eyes, the bittersweet suffering hiding behind the joy of success, they know it's with good reason. We won, but I've lost.

Ginger, Summer, and I band together, blinded by the flashing cameras of agents that declare we've saved the world. Maybe. But the victory feels insincere. Ingenuine. Like any second the glass will shatter and we'll fall through. I push my fear aside and revel in the so-called end, despite the fact that I fear this is only the beginning.

EPILOGUE

A few weeks pass before I finally work up the guts to stop by the infirmary. I can't help but feel a pang of regret every time I think of that moment with Archer. The last time I saw him, I kissed him. I'm not even sure I mean it. I'm not sure I *didn't*, either. But it happened. I can't ignore it. Can't run from it. But I *can* apologize.

And that's what I intend to do.

When I walk into his room, Archer is slumped against the pillows of his hospital bed, picking half-heartedly at a plate of green Jell-O. His sharp eyes turn on me and he immediately seems to perk up, a smirk tugging at his lips.

"'Bout time you showed up, Crane."

"Yeah." I shrug. "Had to make sure the American hospital food didn't kill you, didn't I?"

"Halfway there." He pokes the Jell-O with his fork. "So why are you really here, then?"

"To say sorry."

"Sorry? What for?"

"For kissing you." He looks hurt, laughing softly and shaking his head to mask the pain. "It's not that I didn't enjoy it. I did. I think. But um, there was a lot of misplaced emotion and I'm—"

"It's alright." He nods.

I take a few steps closer. Weakly, Archer reaches out for my hand, letting out a little grunt and holding his other hand to his stomach, where they probably had to do surgery to prevent him from falling apart like the Scarecrow from *the Wizard of Oz*.

Slowly, gently, my skin brushes against his as his hand grips mine with whatever strength he can muster.

"I didn't want to force anything on you. It was my fault, and it was uncalled for."

He shakes his head. It takes him a second or two to accomplish what he wants to, but he manages to scooch over enough so that I can sit beside him on the narrow hospital bed. Both of his hands clasp mine, his larger fingers weaving through my smaller, shorter ones.

"I didn't mind it all that much." Archer chuckles. He lets go of one hand and reaches up to brush the hair out of my face.

What Archer does next, I'm sure it's in the heat of the moment. It's an emotional I'm-in-pain-please-make-it-better gesture. It doesn't mean anything. Or at least, that's what I'd like to believe. Unlike the last time, this is slow, agonizingly so. His breath flutters across my cheeks. Thick eyelashes close over his green eyes, his lips part. I make no effort to stop him, frozen in place.

And then he kisses me.

ACKNOWLEDGEMENTS

Of all the stories I've written, L.O.S.T. and F.O.U.N.D. has a special place in my heart. The story itself has been with me since the summer between my freshman and sophomore years of high school when I went to the ice cream shop and decided to drop my Work in Progress of the time to pursue a story about a teenage spy and her clueless civilian boyfriend.

And god, has it changed since then.

This story and these characters have come such a long way. They've been renamed, reworked, created from scratch a few drafts in, and I love all of them as though they're my children, even the evil ones that I love to hate.

Through all of the changes, there have been so many people with me on this journey that I really couldn't have done this without.

First of all, Maddison, who was physically present the night I started writing this book, who read the first chapter and suggested the first character name change, from Eli to Dave. Let's thank the gods for that.

Mom and Dad, thank you so, so much for supporting this crazy dream of mine and putting up with my author rants and huge poster boards and the long periods of time in which I laid on the floor for a bit until things started to make sense. I never said I was normal, but you've tolerated it all and have been super supportive all the while.

A special thanks to SelfPubBookCovers for making the book cover process so user-friendly and helping the rerelease of my novel look like the book of my dreams.

To all of my friends and beta readers, you are amazing, wonderful people and I love you all more than words could ever describe. All of your input and reactions have influenced the content and quality of this book more than you could ever know, and for that, I thank you.

And finally, I thank you, dear reader, for giving me—and this book—a chance.

BONUS MATERIALS

MEET DAVE

The story of how Mia met Dave...or how they originally met, anyway.

THE ALTERNATE ENDING

Believe it or not, Dave's fate hasn't always been the same. The story used to end a little like this...

FINDING L.O.S.T. AND F.O.U.N.D.

How the story in these pages went from an idea to a book and everything in between.

OPERATION OLYMPIAN SNEAK PEEK

Not done with Mia and the wonderful world of F.O.U.N.D. just yet? Take a look at what's next in this exclusive sneak peek of the sequel to L.O.S.T. and F.O.U.N.D.

MEET DAVE

David Bowen was not always named David, and we'll get into that later, but in the early stages of L.O.S.T. and F.O.U.N.D., there was always a scene at the beginning that chronicled the story of Mia and Dave and how they met.

In the first draft, and even in the final version, Dave works in an ice cream shop called Lucky's. It's mentioned in the published cut, but it's certainly not as important as it was in the first draft. Hell, in the first draft, Ginger didn't even exist (which is why she's absent from the following scene, but we'll get into that later too).

Anyway, this is the chapter (or at least part of it) that started it all.

TWO YEARS AGO

Let's rewind to the day I met my boyfriend. The day started out as any other day did back then. I was fifteen. It was the summer between my freshman and sophomore years of high school.

The sky was a bit cloudy, overcast. The air smelled of rain, and at this point, a bit of downpour was inevitable. My best friend Summer (a fellow agent and my assigned partner since we were six) and I had just finished a mission and were riding our motorcycles back to Headquarters to fill out post-mission paperwork. It was then that we passed a little ice cream shop.

"Did you see that?" Summer asked through the headsets in our helmets. I glanced at her as she rode next to me. Our motorcycles hummed quietly as we rode down the smooth streets through town.

"The ice cream place?" I asked, looking back at it. The sign out front had a large green three-leafed clover painted on it. In fancy gold letters, 'Lucky's Ice Cream Shop' was written.

"Yeah," she paused, "up for some victory sundaes?"

"Can we? Sheila wanted us back to file our paperwork,"

"I'll call and ask," Summer decided. We pulled over to the side of the road as she called Sheila through the headset in her helmet.

"What is it now, Summer?" asked Sheila as soon as the call got through. Sheila is our advisor, a forty year-old Australian woman. From the tone of her voice, I could tell she wasn't in the best mood.

"The mission was a success." Summer gave her the good news first. "We're requesting victory ice cream,"

"You passed the little place in town, didn't you?"

"Maybe..."

"Fine." Sheila gave in, taking me by surprise. Perhaps it was fate that she said yes to a request she would normally shoot down. "But you're both staying overtime to finish your paperwork,"

"Deal," Summer agreed quickly before she hung up. "We're good to go."

"Sweet." We took off and turned around.

Our bikes looked a bit out of place in the parking lot, but no one seemed to notice. Not that there was anyone there to notice. If it had been sunny and warmer outside, there would have been a flock of people there, but on a chilly cloudy day like that, the place was deserted. Not to mention the fact that it was late-ish and the according to the sign out front, it was fifteen minutes to closing time.

We took off our helmets. A cascade of messy chestnut brown hair fell into place around my shoulders, completely and utterly messed up by my helmet. I raked my fingers through my tangled locks, doing my best to make myself at least look somewhat presentable (not that I really cared) and followed Summer through the front door.

A little bell jingled overhead as we walked into the cool air-conditioned building. The rush of cold was much appreciated. As protective as the agency uniforms were, they were hot. Black leather isn't exactly pleasant in the summer months, even on chilly days, but the bulletproof padding is absolutely necessary in my line of work. I'll take safety over comfort any day.

The first thing I noticed when we stepped through the door, despite the wide variety of colorful ice cream, was the guy standing behind the counter.

He had a head of curly brown hair, pale skin, and clear blue eyes that were magnified by thin-framed rectangular glasses that sat on the bridge of his nose. It wasn't like he was the hottest guy I had ever seen. He was more of what I would call...adorkable.

He was wearing a light yellow polo shirt under his dark green 'Lucky's' apron. His shirt was a bit tight, hugging the arm muscles that I could only assume he had built by scooping ice cream all day. My eyes jumped to the name tag on the corner of his apron. David. His name was David. And Lord Almighty, was he cute...

"Mia," Summer touched my shoulder, pulling me out of my daze. "You alright?"

"Yeah, I just—"

"Hi, can I um...can I help you?" asked David nervously. His blue eyes flicked to me, his cheeks flushed a light shade of pink, and he smiled sheepishly before looking away.

"Two hot fudge sundaes, please,"

"Coming right up." After he poured the hot fudge over the scoops of vanilla ice cream, he dropped a cherry onto each and handed them to us. "Is that all?"

"Yep." Summer pulled out her wallet as he rang us up.

"That'll be $5.58," Summer handed him a ten and put the change in the tip jar. We walked out the door.

There was a long pause before either of us said anything. I still felt like the world was spinning, and I wasn't really sure why. I never got nervous around guys. It was just something I didn't do. I didn't really even know the guy, and yet I had an itching feeling that I should go back in and talk to him.

"So...you want me to get his number for you?" asked Summer with a mischievous grin. "I forgot to grab us spoons anyway."

"You could tell?"

"Mia, for a spy, you're pretty damn easy to read."

"Fine," I surrendered. Summer sauntered through the door, looking smug. I only shook my head and rolled my eyes as I found a spot to watch her from outside the window.

There was a smirk on her face as she told him something along the lines of 'I need two spoons and your number for my friend. She thinks you're cute.' I watched as his eyes darted around. He looked as bewildered as a deer in headlights as he asked 'Really?' Summer nodded and smiled, her eyes twinkling.

I couldn't help but blush as his gaze found mine outside the window. My heart was racing a mile a minute, and I was powerless to do anything. His cheeks flushed as he picked up a pen and a napkin. I watched as he scrawled something on it nervously. He handed Summer the spoons and the napkin, and she was out the door in seconds.

Summer shoved the napkin into my hand, looking pretty pleased with herself. Scrawled on it messily in blue ink was the name 'David Bowen' and his phone number. A small smile tugged at my lips.

"He's all yours," she sing-songed.

I folded the napkin and tucked it into my pocket. I planned to text him later, or something. Well, I would once the butterflies in my stomach decided to calm down.

294

"He got sooooo flustered. It was super cute. It's almost as if no one's ever asked for his number before."

Summer and I sat on a bench outside the ice cream shop and enjoyed our sundaes. I checked my watch. Nine o'clock. David flipped the sign on the door, locked it, and walked outside. He stood on the sidewalk for a little while. Then his phone buzzed.

"Dammit," I heard him mutter. Summer and I were already strapping on our helmets and getting ready to leave. We rode up to him.

"Something wrong?" I asked, raising the visor of my helmet so he could see my face.

"My, uh...my ride bailed..." he stuffed his phone into his pocket, a defeated look on his face. At that moment the clouds surrendered and it started to rain. "Perfect..."

"Need a lift?" I offered.

David sighed. "I'm not worth the trouble." He glanced down the street. "I guess I can walk..."

"Mia, I'll take care of the paperwork. Take him home before he catches a cold." Summer rode away without another word.

"Hi, I'm David," he introduced officially, offering me his hand. "But most of my friends call me Dave."

"I'm Mia. Mia Crane. Here." I opened up the compartment under the seat of the motorcycle and pulled out my spare helmet. Our fingers brushed when he took it from me. I sat down and patted the seat behind me. "Hop on."

He strapped on the helmet and hesitated before he sat down. I felt his arms ever so gently wrap around my waist.

"You're going to need to hold on a bit tighter than that if you don't want to fall off," I warned, the smile on my face coming through my voice.

"Whoops," he said softly. I heard him chuckle nervously as I pulled his arms further and tighter around me. "Sorry."

"Ready?"

"Yeah."

I revved up my bike and took off, practically flying down the street. "So, where am I headed?" I asked. "Directions would be helpful at this point."

"Oh right. I live on the corner of Birch and Maple."

"You were going to walk to the other side of the bridge in the rain?" I scolded playfully, laughing a little.

"Well..." he paused, "thanks. For this."

"Don't mention it."

We rode down the roads and across the bridge. We talked the whole way there. I almost missed his house, drove right past it. But I turned around and rode up into the driveway.

I killed the engine and he handed my helmet back. I tucked it back into its spot inside the base of the cycle and then took off mine and tucked it under my arm so I could give him a proper goodbye.

"So uh, do you want to maybe, I don't know, go out sometime? Or something?" David looked at me timidly.

I mulled it over, but I already knew the answer was yes. "I'd like that," I replied, laughing a little at his meek invitation. "A lot."

"Thanks for the ride Mia," he walked up the steps and opened the front door. "See you around."

"See ya." I lowered my visor and drove off, replaying the event over and over in my mind as I made my way back to Headquarters.

THE ALTERNATE ENDING

Believe it or not, Dave wasn't always fated to die in my cruel hands. In fact, the original ending set up a much different sequel. Prepare to have your hearts broken – again.

Some background information, though: in this version, some parts of the third act were the same...up until Dave died. He lived through the hospital scene and woke up to find he had super powers (this wasn't established until after he was rescued) and therefore became a F.O.U.N.D. agent and helped in the final battle (which is VERY different in the first draft, so I'm not even gonna go there.) But L.O.S.T. still, for lack of better word, lost, and the F.O.U.N.D. agents still threw a party to celebrate. That's where this picks up.

Also, Mia (obviously) did not kiss Archer in the version where Dave lived, but Archer still got shot.

The 'Goodbye L.O.S.T.' party was one for the history books. Agents from just about every wing got together to celebrate an end to the Orvilles and their evil schemes.

But as we danced into the night throwing the biggest agency bonfire of all time, I couldn't help but feel kind of bad about Archer, so I stopped by to see him the next morning.

"Enjoy the party, Crane?"

"I did." I told him. "How are you holding up?"

"Doc says I'll be back in action in a few weeks." Archer sighed, dark bags evident beneath his tired green eyes. It was obvious he was in pain, but he was gonna be fine. "I got a transfer slip from Hodge. They found my former partner John Jacobi driving one of

Orville's trucks and arrested him for treason. And seeing as I'm in need of a new partner..."

"So you're staying here then?"

"Yeah." He nodded, folding his hands over his stomach. "It takes more than a shot to the gut to get rid of me."

"What a shame." I laughed. "Well, for what it's worth, Dave doesn't officially have a partner yet either."

"Are you saying—?"

"Yes. Yes I am."

After I checked up on Archer, I went back home to help Dave unpack some boxes. He and his mom moved into a house in F.O.U.N.D.'s spy suburbs, or as Dave likes to call it 'the Spyburbs'. Twenty-seven identical houses all home to families of spies. He's in the safest neighborhood around, and only a ten minute drive from the mansion.

Lots and lots of agents pitched in to help rebuild the bakery and the other buildings that were damaged in the bombings. Most of the injured agents are making a wonderful recovery, and the ones that didn't make it are being remembered each and every day by those that did. Greta took it hard, losing so many of her bakers, but I think she's going to be okay.

The Ivanovs went on trial, but were found not guilty due to the fact that they were being threatened and they provided us with Orville's location. Since the trials, they were recruited by F.O.U.N.D.'s base in Moscow, close to their home. Even though they're miles and miles away, I can't help but get the feeling I'll see them again.

Life after L.O.S.T. fell has definitely been easier. I think Sheila's decided to give us a much-needed break. It's appreciated, especially considering that school starts in a week and I haven't even touched my Latin homework. Or my AP Lit homework. Or my World Studies homework. But you know, I'll take care of it. Hopefully.

I was thinking about the new path I'm headed down and the new experiences and chances that lay ahead, and honestly, I'm pretty excited. The things I once dreaded, as far as telling Dave about the agency and him dealing with this whole new world, they really aren't that big a deal anymore.

He knows I'm a spy. He knows I can speak Russian fluently and kill a man with my bare hands. He knows that I can fire just about any gun you put in front of me and throw knives as easily as he can throw a ball. He knows I'm a weapon, raised in a family of spies and trained by the best in the business.

And the best part? He doesn't care.

After everything we've been through, everything we've lost, and everything we've found, I couldn't be happier with the way things turned out.

"So what happens next?" Dave asks on a warm summer evening. We're lying on the beach, our bodies entangled as we gaze at the stars. "Now that L.O.S.T. is over and Orville's gone, I mean."

"Sheila gives us a few weeks off, and we start fresh with the next case that pops up." I tell him.

"Are all of your summer vacations as crazy as this one?" He chuckles, his blue eyes fixed on the sliver of the moon surrounded by the glittery stars.

"You think that was bad, just wait for Christmas break. You haven't seen anything yet,"

"I hope you're kidding,"

"I wish I was,"

"And I thought all of the initial craziness of my girlfriend being a secret agent was over."

I shake my head, thinking about everything ahead of us. The possibilities are endless, the missions are limitless, and the dangers are infinite.

"Brace yourself, Curly. The chaos has just begun..."

MORGAN M. STEELE

FINDING L.O.S.T. AND F.O.U.N.D.

The story of L.O.S.T. and F.O.U.N.D. taught me not only a lot about the writing and publishing process, but I learned a lot about myself along the way. As Mia grew, I grew. When I originally wrote the prologue, where Mia was fifteen, *I* was fifteen. And by the time I originally published the book, I was seventeen, Mia's age.

Mia coming out as bisexual was sort of my coming out as bisexual. It's one of the very few things she and I have in common. Finding Mia and getting to know her voice helped me get to know my own, and I doubt I'd be the person (or the writer) I am without her.

I, personally, have come a long way since then, but so did the story and the characters in it.

L.O.S.T. and F.O.U.N.D.E. (not a typo. Different acronym. Long story.) was once the story of Mia *Carver* and her civilian boyfriend *Elijah* Bowen. It was originally going to be about a former spy from a family of spies who had to come out of retirement to rescue her captured love interest before it was too late. In some ways, things are still similar to that idea. In other ways, the book is a completely different story than that.

It was after a trip to the local ice cream shop (Lucky's is a not so subtle reference to a place called Shamrock's in my hometown) that I finally got the ball rolling and sat down and wrote the first chapter. It got changed a million times and then eventually cut altogether, but without that first tiny attempt, I wouldn't be here.

In fact, the first draft of L.O.S.T. and F.O.U.N.D. was practice for my first ever year participating in National Novel Writing

Month (NaNoWriMo). I ended up liking L.O.S.T. and F.O.U.N.D. a lot more than the other book I wrote, so I poured more time into polishing it until I was pleased with it.

This was a lot harder than it sounds. As they say, you are your own worst critic, and I learned very quickly that this was the case for me. It was so bad that I ended up sitting down, taking the entire book apart, outlining it again, adding new scenes, new characters, and changing others entirely.

In the first draft alone, six characters had their names changed. The Cranes were the Carvers, Dave/David was Eli/Elijah, Viktor Ivanov was named Alexei, Brian was Albert, Mateo was Roberto and then Antonio, and Isaac was Jeremy and then Aaron before I settled on Isaac.

My main issue was that I had five male characters who all had names beginning with 'A' and I thought it might get confusing. In the end, the only one who got to keep his name was Archer because it sounded the coolest and I wasn't able to find another name that stuck for my favorite British agent.

And then, once I took it apart and reworked the whole book, I broke ground on the second draft. Just when I thought things were done changing, almost *everything* changed. It still felt empty.

So, on a sunny afternoon, Ginger Williams introduced herself to me, fully realized, and I fell in love with her instantly. Because I wanted her to be an important character, that meant any spy scene had to be rewritten. I also added in Nikki, Jace, and Ethan, none of whom existed previously. Some of the new scenes include some of my favorites: The 4th of July, Summer's birthday party, shopping for Summer's birthday presents, the Spy Party, and the adventure to Caillte. Additionally, Dave lived and therefore, Mia never had a romantic relationship of any kind with Archer.

All of these changes required basically an entire rewrite that added new features to the already existing characters. Mia became hard of hearing and because I had learned I was bisexual, I made Mia bisexual too. Dave got some social anxiety and became colorblind, Brian was revealed to be diabetic. None of these were in the first draft, but helped give my characters depth and feel more like real people and less like ink words scattered over paper.

So if you're an "aspiring author" with dreams of being published but you think your writing isn't quite up to snuff, keep writing. And after that, write some more. Write in your free time, write during your lunch break, write in your study hall. Write in your head, write out loud, write in the notes on your phone, write while you're lying on the floor, staring at the ceiling, waiting for everything to make sense.

Just keep writing. Because if you really love it and care about your characters, it doesn't matter how long it takes, it doesn't matter how many breaks you take, you'll come back. And when you do, they'll be waiting right there for you to welcome you home.

After all, the only person who can tell their story is you.

OPERATION OLYMPIAN

Though the sequel to L.O.S.T. and F.O.U.N.D. is still very much a work in progress, here's a sneak peek at the first chapter

CHAPTER 1

Senior year, despite it all, has been off to a good start. So far. Halfway into the year, and yeah, not much has happened. Senior Homecoming was supposed to be more exciting, I guess. But it was normal. I guess I shouldn't be complaining about the normality of it all.

After all, I used to be a girl who longed for normal.

It took a while, but finally, "Mia Crane the Almighty L.O.S.T. Slayer" became another face in the crowd. The younger agents started to see the pain in my eyes when they asked for an autograph, so they stopped. And the agents above me moved on too. There were bigger problems to handle than a teenage agent that got lucky.

So I've been free to enjoy my senior year. The last year before F.O.U.N.D. ships me off to wherever they decide. Just like Nikki, Jace, and Isaac, I too will be shoved out of the nest. The house has been quiet without Isaac's silly antics. It's weird. Just when you get used to things, they change.

We keep in contact, though. My idiot older brother got shipped off to Golden Ridge, California. A long ways from Great City. I miss him a lot, but Christmas is coming up soon, and with Christmas comes the yearly Winter Evaluation. Usually, these haven't meant much, but because this is my last year before my eighteenth birthday, this Eval is for all the cookies.

It will make or break my career as an agent.

Archer says not to worry. That I'll do fine and they'll find a good spot for the agent that saved the world. But did I? Did killing Louis Orville solve all of the world's problems? Did it end war? Hunger? No. Killing Louis Orville only postponed the inevitable.

I'm living in a lie. And I'm loving every second of it.

With all of the double-agents that had to be rooted out of F.O.U.N.D., obviously, there are positions to fill in every department, which leaves Summer, Ginger, and I on application duty. We don't currently have an open field mission, therefore making us Sheila's temporary assistants. We basically get to do whatever she needs us to do while we're on the clock. And seeing as the new and improved Sugar & Spice doesn't open until spring, we've been stuck at Headquarters for the most part.

"Shelby Marks. Sixteen. Skilled with mathematical equations and physics," Ginger reads from a sheet, her eyes narrowed at the lines of text detailing the F.O.U.N.D. hopeful. "Do I stick her in the science wing or in the tech wing?"

"Math and phys sounds more tech than the science wing." Summer taps a pen against her pink lips, staining its plastic cap with her favorite lip gloss. "You know, building things and stuff."

"You're right." Ginger sets the application in the tech pile and grabs another.

We've been at this for almost three hours and we haven't even made a dent in the mountain of papers. I have four paper cuts and counting. You would think with F.O.U.N.D. being F.O.U.N.D. and all, they would have an algorithm to do this for us, but paper files are a lot harder to hack. They don't put anything into the system until the applicants are approved and have signed their lives away to the agency.

"Kaleb Clarke. Fifteen. Physically gifted," Summer reads. "Gifted with a capital 'G'."

"As in...Enhanced." I walk over to glance at the paper. He wasn't one of the Thirteen. I would recognize him. But we've only scratched the surface of Orville's would-be army. I get the feeling there are plenty more where that came from. "Stick him in the field agent pile."

"Yep."

The next application I pick up is Kaleb's sister Kennedy. She's a year older than him, but also Gifted. I set her paper on top of his and pick up an application that makes my stomach drop.

Mark Cho. Eighteen. Great with mechanics and geometry. The picture attached confirms what I already know. This is one of Dave's friends.

Shit.

"Hey, just a quick question..."

"What, babe?" Ginger pushes a large pair of glasses up the bridge of her nose. It's a new thing she's picked up, sometimes wearing a pair of lens-less glasses for the sake of fashion. It's a good look for her, though. I guess it's for when she's not wearing her Brian Martin Mobile glasses. The ones that have pop-up fun facts every time you look at something remotely interesting.

"Do you know where the applicants are?"

"Why?" Summer gives a suspicious glance. "What are you do-ing, M?"

"It's important."

Summer and Ginger look at each other and then at me again. They know I've been acting a little different since everything went down, but they're still my best friends. I'm still their Mia Crane.

"Down in the novice training facility, I think. The field agent hopefuls are testing in the big room, and everyone else got shoved into Lab Zero." Ginger glances at the door. "I would get down there before Sheila gets back, though. She probably wouldn't approve."

"Thank you."

I take the file and a clipboard and book it from the administration department. When the elevator doors close behind me, I'm finally able to breathe. Messing with the recruitment process is sort of frowned upon. And by sort of, I mean it's basically the fourth unwritten rule of the agency. Maybe fifth after 'never interfere with another agent's mission'.

The lower floors of the building are not as high-tech as the upper floors, that's for sure. The higher you go, the deadlier (and cooler, let's be honest) it gets. When we were younger, Ginger, Summer, and I would dream of the days when we finally got to go up to the higher floors as more than a Spy School Field Trip. But now that I work up here regularly, it doesn't seem as glamorous.

The door to the big training facility is shut tight, but I can still hear the clangs, bangs, and booms of weapons through the 'soundproof' door. The new field agents are a promising bunch.

A few doors down is Lab Zero, a large silver oval painted on its smooth white surface. About a hundred hopeful F.O.U.N.D. scientists and inventors are hard at work building little trial gadgets or taking the standardized admissions test. I spot Mark, but luckily, he's too absorbed to notice it's his best friend's ex-girlfriend standing in a field agent uniform.

In the front of the lab sitting at a long desk are a handful of F.O.U.N.D. agents wearing lab coats, goggles, and rubber gloves. They're monitoring the test, but it doesn't stop them from working on their latest projects.

Sitting second from the other end, broadcast by a head of fiery red hair, is none other than Brian Martin, by far the brightest brain of the bunch.

"Bri, I need a favor." I whisper it as quietly as I can, but the other agents all shush me anyway.

Brian peels away from his work and turns to look at me. After thinking for a second, he motions towards the door. Once we're in the hall and it's closed behind us, he asks, "What are you doing down here?"

"I need to pull out one of your applicants."

"Did Sheila send you?"

"Not...exactly..."

He lowers his voice. "You're going Rogue again, aren't you?"

"Kind of. One of the guys in there is one of Dave's friends." I hold up the file in my hand.

He skims over it and his expression softens from concerned to understanding. He opens the door a little and says something to the guy sitting on the end of the table. Then, that guy says something and then there are footsteps and the door opens to the sight of a very panicked Mark Cho.

"Did I do something wrong? Agent Martin, I didn't mean to—

"Mark, you didn't do anything wrong. Agent Crane is just...taking you for a...I suck at lies. You do it. You're better than I am."

"Please don't kill me! I have a family! I have a little sister!" Mark has obviously watched too many spy movies.

"Look at me." I snap my fingers in his face, and for the first time he looks up at me, recognition flashing across his features. "You're not gonna die. That's not what we do here."

"Oh." Then, after a pause, "You...you're Mia..."

"Come on. We can talk about it on the way."

"On the way to where?"

"Surprise." I shrug. "Thanks, Bri. I owe you."

"I was hoping you'd say that, actually. I need to talk to you about something I've been working on for Summer. It's this really complicated pro—"

"I'll catch you later, alright?" I don't have time for a Brian ramble right now.

"Right. Later."

The door clicks behind him as he retreats back to the testing room. I guide a wide-eyed Mark down the halls and finally to the parking garage.

"So you're a field agent."

"Yep."

"How long have you been a field agent?"

"Since I was five."

"Did Dave—"

"Let's not talk about that right now." I'm quick to cut him off, my stomach dropping at the mention of the curly-haired dork.

"Oh, okay." Mark doesn't say much after that. Well, until we're standing in front of my motorcycle and I hand him one of the helmets. "Is this a test?"

"No." I get on and pat the seat behind me.

He pulls the helmet onto his head and sits down, arms tentatively wrapped around my waist.

"You're gonna need to hold on tighter than that."

We ride out of the garage and through the modern Metropolis that is Great City, New York. The skyscrapers and billboards are still the same as they were. Even though my life feels like it's so much different than it was, it's really not. There are just pieces missing.

People missing.

We manage to get to Crane Manor without too much trouble. In the middle of the afternoon, the only real traffic is tourist traffic, but with it being so cold out, even that has dwindled. The mansion is waiting on the hill like it always is.

"Woah, who are we meeting here, Batman?" Mark doesn't realize there's a microphone in his helmet.

"Not exactly."

"Woah! You can hear me in this thing?"

"Yes. I can. There's a mic."

"Oh, sweet."

I park in the garage and walk up the stairs, through the door into the kitchen. "This is my house."

"You LIVE here?"

"Yeah. I don't think my parents are home, but I'm not exactly supposed to be here right now." Once we're in the foyer, Mark looks around in awe. "C.A.I.T.L.Y.N., deactivate outsider mode."

"Welcome home, Mia. Is there anything I can assist you with?"

"Oh my God! You have AI?"

"Mark, this is C.A.I.T.L.Y.N. She's our Caretaking Artificial Intelligence and Logistical Youth Nurturer. Basically a robot babysitter without a body."

"Hi, Mrs. C.A.I.T.L.Y.N., nice to meet you." Mark waves at the empty room, a bright smile on his face.

This is what Dave would have done, I realize. But Dave never met C.A.I.T.L.Y.N. He was too dead to do that.

"This way. Haven't got all day to screw around in the foyer." I drag him towards the elevator and we get in.

Pressing my hand to the biometric scan enables me to bring us to the Archive. It's kind of like the Trophy Room, but not as grand. There aren't any shiny medals or plaques down here. Just pictures and files. It's a colder place. More distant. Where the trophy room has warmer toned wood and yellowish lights, this place is almost white, stark, like a hospital.

Pictures hang on the wall. Not very many, but the beginning of a collection. They range from the forties on, dating as far back as the beginning of F.O.U.N.D. The more recent ones are near the bottom of it. And at the end of it all is Dave. And me.

"These are the agents in my family." I skim my fingertip along the rows of photos until it lands on the little square photo printed out of Dave's old Polaroid.

I remember that day. The trees were alive with the colors of fall. We had just gotten together at that point, and Dave insisted on getting a snapshot of the two of us together.

"Dave was an agent that whole time?"

"No. He wasn't." I cut him off.

Mark raises an eyebrow and opens his mouth to ask a question, but then stops and lets me continue.

"*I* was an agent that whole time. I have been basically all my life. My parents are agents, my grandparents, my great-grandparents before them. I'm a fourth generation, but Dave never knew that. He never knew any of it. And as soon as he found out, he died." I didn't think I was going to cry today. I was wrong. The tears are hot and fast, running down my cheeks faster than I can catch them. But the emotion doesn't carry into my voice. I still sound cold, removed. The wall I spent five months building is stronger than my sudden surge of emotion. "Dave died because my job put him in danger. I'm not letting the same thing happen to you."

"You really loved him, right?" Mark looks away from the picture of Dave and I and finally looks at me, at the tears streaming down my face.

"Yes." I manage to muster a soft smile. "I really loved him. But I couldn't protect him. So let me protect you."

"I think I can do that." Mark stares at me for a long moment, and it looks like he's deciding whether or not to hug me. His decision is made clear enough when I find myself trapped in his embrace. His hand rubs a large circle on the fabric of my F.O.U.N.D.-issue winter coat. Then he whispers, "I miss him too."

ABOUT THE AUTHOR

Morgan Marie Steele is an author from Michigan. She lives with her Mom, and her miniature schnauzer, Maggie.

As you can probably tell by this point, she's a huge nerd obsessed with super-heroes, *Star Wars*, and spies. She spends the majority of her free time playing Skyrim, watching the *Back to the Future* movies, and working on her next novel.

Morgan graduated from Grand Valley State University in 2022 with a degree in Film and Video Production and minors in Writing and Women, Gender, and Sexuality Studies.

For updates on her upcoming books, you can follow Morgan on her social media:

Twitter/Instagram/TikTok: @msteele1212.

Facebook: Morgan M. Steele Books

Goodreads: Morgan M. Steele

Support the

Author!

Leave a Review